My Teeth
Become Weapons

Daniel Bishop

Lisbeth & Luna Publishing, LLC
St. Louis, MO

MY TEETH BECOME WEAPONS
© 2024 DANIEL BISHOP
All rights reserved. This book or any portion thereof may not be reproduced or used in any manner whatsoever without the express written permission of the publisher except for the use of brief quotations in a book review.

For information about permission to reproduce selections from this book, please contact lisbethandlunapublishing@gmail.com.

First printing: 2024
This book was created with help from Editwright.
Visit editwright.com for more information.

Creative direction by Andrew Doty
Cover illustration by Rachel Yamnitz
Book interiors by N-K Creative
Copy editing by Allison Janicki
Published by Lisbeth & Luna Publishing, LLC

Typeset in Sabon LT Pro and Caveat

ISBN: 979-8-218-36535-6
Library of Congress Control Number: 2024912800

BISAC
YAF062000   YOUNG ADULT FICTION / Thrillers & Suspense / General
YAF031010   YOUNG ADULT FICTION / LGBTQ+ / Bisexual
FIC030000   FICTION / Thrillers / Suspense

TO THE PEACEMAKERS FUELED by the simple notion that we have much more in common with one another than we are led to believe, this book is dedicated.

TO THE YOUNG PEOPLE who must compromise on a daily basis between the person they wish so painfully to be and the person they must be for their well-being, this book is dedicated.

TO THOSE WHO CHOSE to stay true to themselves in a weary world and suffered a personal cost, this book is dedicated.

Acknowledgments

I'D LOVE TO EXPRESS deep gratitude to the first three individuals I entrusted with the first draft of *My Teeth Become Weapons* and whose services are inseparable from the final product: my three trustee beta readers, Jas, Iman, and Oskar. I would also like to acknowledge and express thanks to the fine people at Editwright for their meticulous attention to detail and months' worth of time and energy put towards fine-tuning the novel the reader holds in their hands at this very moment. Any educator knows creativity can only flourish if it's encouraged, so I would love to thank all my previous teachers, directors, professors, and mentors through my youth in Jerseyville, IL, to my collective enrollment at DePaul, SIUE, and Webster. I would love to thank the friends, present and dearly departed, who have encouraged me to live truthfully and passionately. Finally, my deepest gratitude is reserved for my extended and immediate family members.

Mom and Dad, you will always be my first and greatest audience and the one I work hardest to make proud.

Author's Note

THIS BOOK CONTAINS SENSITIVE material related to alcohol/drug overdose, homophobia, transphobia, Islamophobia, xenophobia, conversion therapy, gun violence, child abuse, spousal abuse, suicidal ideation, homicidal ideation, and grief. The author is hopeful readers will pace their reading mindfully and provide themselves ample grace and patience as the story progresses through rocky terrain.

Love and solidarity,
Daniel

One

I CAME OUT TO my class via PowerPoint in the fourth grade. Accidentally.

It was Valentine's Day, and we were supposed to pick a fictional character we'd take on a Valentine's Day date. At this point in time, *Wonder Woman* had just been released in theaters and our school copies of the novelization were promotional versions with Gal Gadot on the cover. Naturally, boys my age picked Wonder Woman or Hermione from *Harry Potter* or Keira Knightley in *Pirates of the Caribbean*. For my presentation, I thought back to the film my mom watched religiously despite having released in theaters 17 years prior: *A Knight's Tale* starring Heath Ledger (I thought I'd lead with the movie title so you didn't instinctually think a child was exposed to *Brokeback Mountain*). I did not want to take my eyes off him at all. His ruffled blonde hair and boyish profile had me in a trance I couldn't even define as romantic or sexual, it was just his charisma. It was gravitational.

You'll be happy to know nothing inherently sexual was demonstrated during the presentation, it was basically just, "This is X, here's what my Valentine to X would be, here's what our date would look like." I'd get Heath Ledger new jousting gear and we'd go to a picnic under the stars. The weird part? Maybe a quarter of the kids were stunned or confused by my presentation. It wasn't the '90s anymore, but by no stretch of the imagination were things where they could be.

But especially not in Anthem, Tennessee.

To save you the suspense, I was the only boy who picked a male character. At this point in time, Millennial teachers were getting drafted into classrooms for the ongoing battle of what portions of tomorrow could be taught today, in this case, queerness. But they learned that day what nearly every teacher inevitably does, and that's the line between what teachers teach and what parents would prefer they didn't.

Parents complained. They didn't think teachers should be monopolizing the "delicacy" of the conversation on sex. But the real irony was a child was expressing their interests like every other kid and teachers weren't weighing in at all. Parents said such a discussion at that age would "confuse and even scare" a young child. I tried that very same argument for banning fractions from math class, but I'll be damned if I wasn't forced to learn them.

In full honesty, I don't look back and resent much of anyone outside of the ignorant parents who beat their chests and filled their kids with their own faults and the "little extra" just for them, to quote Philip Larkin. The words "gay," "queer," and "coming out" were absent from my PowerPoint, but nevertheless, my school district used my presentation as a precedent on what is and what is not palatable for young minds. Either that or they're just Rob Pattinson girlies. If I really truly did feel bad for anyone involved in Ledger-Gate, it would be the two classmates who had gay parents.

Parents and teachers reading this already know kids go to school with their own measuring sticks for normalcy from their households and often hold them up to their peers with a bottomless pool of inquisition. So when classmates began speaking up with lines like, "It's really gross that you'd wanna kiss a guy!" Gloria (who had two gay uncles in Pennsylvania) turned red and sunk low in her chair.

If we didn't grow up in a Catholic school where uniforms were mandatory, my guess was Gloria would be the most fashionable, given the source, or at least that's the stereotype nine-year-old me fell victim into believing. When you realize you're queer (or rather, the entire school district makes you well aware), your only prayer at finding your bearings at that age are, sadly enough, *stereotypes*. And no, shedding the shackles of common preconceptions of your sexuality at a young age is not the "liberated Andy Dufresne standing in the rain in *Shawshank Redemption*" moment you might picture it being.

I still loved sports. My fashion sense was still plaid cargo shorts. Nothing really changed in the tenor of my voice or mannerisms and believe me, I was vigilant. I felt like Peter Parker after being bitten by the radioactive spider, but the superpowers were the last thing I wanted. And miraculously enough, the more I hyperfixated on my sensibilities and attractions, I still liked girls. And if you think this was supposed to reassure me that LedgerGate was merely a phase, just know my attraction to boys didn't get canceled out by this phenomenon.

Looking back on that chapter now as a sophomore in high school, there were advantages and disadvantages in navigating queerness to nine-year-old me at the time. Do kids that young have the nuances of sexual identity handed to them at Scholastic Book Fair night? No. But did a digital native like me need to depend on it being the case? Nope! One Google search and all I needed to know on the subject was delivered in a millisecond. But as most digital natives reading might know already, immediate accessibility to literally all information in the world comes with a cost of your innocence depending on how far your curiosity takes you.

But was there ever a moment in your youth when your curiosity was met with punishment? To me personally, it seems like a cruelty reserved specifically for children. Adults typically have curiosity rewarded because adults are unassuming of one another — well, to a moderate extent, at least. Children and curiosity are a relationship as old as humankind, but only as old as the repercussions which follow suit. Kids who followed the curiosity of who they were attracted to in the books I've read were almost always punished by peers, parents, teachers, priests, churches, nature, society . . . the list goes on.

The risk/reward ratio of following your curiosity can depend on your surroundings and environment as well. In a small town like Anthem, Tennessee, the town I've grown up in, curiosity is usually placated by an endless supply of gossip and rumors. However, if you're like me and you see how trite and shallow gossip truly is, your questions need deeper, more complex answers before they can be truly put to rest. But if you've ever openly pursued deeper answers to the wrong questions without punishment, that means you were never sent to Revival Church Camp for a summer.

Two

"TWO MORE FUCKING OVERDOSES last night," my mom Carol said, slamming the front door behind her. It was a household ritual for her to storm in through the front door after her shift was finished at St. John's Memorial Hospital. There were only two consistencies when Mom stormed through the door home from work. The first was if it was deep into the a.m. last time, it was deep into the p.m. this time. The second was an announcement relating to the weekly toll of overdoses in the hospital, almost predominantly teens and young adults. While other parents and kids count down the days to Halloween, such rowdy and debaucherous occasions prove to be hell for round-the-clock hospital staffers like Mom.

I never had to ask what age group the patient was. I had developed an internal compass which clocked Mom's general mood, and the more south things looked, the younger the patient was. Sometimes they'd recover, sometimes not. Again, deep in the a.m. or deep in the p.m.

"And you don't think it's just idiot kids bored out of their minds in a shithole town?" I asked.

"My entire *graduating class* were idiots bored in a shithole town," my mom shot back. "We did bored shithole drinking. This is never bored shithole drinking."

This was typically the part of the conversation where I knew I'd only be asking questions she gave up finding answers to years ago.

Mom said, "This town can raise $8K for church trips to Peru, you'd think half of that could find us mental health professionals who knew what the fuck they were doing."

Anthem didn't have mental health professionals, they had pastors and priests. We didn't have AA or NA meetings, we had prayer groups. And no, an aspiring author like myself can't ignore the irony of the first AA meeting being a prayer group in the 1930s. But things change in a century. People and the reasons they drink, smoke, snort, and shoot up change. Teenagers change. Adults see the world and oftentimes they don't understand what they see, but they know for certain it's worse. They want children thinking critically and constantly self-assessing, aware of their principles, and aware of their goals. But in Anthem, teens are bored, and the time required to navel-gaze properly is offered in abundance. Adults think children become *less* inquisitive and ask *fewer* questions as they age into teenhood because their intelligence is expanding, and for digital natives, answers are in your pocket. However, teenagers still *do* have questions about the world and about themselves, but answers aren't given to shut them up anymore. That no longer works as well as it used to.

"I'm sorry, Ill," Mom said, "you're a teenager, that's soul-crushing enough. How was your day? How's school? How's the story going?"

"It's okay and thank you for asking," I said. "School was okay. Rox ditched school early again."

Mom's fake smile dropped. "*Again*? And you didn't stop them?"

I replied, "It's always when my head is turned. They've gotten craftier the past month. It didn't even occur to me they were gone until seventh period."

Mom *loved* Rox. She's spent the past three years telling me to hold onto Rox tight because they're "no bullshit." I didn't understand what she meant when I was young, and I might understand better today, but it's felt like with each passing day, the less I really know Rox like I used to before this summer.

If I can sum Rox up in a thousand words or less, they're the type of friend you have to build a new bridge to on a daily basis. What bridge was that in our friendship? Creative writing. Fiction. We would spend hours after school swapping story ideas, acting them out, and discussing which genre we would one day be published in. But even in this shared world of storytelling, Rox and I had our differences. While I punished the protagonists of my stories with trials and tribulations for a sense of control, Rox sent their protagonists off on life-affirming adventures that both lifted up and affirmed the protagonists for their own sense of control.

Please don't mistake the punishment of my main characters as a form of sadism, it's just a personal belief of mine that characters need to be tested on their principles and core values before they can have a resolution. Samwise Gamgee had his loyalty to his master and lover — sorry, "friend" — tested to its deepest root before the Ring was cast into the pit of lava and destroyed. Rox, who has been provided more than their fair share of torment and trial, is naturally inclined to retrieve a protagonist from suffering at the start and show the fairer side of things. Like any parent determined to break the generational curse, Rox works tirelessly to provide their creations that which was unprovided to them.

Rox doesn't tell anyone about the four months they spent away at Revival, not even me. If you knew how much their usual energetic self had been done away with so efficiently, those four months away spoke for themselves. Rox was hardly the only child in Anthem, Tennessee, sent to Revival for four months, as the issue at hand had become a municipal nuisance the past decade. The only reason I wasn't sent away following my PowerPoint presentation was my mother's alternative wishes for my well-being coupled with an obligatory promise to the school to "let faith lead the way."

Mom's consensus was that faith was leading the way for enough people in the state and the youth were no better for it, due largely to places like Revival and those sent there for four months in the summer. If faith *was* indeed leading the humble township of Anthem, overdoses were close behind.

Circling back to the subject of *bored teens in a shithole town drinking*, if I were going to find Rox anywhere tonight, it would be a party. A party with alcohol. Drugs? Give or take. Rox was crafty enough to sneak wine coolers from gas stations but hated drinking alone. When Mom would drive me past taverns, she'd point inside and say those were the guys who drank to forget because whatever demons would surface the drunker they got, company would offer proper distraction. I suppose Rox had a similar experience. Rox was a beggar but not a chooser when it came to both poison and company, otherwise they wouldn't be caught dead at high school functions.

But if Rox didn't suffer fools, they suffered bullies even less. Our freshman year of high school, a classmate of ours named Colin was transitioning and changed her name to Sybil. Despite her protests, the school refused to change the name in the class roster. Each morning when her deadname was barked across the classroom, Sybil refused to adhere and was sent to in-school detention every day. Rox took it upon themself to right this wrong by teaching themself to hack the mainframe of the school computer system to change Sybil's registered name to the name she now owned for herself. Rox earned themself a three-day suspension in the process. When I asked them how they found the time to learn how to do such things, they said they never let school get in the way of their education.

Both students and teachers at Blount High School knew the football team hosted a rager immediately following Senior Night for players and cheerleaders alike. Tonight it was at quarterback Torrie Coates' house out in the country. While I personally never cared for ragers and was never much of a drinker, I didn't want Rox to feel alone. Wherever Rox's head was at these days, it was 100 percent possible to feel completely alone in a house full of people.

"Torrie Coates' house? As in *toxic-masculinity-poster-child* Torrie Coates? Have you completely lost your mind?" my friend Sasha asked while trimming her unibrow in the mirror. Sasha's parents were immigrants from Pakistan and had pause allowing a boy into their daughter's bedroom, so the door was required to be cracked open.

"You know Rox is gonna be there for one reason and one reason only," I said.

"Yeah, to get shitfaced and spend the next day at school blaming us for not intervening," Sasha snapped back. "It really hasn't dawned on you that not going at all is seen as *less* of an offense to them than going and knowing better than to stand in the way of their self-destructing?" Sasha had a knack for making common sense land like a hydrogen bomb, but she had a point. She shifted her fashion options to crop tops and leather pants once she internally accepted where the evening would take us.

All friends have their differences between one another, whether it be their interests or opinions. Although Rox and I had our differences from time to time, they paled in comparison to the differences between me and Sasha. Chief among these differences was the type of credit that doesn't quite stand out to others the way it does to queer people, but especially in a social setting: the credit of straightness. The credit of straightness requires no real effort or skill, but it *does* require the pure dumb luck of happenstance. On the other side of the coin, having to accommodate the "luck" of being queer in a town like Anthem requires constant skill, vigilance, alertness, and caution. Caution of who would kiss and hold you in the privacy of their own room but would never want to be seen dead with you in the hallways. Caution of who was showing interest in you as a prank or some cruel gimmick for his buddies. Caution of a strategically placed video in a classmate's social media algorithm painting you as society's gravest ill in desperate need of stomping out as soon as possible.

One of the strangest beauties of this difference between me and Sasha was her complete obliviousness to the delights of straightness 99 percent of the time, but never was it more clear to me than when she was acquiring a commodity so abundant yet so elusive to me: male attention. In all fairness, I considered Sasha to be the single most beautiful girl in the entire school and I was not alone in the sentiment. Attendance in volleyball games grew as she rose through the ranks of the team, as Sasha had a beauty undeniable enough to keep boys interested and keep girls jealous. And in the strange calculus of high school social synchrony, female jealousy meant female friendship.

Sasha always says that beauty is subjective, but the attention she received from both guys and girls was not something she could rationalize.

I said, "Rox needs their friends now more than ever and beyond that, they need company tonight that won't make them feel like even more of a freak than they already feel they are."

"Ill," Sasha snapped, "if you haven't noticed or you don't want to, Rox's friends *have* been at their side and have been since the day they got back. I literally offered to take them off campus for lunch on my own dime to talk to them, and they shoved me off. They were only, what, the *sixth* student this year to get shipped off to Revival? A few psalm verses around a campfire and rosaries to pray the pronouns away for a whole summer. Do they want a parade for their service?"

Sasha won't be a *spoonful of sugar* mother by any stretch of the imagination. But it would be unfair of both you and me to hold her up to the relationship Rox and I share and the deeper understanding therein. Sasha didn't read Rox's stories and didn't witness firsthand the drastic change their approach took following their return from their four months at Revival. Rox protected their protagonist, almost to the point where the overall plot progression suffered.

Why protection? Why now?

"If you go with me tonight, I promise I'll take care of your midterm research paper for English," I said.

"Does that include the lit review?" she asked.

Goddammit.

"Yes," I replied begrudgingly.

"Deal!" Sasha said, stretching out to shake my hand. If you made a deal without breaching some academic/ethical gray area, it wasn't a deal with Sasha Dehwar.

Sasha's parents arrived from Pakistan in the early 2000s in the wake of Operation Enduring Freedom. Her father was invited to work at a manufacturing plant outside of Knoxville as his background in Pakistan focused on engineering and construction. As the demand for manual labor began increasing as trade schools began shuttering at the turn of the 21st century, a wave of Islamophobia and xenophobia swept the country at the same time following 9/11. Suffice it to say it was difficult to assess whether Sasha's parents arrived in the States at a better time or a worse one.

Three

ONCE SASHA AND I drove well over 20 miles into God's green creation, we had made it to Torrie Coates' farm where at least 30 blackened silhouettes surrounded the two-story farmhouse. The sound system was blasting music loud enough to be audible for at least three miles in any direction. Sasha was still applying her makeup in the visor mirror of the passenger seat while I clung onto every remaining second spent *not* walking towards the vast sea of silhouettes dimly lit by the orange glow of the bonfire.

I hated parties. My heart was racing so fast I was certain Sasha would have heard it if her hearing was attuned to catch just a decibel or two extra. My eyes were pulsating while they gawked at the congregation of partygoers when a faint glisten on the steering wheel caught my eye. A single drop of sweat streaked down the surface of the left side of the wheel. My palms were pools of sweat.

"Alright, let's fuck shit up," Sasha said, clamping her foundation container shut loud enough to startle me out of my trance. She grasped both my hands immediately without being perturbed by the sweat I had accrued, since this was hardly an unfamiliar sight for her. She looked directly into my eyes and delivered the routine missive, "Ilya Burkhart, you are going to wipe the sweat off your hands, look in the rearview mirror, and remind yourself of that bad bitch you are. We are both going into that Podunk party and we are both gonna be the baddest bitches in sight. Right?"

"Right," I said sheepishly.

"Sorry, my hearing must be getting shot by the shitty trap music blasting out of those shitty speakers . . ." Sasha had my number for making me pig-snort laugh at any moment. ". . . RIGHT?!"

She shouted so loud it caught the attention of nearby partygoers.

"RIGHT!" I shouted back, smiling like an idiot. We grasped each other's hands and brought our dumb, smiling faces within an inch of each other.

Sasha said, "Let's tear this hillbilly bitch UP!"

We were both immediately hit with the smell of vodka and vape smoke (grapefruit, I think) once we entered the front door into the crowded living room. Mathlete Alexa Fuller was seated on top of stoner Max Volpe as they made out on a love seat in the corner. It wasn't terribly uncommon to see these types of matchups at ragers for a handful of reasons:

1) The couple is typically under 21 and they don't have fake IDs, meaning ragers are the only venue where they can get properly drunk enough to make out like codfish.

2) Everyone is too drunk, stoned, crossed, or sad to remember who kissed who so it becomes lost in the deluge of hearsay anyway.

3) Billy Joel was right, Catholic girls start much too late.

Since I was designated driver and couldn't rely on liquid courage, I set my sights for Rox and figured they would be in the basement. The criteria for scoping out Rox was simple enough since they preferred being close to the crowd but not in it. It didn't occur to me how long I had stood in place until I lifted my feet and residue unfastened from the bottom of my shoes and the wooden floor. My shoes' unfastening from the sticky floor was loud and sudden enough to alert nearby partygoers who shifted their attention towards me instantly. My face turned bright red, and I hurried past the crowd towards the basement door as onlookers chuckled at my expense. Did I mention I hate parties? I descended the stairs past a line of couples waiting anxiously to "use" the guest room (especially the guys, liquid courage only lasts so long). I made my way to the common room where a group of the wrestling team was playing air hockey and a group of band kids was playing an old Nintendo 64.

No Rox.

I asked, "Hey, has anyone seen Rox tonight?"

"Who?" Gary Flowers, a wrestler, asked without looking up from the air hockey table.

"Green-haired dude," his teammate Thomas Brockman replied.

"They're *not* a dude," I fumed.

"Jury's out," Brockman said.

Assholes.

Gary said, "Yeah, she was headed to the backyard by herself, took some Jameson with her." I didn't bother correcting him, it'd just be to their satisfaction at this point. I was headed upstairs past the brothel line when I saw Sasha with her volleyball friends in the kitchen. Sasha didn't drink since alcohol was haram, but she struggled with FOMO. Her shot glass usually held water.

I ventured out into the smoke-littered dark of the backyard where a large assortment of partygoers was gathered around the bonfire, some taking in the respite of a cigarette. Half the school must have been there as one frenzied conglomerate which, in retrospect, played a massive role in the events which would play out the same night.

I shouted, "Rox! Are you out here? Rox?" No answer. I hated drawing any attention to myself but was beginning to feel more nervous with each square footage of the yard I scoped out.

"I thought you hated parties. They make you anxious," I heard from behind. It was Rox's voice. I turned to find them wearing a blue hoodie and black skinny jeans while smoking a cigarette. They had dyed their hair green since I saw them at school two weeks ago.

"I do," I said, "but when my friends need my help, I tend to make an exception."

"I don't need you or *anyone* else to be worried about me." Rox sneered.

"That's not how friendship works, Rox. It's not a faucet you turn off. You're ditching school, not talking to your friends, getting drunk —"

"I'm *not* drunk," Rox interrupted.

"Why else would you be at this shit party?"

"I like being sociable."

"Oh, so just as long as it's *not* the people who actually give a shit about your well-being?"

Rox's nose scrunched up, their official symbol of when things have gone too far but they won't say as much. I noticed out of the corner of my eye a handful of partygoers had taken notice of our squabble.

"I just wanna have a fun night and forget about all the bullshit," Rox said. "If you cared about me, you'd let me enjoy myself, but since that doesn't involve you coming to my rescue, it's no wonder you're throwing a bitchfit about it."

This drew some verbal reactions from the crowd including various exclamations of "ohhh!" and "daaamn!" I could feel my forehead and cheeks becoming flushed.

I replied, "I'm not rescuing anyone, Rox. All I want is for us to talk since we haven't in months."

"Talk about what, exactly? Our bullshit stories? Campbell's hero's journey? Here's something you might not know, Ilya. While you're at home penning some John Green offshoot, these people are actually *living* stories they can tell their kids one day. Stories where they made actual friends and actual memories." At this point, anyone within earshot was watching our battle of wits.

"We *did* make memories, Rox," I said as a lump formed in my throat. "We *were* friends and we still *are*."

Rox scanned the crowd which had formed at the last minute. "I'm getting another drink. Don't put this in your fucking story."

My ears were hot more out of embarrassment than anger, and I was suddenly sick to the pit of my stomach. The aroma of weed and bonfire smoke wasn't helping my condition, and if half the school was indeed here, a quarter of them just watched me make an asshole of myself in front of my best friend.

———

I stormed back into the house, took an immediate left turn into a crowded hallway, and threw myself into the nearest bathroom, jumping at least three people waiting in line. I sat myself on the fuzzy toilet seat cover and started bawling my eyes out while fists began raining on the wooden door and obscenities were shouted at me from the other side. I felt like a complete idiot sitting in that disgusting bathroom. The banging on the door and the shouts and insults hailing from outside didn't bother me nearly as much as the thought of losing my childhood best friend after wanting nothing less than to help them. Sasha was no doubt making out with some random jock at this point in the night, meaning I was truly alone in a sea of high schoolers, dozens of whom I just embarrassed myself in front of. My sobs became even stronger when I realized that Rox was just as alone as I was that night, and I ruined any chance of them having company that didn't laugh at them behind their back.

"Yo, Ilya, is that you?" a voice from outside said. A male voice.

"Please go away," I shouted back.

"Ilya, it's *Jordan*." Jordan Flores, a.k.a. the only athlete at Blount who would give me the time of day unironically. "Listen, Ill, I'm sorry about whatever happened. I really am." He really was. "But people have a right to throw up and cry in private just as much as you."

This quip resulted in my first genuine smile since getting out of the car with Sasha. Without saying anything, I flushed the toilet (no idea why) and headed towards the door. Jordan was waiting for me and gripped my right shoulder before he led me down the hall to a private room past the irked crowd I had jumped ahead of. Before you get any ideas, just know Jordan has been a big brother to me since he was my neighbor growing up. But I would be lying if I said I hadn't had a slight crush on him since my freshman year, as did most underclassmen. He sat me on the bed and handed me a red Solo cup of water.

He said, "I saw what happened between you and Roxanne. I'm really sorry. I know you, and I know you were just trying to be a friend." I nodded in agreement as I emptied my red Solo cup in two massive gulps.

"Thank you for saying that," I said, "and for what it's worth, I don't see Rox as some sad puppy in the rain who needs rescuing. I never did when we were kids, and I never will."

"It's fascinating, though. She's always come off —"

"*They*," I interrupted.

"Right, sorry, *they've* always come off as so . . . hard-boiled and rough-around-the-edges at school that I never saw them as anyone who couldn't take care of themself. I don't know, maybe that's exactly what they want us to think."

Jordan was more right than he knew. I knew Rox better than anyone and I knew their efforts to throw people off their scent only surfaced when they needed attention the most. Their stories told me more than their haircut and black pierced jeans told the school, even before Revival.

Jordan said, "Believe it or don't, my cousin Jozie went to camp with them this summer, actually."

"*Revival?*"

"Yeah, coincidence, no?" Jordan's reply was casual but his eyes dropped and began darting across the floor. It was odd. Jordan was the charmer of the halls at Blount, and I'd never seen him lose his cool.

I mumbled, "Was Jozie . . ."

"Jozie was . . . *something*, yeah." The tone of his voice was dropping off. "She loved the outdoors, though, and jumped at the opportunity for a summer full of outdoors and fun. They make it no secret in the brochure that it's a church camp, but she didn't care. My mom and dad grew up hearing Revival stories and even had Revival kids as classmates. They never told me their feelings on the subject, all I know is they freeze up when I ask about my uncle Marty and aunt Dottie."

"Jozie's parents?"

"Yeah." Jordan's eyeline had not left the wooden floorboards since the discussion on Jozie had erupted, and it wasn't until I gulped that I noticed how dry my tongue and throat had become in the three minutes since I devoured an entire cup of water.

I asked, "Have you seen Jozie since?"

"No, but my Snapchat streak with her ended sometime in August."

"They don't take their phones away at camp?"

"She told me they can use them for a minute or so before lights out, but our streak had been going for *four* years, ever since the day she started using Snap. But then again, she's in the seventh grade and I remember shit getting rough for me at that age anyway."

My mind was spinning with a cacophony of questions I knew better than to ponder, much less ask Jordan for myself. Before I had a chance to further investigate, Sasha suddenly materialized in the frame of the door with a look of hot panic in her eyes.

"We need to go NOW!" She trembled.

"Cops?" Jordan asked, standing.

"No," Sasha said, "but there *will* be soon, and we can't afford to be seen here." Before I had time to process, my left arm was thrust onward by her grip, and I was being led into a manic swarm of partygoers darting every which way.

"Is it Rox?" I shouted.

"No," Sasha shouted back, scanning for a hole in the motioning mob. The two of us were swallowed up by the frenzied horde and were involuntarily thrust to the front door like a riptide had been angrily awakened. It was a hellish scene watching the same darkened silhouettes from earlier in the evening now racing to their cars, some tripping and sliding on the gravel. It wasn't until Sasha and I had made it to the Jeep that I started hearing girlish sobs from the front lawn. Every other sob was interrupted by a panicked yelp which sounded like a hiccup from a dried throat. The sounds only made the picture feel all the more nightmarish.

"Get us the hell out of here!" Sasha barked as we jumped in my car.

My senses had not caught up with me until shortly after the key had been turned and the gear shift thrust forward. I could finally process the blur of police lights barreling towards us and the hellish picture we were leaving behind us.

As I lay in bed waiting for updates from Sasha, I was thinking about Rox, Jordan's cousin Jozie, and the previous generations who passed through Anthem with the misfortune of being queer or trans. I knew Revival had a troublesome reputation during my mom's time in the '90s, but when testimonies from the teens and parents weren't lining up, no civil case ever materialized and the community was assured it was an "anti-Christian campaign" fueled by a "liberal tidal shift" in society. Since Anthem had a church of every denomination on every street corner, speaking out against Revival was speaking out against the community.

It was common knowledge at Blount that Revival had toned down the queer-bashing since the previous pastor was sacked in the '90s. In fact, campers would come home at the end of summer with nothing but positive things to say about the experience. I kept repeating in my head what Jordan said about teens being depressed and moody anyway. Rox has always been an up-and-down friend since I knew them. In fact, memory served too well for me to forget moments in our friendship wheen they weren't at some point moody, distant, and combative.

I was remarkably close to feeling reassured enough to make even a feeble attempt to fall asleep before my room was flooded with white light from my phone. It was Sasha.

I answered, "Hello?" I heard nothing for seven straight seconds but muffled sobs before Sasha gave me a reason to be grateful my mom was off shift tonight.

Four

I DON'T KNOW IF you've ever had the misfortune of walking the halls of a high school in the wake of a student's death, but it's even more sobering than it sounds. You realize how petty and fruitless teen drama was all along when the halls are completely silent with the exception of pitiful footsteps and sobs from students and teachers alike. A sickly sensation formed in the center of my gut as I walked past a soldiering queue of pale faces. Whether they had hundred- or thousand-yard stares, they all eventually circled back to the loss of senior Brent Cushman. I was too young to have formed any noteworthy rapport with Brent, but everyone at Blount knew they would be hard-pressed to find a student more impassioned by his faith in both God and in other people, even strangers.

Anthem was never short of its fair share of bible-thumpers, but Brent brought a mixture of unconditional kindness and generosity to his approach that would make even the most staunch atheists of the world second-guess their convictions. Students and teachers would be equally as hard-pressed to find a single reason why such a soul as Brent would be driven to drink himself to death in a classmate's basement during a rager. Although no suitable answer would materialize in this lifetime, the entire student body of Blount and two-thirds of Anthem were nonetheless siphoned into the school's gymnasium for some semblance of direction that Monday morning in October.

I found Sasha high up in the stands seated next to her volleyball friends. The gymnasium floor and its usual mustard-colored and eroded wooden panels were covered by black tarp, and the mobile stage typically reserved for graduation and the Veterans Day assembly was wheeled out to center floor. To the left-hand side of the floor, I noticed Brent's mother and father conversing with none other than Anthem's very own Pastor Erick Neary, a heavyset man in his mid-30s with red hair and a beard.

Pastor Neary was one of the few figureheads in Anthem to be completely engulfed in mystery, as choosing to be anything but overbearingly transparent in a town like Anthem earned you immediate suspicion and equally immediate dismissal from circles. Typically, it was Catholic priests who had a shield of enigma built into their line of work since they couldn't marry or have children. But Pastor Neary was not a priest nor did he have a spouse or any children, and since priests and pastors alike were shrinking in numbers, Anthem knew better than to beg *and* choose. Pastor Neary was not fire-and-brimstone by any means, and his Millennial status bought him just enough good faith (no pun intended) with young people to keep youth groups active and afloat.

Personally, I never minded Pastor Neary. I thought he had genuinely good intentions and walked the walk when it came to practicing what you preach. If he had an issue with Adam and Steve, he knew better than to broadcast it, but especially with regard to the impact it would have on the liberal sensibilities of his youth groups. Sadly, I could not attribute the same spirit of allyship (or even neutrality) to other faith leaders in Anthem, but as far as I knew, Pastor Neary was aboveboard. But even after his decade of service towards his parish and his community, Pastor Neary could never shake his reputation of being a Rubik's Cube that scurried back into hiding before you could crack it.

The juxtaposition between the usual electric fervor of the crowds at pep rallies, basketball games, and volleyball games in that very gymnasium and the subdued murmur of voices on that Monday morning was too sobering for words. A handful of Brent's senior photos were displayed across the mobile stage, and the wooden podium usually reserved for graduation awaited Pastor Neary and whichever other poor souls had the misfortune of addressing the better part of Anthem.

"It's fucked up how much this looks like Brent's graduation, doesn't it?" Sasha asked.

I replied, "Holy shit, you're right. With the senior photos and podium?"

"Exactly, not to mention the whole freaking school and town being here. It feels so . . ."

"*Ominous?*"

"Yep, that's it. It's kind of giving me anxiety, not gonna lie."

It wasn't until Sasha mentioned anxiety that I noticed her right hand was stretched out and shaking, palm-side up. Sasha once joked I was her human Xanax pill. I took her hand in mine and braced myself for the usual white-knuckled squeeze.

"I definitely don't envy the pastor," I said, keeping Sasha's mind distracted.

"No doubt," she replied. "I would feel like a news anchor who just got told the world was ending. What do I even say to the people watching, y'know?" I nodded in agreement while I scanned the stands. No Rox. I had not heard from them at all since our encounter at the rager on the night which will live in infamy.

"What happened with you and Rox?" Sasha asked. "I heard there was a fight or something?"

"It was not a fight. They just bitched me out for trying to be their friend is all. Y'know, Rox stuff."

"Did I tell you to expect anything less? This is just their weird, manipulative cycle, and for some reason you keep going back for more."

I replied, "Mom says a true friend can only be measured by how willing they are to stick by your side on your worst days."

"Bad days are one thing, Ill. Letting someone drain you of your energy by making you liable for their own shit is another."

"I get where you're coming from, I really do. But it's not like this has been Rox's MO since I met them. They've *changed* since last summer, and I'm getting to the bottom of why one way or another. Mom didn't raise a fair-weather friend even if you'd prefer I be one."

Sasha's eyes cast downward as the side of her lip scrunched up. She mumbled, "I miss Carol a lot, believe it or not."

I smiled for the first time in 48 hours. I replied, "She misses you too."

"Promise I can spend the night soon for wine-and-movie night?"

"Of course, just promise you won't pee your pants on my mom's duvet again," I replied with a smirk. Sasha was about to feign anger and rain fists down on me before the booming sound of a mic test silenced the room in a split second.

"Attention, folks," Principal Perdun said, "we're 'bout ready to get things goin'." Perdun's voice sounded gravelly, the way mine would sound the morning after going to a concert. He resumed, "Good morning, uh . . . Blount students and faculty . . . as well as the great city of Anthem. We are, of course, gathered this morning to mourn the untimely and *immeasurable* —"

The way his voice reached a peak in tone before his lips sealed shut will never leave my memory. Pastor Neary firmly grasped Perdun's left shoulder before he flung into the pastor's open arms in front of well over two thousand people, bursting into hysterical sobs. Since I had lived with a single mother since I was four months old, I could say with confidence that I had never seen a grown man cry with my own eyes until that day, at least not one that wasn't acting in a play or musical. Principal Perdun cried for what felt like five whole minutes, although he more than likely hadn't broken the plane of 30 seconds.

Perdun spoke. "I'm sorry, I'm sorry. My wife told me to speak from the heart and mind alike. The heart because it knows the truth and the mind because it knows what I can bear saying without bawlin' like a baby." This got a pitiful laugh from roughly half the crowd. "But the fact of the matter is, we lost a true one-of-a-kind soul over this weekend. Brent Cushman understood the impact people could have on this world merely by the most ordinary and even mundane acts of kindness. He understood as well as anyone in Blount High and all of Anthem the power each of us has to do right by each other through generosity and unconditional friendship."

It wasn't until this point in the memorial that I caught from the corner of my eye Sasha wiping away tears with the cuff of her hoodie sleeve. I instinctively put my left arm around her shoulders before she wrapped herself around me with one arm on each side of my chest and hugged me tightly. Nearly all of my friends were not huggers, but Sasha was a *big* hugger, and fortunately for her, so was I. Pastor Neary promptly relieved the principal of his post and took over emcee duties as Perdun collected himself.

"Psalms tell us that the Lord is near the brokenhearted and saves the crushed in spirit," Pastor Neary said, his voice booming through the PA system.

Sasha lowered her head in prayer. She was Muslim but was still respectful of other faiths. The loss of a child has a knack for bridging gaps.

Pastor Neary powered through. "Why should we as God's children ask for His comfort after he removed a soul such as Brent Cushman from this world? If a follower of God's will such as Brent has no place in His plan past an age so young with so little of his potential fulfilled, why should we continue to teach God's will?" One of the reasons I respected Pastor

Neary was his critical approach to faith. He was never one to accept things as they were but rather questioned them and inspired young people to do the same. He was something of a rogue.

The pastor continued, "Instead of wasting our precious time on this Earth searching for answers we will never find, I implore friends and family of Brent to take solace in the fact that a soul such as him can choose kindness so consistently in a world that seems hell-bent on hardening us. From working triple shifts at soup kitchens in Kingsport during the holidays to spending his summer this year as a counselor at Revival, Brent could never bring himself to enjoy times for leisure when he knew other souls were suffering."

My blood went cold. Brent worked at Revival? The silence of the room was punctured by a murmur of whispers of students talking amongst themselves. The pastor's speech summoned a great enthusiasm in the stands of the gymnasium but surely not the way he intended. If Brent Cushman was the poster child for all things Christian, why was his spending a summer at a *faith* camp such a cause for conversation now?

"Please, if we could bring our minds and hearts *back* to the celebration of Brent's legacy," Pastor Neary pleaded, desperate to curtail his evocation of Revival. But it was clear in the pastor's tone that he knew there was no closing this Pandora's box.

Neary steadied on. "Surely there are strong emotions related to the . . . *untimely* loss of Brent and all he leaves behind." His efforts to move the conversation onward only fueled what started off as mild intrigue into instant furor in the student body. As much as the author in me hates clichés, suffice it to say, the cat was out of the bag.

"Please," the pastor pleaded, "if I know Brent like we all did, he would not want us to turn to —"

"YOU FUCKERS KILLED HIM!" a student yelled. This dialed up the uproar in the room instantly. "You fucking *brainwashed* him like every other kid in this fucking town!" Every person above the age of 30 had their sights set on the stands trying pathetically to ease the tumult.

At this point, Principal Perdun had relieved the pastor and stepped in. "Students of Blount High, we beg of you to not let your emotions get the better of you and tarnish the memory of one of Anthem's finest —"

"You're the reason we're all here!" a female student shouted. "You're the reason he and my cousin both drank themselves to death!" The uproar turned to full pandemonium in what felt like seconds, but in that same instant my peripheral vision caught something only I would consider material during the commotion: Rox was sneaking out. I had sights on Rox only for a brief second before my view was obstructed by half the Blount student body rising to their feet in protest of the powers that be who aided and abetted Revival Church Camp.

"If I don't see every butt on a bench in three seconds, you can forget about off-campus lunch the rest of the year!" Principal Perdun shouted, stepping up the authority in his voice exponentially. Although there were a handful of holdouts, Perdun's ultimatum was abided by collectively. The electricity of the gymnasium was not so quick to die down, but the memorial ceremony charged onward as murmurs gradually diminished as Brent Cushman's memory took center stage once again. Even in his memory, Brent was bridging a formidable divide.

Despite the chaos that erupted via the mere *mention* of Revival, the rest of the school day was dull and surprisingly boring. Rox wasn't answering their texts, and nobody at Blount but me seemed interested in locating them, at least I thought as much before Sasha ran into me during passing period in the hallway.

"Any luck finding Rox?" she asked.

"No. But I have an idea of where they might've run off to."

"That's great! When are we going?"

"*We?*" I asked dumbfoundedly. "As in plural?"

This obviously hit a sore spot for Sasha, whose enthusiasm dropped.

She said, "Ilya, I'm sorry for the other night. You were right, Rox is our friend and friends don't walk away when things get weird."

"You don't need to be sorry; I get it. Rox has that effect on people."

"But the difference is we take friends as they are *now*, not who they used to be or who we *prefer* they be for our own comfort." It felt like Sasha's cadaver had been vacated and instantly inhabited by my mother's spirit.

I said, "If I know Rox like I think I do, they're loading up on as many insults as they can to drive us away when we show up."

"I know," Sasha replied, "so who's gonna drive?"

Five

THERE WERE A HANDFUL of unspoken rules in my friendship with Rox, one of which surrounded where they could be found depending on how much they wanted to be. Sasha and I rode in her old green Infiniti to the outskirts of town towards the deeper swells of the countryside.

"And you're *sure* they'll be there?" Sasha asked with her hands on the wheel.

"No, but it'll tell us whether it's a wash to try."

"A lot of gas and energy to waste. You'd think eight unanswered texts would —"

"Rox doesn't work that way," I said. "They play chess. They're complicated."

"*Manipulative* can be said in only so many words."

"I didn't force you to help Rox."

The pause that followed thickened the tension to the thousandth degree.

"I'm not helping Rox," Sasha said. "I'm helping *you*."

"Then what was all that back at school about 'standing by your friends when things get weird'?"

"That was half an ungodly trek through creation and however many gallons of gas ago. Who does this to friends? Who manipulates them through fucked-up mind games and trickery?"

"Rox does. My best friend does."

Sasha let a deep exhale out of her nose. The tone in my voice was enough to let her know I was through fighting with a best friend in the process of locating another.

"We'll find them, Ill, don't worry," Sasha said reassuringly. She rubbed my back with her right hand and continued driving.

In modern-day Tennessee, places like Revival practiced openly for decades and continued to do so, leading to a plentiful amount of unsettling lore discussed mostly in basements, at sleepovers, and during late-night car rides. But even deeper in the state's closet, or rather its *forests*, are remnants of the past left to decay. Remnants such as the Juvenile Rehabilitation Center once inhabited by teens deemed menaces to society that was shuttered during the late 2000s due to lack of funding but continued to embrace troubled teens to this day.

Troubled teens such as Rox.

The cluster of yellow weeds and grass that blanketed the road which once led visitors to the front door of the building was beaten enough for us to follow. Any revenge young people wanted to take against all the three-storied "rehab center" stood for in its prime was more than taken over in the past decade by means of shattered windows and graffitied walls. Nature appeared hell-bent on retaliation as well, as thick, thorny vines climbed the brick walls towards the roof like the tentacles of an angered Kraken taking its sweet, ungodly time to devour. The idea that the same fate awaited Revival made me smile.

"You're worried Rox is ignoring us and *not* worried they died from asbestos poisoning in there?" Sasha asked.

"Not as much as I'm worried about *that*," I said, gesturing upward through the windshield.

Rox towered above both of us, seated on the windowsill of one of the second-floor cells smoking a cigarette.

"Subhanallah," Sasha said, "they told us they were quitting."

"There are worse coping habits," I said dismissively while climbing out of the Infiniti.

"There are better ones too," Sasha said before surrendering and following my lead.

If the hasty calculus in my mind was correct, Rox was open to the comfort of friends but was not letting us off easy by any means.

"Thank you for driving here, Sash," Rox said from above. "I'll recoup your money."

"That's okay, Rox," Sasha said. "I'm happy to be —"

"She didn't exactly come here alone," I interrupted.

"I never said she did, Ilya," Rox snapped. "Just showing some appreciation."

"Appreciation, that's nice," I said. "I'm relieved that word's still in your vocabulary."

Sasha's feigned smile dropped as she closed in on me for a sidebar. "Ilya, what the hell?"

I replied, "I'm taking the scenic route, trust me."

She backed off but was none too pleased. I had to remember she was a novice when it came to Rox management.

"How's the cig?" I asked finally.

Rox replied, "It's alright . . . good blend."

"Blend of what, exactly? Arsenic and formaldehyde or carbon monoxide and tar?" What having a nurse as a mother does to you. Rox stayed quiet but kept smoking.

"You told us you were on an antidepressant," Sasha said. "Dula something?"

"Duloxetine and yes, I am," Rox replied.

"It's not working, then?"

"It *is*," Rox said before taking a long drag. "This is just a nice bonus."

I let out a brief chuckle, but Sasha was by no means amused. I noticed our view of Rox and the dilapidated building were beginning to lose light, which meant dusk was creeping in.

"I saw you leave Brent's memorial service," I said. "It's unlike you to leave during all the excitement."

"There's nothing *exciting* about a good person dying," Rox snapped, taking another long drag of their cigarette, "much less a child."

"He was 18, Rox," Sasha said.

"And?" Rox asked.

Sasha had no instant rebuttal and elected instead to let the awkward seconds of silence ride out. Before I could map out which direction to take to minimize further tension, Sasha decided to throw caution (and subtlety) to the wind.

"Did you know he worked at Revival?" Sasha asked, unaware of how much she jumped the gun.

Rox lasered in on Sasha with a fixed stare before their eyes began lowering until they were staring directly down, almost as if they were scoping out where they would land if they jumped.

"Rox?" I asked.

No reply, and I noticed it had been at least two minutes since their last drag. Before Sasha (a.k.a. Makeshift Perry Mason) and I could investigate further, Rox suddenly retreated into the second-floor cell but not before throwing their cigarette to the spot immediately below them.

God only knows when and where they would eventually exit the building.

"How the hell did they even *get* here?" Sasha asked.

"Followed the creek," I said, "like when we were kids."

"Oh."

"There's so much of them still in there, Sash. That's why I'm here."

"That's why *we're* here," Sasha said before taking my hand in hers.

The two of us accepted defeat and turned back for our sluggish retreat to the green Infiniti. The harsh chill from the setting sun and inching shadows stung our flesh in a climate only the month of October could offer. It reminded me of morning P.E. classes in elementary school when the teacher would tell us to breathe in through our nose and out through our mouths as we ran our laps to "warm the air" before it got to our lungs. I was hopeful Rox would heed the same advice, as it was clear they would be taking the creek back home.

"He found something," we heard from behind. Sasha and I whipped our heads around and found Rox standing not seven feet behind us.

"Who did?" Sasha asked.

"*Brent*," Rox said. "He discovered something this summer."

"What exactly?" I asked.

"I don't know," Rox said, "but I remember around the end of June, everything changed with him. Nobody knew what or why."

Even if Sasha couldn't tell, I noticed this wasn't Rox's usual tone of enigma and faux mystery. Far from it, in fact. They were genuinely as stumped as we were, which was not a common occurrence.

"What do you mean *change*?" Sasha asked. Rox took a pause to process while narrowing their eyes back down to their black laced-up combat boots.

"You need to understand that Brent didn't know a stranger," they said finally. "That bullshit memorial service made it sound like he was the teetotaling . . . spitting image of Job, but it went *so much* deeper than that. It was more than him securing his place in heaven or whatever the fuck."

Rox's eyes began swelling up with tears as they drew their box of cigarettes out of their jean pocket. Whether it be the dropping temperature or their reliving of things they'd rather forget (or a combination of the two), Rox's hands were trembling as they holstered a cig between their quivering lips.

"He didn't see it as 'fixing' kids," Rox said as they drew a lighter from a back pocket. "He told me nobody needed fixing because nobody was *broken*."

This single minute of conversation contained more spoken words from Rox than the past two months leading up to this point.

For someone who considered himself a liaison to Rox's mind, I found myself drawing a blank on how to proceed. Sasha and I were frozen up like children caught in a dark kitchen eating birthday cake by a blinding light from above, switched on by their father.

"What do you think he found?" Sasha asked.

Rox began shaking their head. "I don't know, but I do know there's a direct thread between *it* and *him* drinking himself to death."

"He wanted to forget it," I said, "whatever it was."

"Exactly," Rox said.

It wasn't until there was a distinct quiver in my voice that I noticed my teeth were chattering from the cold. It went from chilly to freezing, and I knew this conversation couldn't conclude in the next two or even five minutes.

"Rox, can we continue this talk in the car?" Sasha asked, taking the words out of my mouth.

Rox's biggest surprise of the day was still in store for us. They smiled and replied, "I'd like that."

One singular question was suspended in the air for the car ride home and lingered there as neither Sasha nor I wanted to risk compromising Rox's improved mood. The conversation in the woods was the most Rox had bridged the gap between us and the events they and so many others endured at Revival. I had become so fucking sick of that word. *Revival.* A word that conveyed promise and hope weaponized by a set of individuals hell-bent on a torment potent enough to drive a decent kid to drink himself to death in a stranger's basement.

The closer Sasha's green Infiniti narrowed in on Anthem city limits, the less real estate we had to investigate further into the goings-on of Rox, Jozie, and Brent's summer. But the silence felt soothing. Not awkward silence exactly, but the type of silence kids in middle school would share after standing up for a friend to a bully's face. After the emotions and adrenaline died down, there would be an invisible tether that bound the juvenile but courageous hearts of the friends together. It was unspoken but felt so tangible, it felt like you could pluck it and watch it waver like a guitar string.

Once we eventually did pull up to Rox's trailer home, my throat suddenly dried up as it dawned on me that I wouldn't know when or where I would see them again after tonight. I had to ask something. I had to *say* something.

"When I would take hikes with Brent, we would talk," Rox said from the backseat, startling both me and Sasha. Sasha and I made eye contact, not certain how exactly to reply.

"What about?" Sasha asked finally.

"Too many different things to keep track, but we always circled back to one subject in particular."

"What was it?" I asked.

Rox's eyes darted from one spot on the floor to the other for five straight seconds.

They spoke rapidly. "His mentorship with Pastor Erick Neary."

Before Sasha and I could process, Rox excused themself from the car in a flash. Nobody would see or hear from them for the next five days.

<h1 style="text-align:center">Six</h1>

IT WAS REMARKABLE HOW much information we received that day at the abandoned juvy center yet how unassured we felt as the labyrinth of Brent's death seemed to grow a new branch with each passing day. The hours in school seemed to crawl as the bottomless black crater left by Brent seemed to taunt anyone trying to move on with their life by giving a single damn about trigonometry or biology. If the cafeteria was dominated either by silence or by the usual cacophony of laughs and voices, we would be better off. But the room seemed to be split between effortful small talk and students with empty glares lost in their own world, barely touching their food. The juxtaposition made it clear that some would be more advanced in their grief than others, or would be so lost in the blissful world of shock that they didn't know what awaited them.

The sound of the bell which marked the end of the school day felt like our torsos were finally released from the talons of some rageful beast. Students would dart through the parking lot as if the entire school property was set to be lifted from its earthly constraints towards the sky like some scene from a Marvel movie. It was becoming clear that Blount High had become a makeshift crypt for Brent Cushman that no sane person could survey or stomach for too long.

I learned early on that adults, but most especially parents, are sometimes at a disadvantage to turn to for guidance, as when they see someone as young as their own child die, it is sometimes difficult for them to discern the deceased from their own.

Nonetheless, the topic was broached as Mom and I were grocery shopping at Sinclair's, a food market Mom was particular towards as she preferred to shop locally.

"Would you believe me if I told you half this cart was less than $20 once upon a time?" Mom asked.

I replied, "Did you know it probably still would be if we were at Walmart right now?"

"There's a noose around this town," Mom shot back. "You shop at some piece-of-shit superstore and you tighten it with every cent you spend."

"You don't think it would be a mercy killing?" I quipped.

It was then that Mom shot me the look of someone who knew they were nearing the end of a lost battle. She could have blown up on me in the middle of that store with every known expletive and it wouldn't have spoken *half* of what that exhausted stare did.

"I'm sorry," I said sheepishly.

Mom directed her attention back to the shelves of tomato sauce and resumed her shopping. I felt sick to my stomach and knew from childhood the feeling wouldn't leave until she broke the silence herself.

Finally, she spoke. "The kids that get wheeled into my wing aren't just there because of their stupid friends or unstable parents. It's because someone somewhere behind some desk decided this town and the people in it were no longer worth the investment. Because all the sickness and suffering in the world pale in comparison to things like 'low patient volume' and 'operating margins.'"

"That's fucked up," I said.

"Yes. It is *fucked up*."

"Do you think that's why Revival is still open?"

As nonchalantly as I tried to make the pivot, Mom's affect shifted on a dime.

"They came to the door again, didn't they? Those fuckers!" Mom sneered, her voice springing in volume. Bystanders took notice.

I said, "No! No, they didn't, I swear to God —"

"I told them if they ever came near our house again, I'd take a fucking flamethrower —"

"Mom, I swear to God they didn't bother us," I said frantically. "Nobody came to the house or called, I swear."

This diffused her suspicion but not by and large. "What about that hellhole?" Mom asked as she reached for tomato sauce.

I knew I had stepped in it badly but had to make it worthwhile.

"Brent was a counselor there," I said.

Mom's face scrunched up in confusion. She asked, "Brent *Cushman*? What the hell was a kid like that doing there?"

I said, "I mean, Christianity was sorta his thing, so it —"

"Revival is *not* a Christian institution and don't you forget it."

"Then what *is* it?"

My question had slipped out so involuntarily that it hadn't occurred to me that I had even asked it until Mom's death glare snapped me back into reality. Once her eyes cast downward towards the tan floor below our feet, it had finally occurred to me that the grocery store of a small town was the last place for an inquisition. In a small town like Anthem, beneath every unassuming townsperson who appeared to be minding their business was a vulture hankering for gossip and scandal embedded in the otherwise trivial conversations that inhabited grocery aisles, hair salons, and church pews. But if the look in Mom's eyes relayed anything, it was that this was no trivial conversation, and the subject of Revival transcended the mill of usual small-town gossip.

"I'm sorry, it's not my place to bring it up," I said, finally breaking the silence.

"It's not that," Mom said. "It's a complicated situation is all. There's a lot of conflicting opinions, and it was wrong of me to get it in your head that the place is . . . *evil* or some-thing. That's just the teen in me jumping out, and that was a *much* different time. I'm sure it's changed for the better since then, especially if someone like Brent deemed it worthy of his time and energy."

"Maybe he did at the start."

"Yeah, maybe he did," Mom said with a new tone of irritation. "Can you grab the guac spread I like, please? It's in aisle seven."

Strike three.

Whenever I was over at Sasha's house, I always pondered the same question. If a child with one arm was homeschooled for the first seven years of their education and arrived at a school full of two-armed children, would they feel deprived? Would they feel cheated, or would it really make a difference since having one arm was their accepted reality during their most formative years? It was typical for me to ponder such a thing when I spent time in Sasha's household where a nuclear family posed for Norman Rockwell on a daily basis. Since my father left when I was a baby and Mom was an only child whose father died in a car crash during her college years, I had no true impression of a father outside of film, television, and Sasha's household. I loved Sasha's parents, and they returned the favor by treating me as if I were one of their very own. And if it wasn't abundantly clear already, I'm slightly ashamed to admit that the predictability of Sasha's home was somewhat an oasis for my mental health and sanity over the last six years. Predictability such as a plate of freshly cut strawberries and a bowl of dates waiting for guests when they walked through the front door.

Sasha and I were painting each other's nails in her bedroom with clay masks on as her lo-fi playlist hummed in the background. We had to keep our voices down as afternoon prayer was a landmark in the Dehwar household. "A few of us at clinic today were talking during break, and according to Jami, Brent's parents are thinking of suing for manslaughter," Sasha said.

"Suing *who*, exactly? Everyone who was present that night?" I asked.

"That's what Lexi asked too. I don't really know, to tell you the truth."

"I mean . . . I guess they'd have a case if he was forced to chug or something."

Sasha said, "That's the thing, none of his buddies wanna talk, and nobody can really get a clear story of what was going on in the basement."

"That's honestly pretty messed up," I said. "His parents deserve closure at the very least by knowing what the hell happened. You'd think his friends would want that for them too."

My phone timer went off, letting the two of us know it was time to wipe our masks off.

"Mary said he was alone," Sasha said, climbing off the bed towards her bathroom. "It was so unlike him to be by himself, and he was never much of a drinker until this year."

"It's gotta be Revival," I said to myself.

Sasha must not have heard as she was wiping off her mask with the sink running. She began moisturizing and asked, "Have you heard from Rox lately?"

I smirked. "What do you think?"

"Me neither," she replied. "Every Snap and text I send them that goes unanswered just makes me feel like a bigger and bigger idiot."

"Same. Eventually, you come to accept the fact that they'll come to us on their own terms."

"Do you ever wonder if their being mysterious and cryptic is some kind of facade?"

"Rox has always had a darker side," I said, making my way to the bathroom as Sasha finished up moisturizing. "But they've definitely upped the ante this year."

"I swear this school year feels like we all woke up on another planet," Sasha said from her bed. "There's been some kind of . . . insane *vibe shift* I can't put my finger on. Everyone at clinic today was saying basically the exact same thing."

If gossip was an Olympic sport, volleyball girls would run gold, silver, and bronze.

I had just begun moisturizing when Sasha asked, "Is it any coincidence that Rox and Brent were both at that weird camp this summer and now all this craziness is happening at once?"

My heart skipped a beat.

"You think they're connected?" I asked, feigning casualness to the best of my abilities.

Sasha continued, "I mean . . . we *both* grew up hearing a million different stories, no? About hypnotherapy and sleep deprivation —"

"You don't really believe that, do you?"

Sasha shrugged. "Well . . . most of the stories predate both of us being born. And God knows no scandal in this hick town goes to waste. Do you remember Sabrina from volleyball last year? It was her senior year."

"Yeah, I think so, why?"

"Apparently, her older brother got sent to Revival when he was 17."

"Was he queer or trans or nonbinary?" I asked.

"I'm not sure, but I do remember he was switching up his outfits around his junior year. It wasn't a great year for him. A bunch of bullying, things got ugly on social media, and it was basically impossible for him to use any bathrooms since the only private restroom was in the teachers' lounge."

"So he was *trans*, then?" I asked.

"I truly don't know. And a lot of people were telling Sabrina it was just a phase and it was all only for attention, but if it was, he was a true glutton for punishment."

"When did Sabrina tell you all this?"

"It was in the hotel room when we all went to State. It was basically one big sleepover, and I guess Sabrina never got to vent it to anyone else since her parents wouldn't even touch the subject with her."

"That's awful," I said.

"It really was, most of us were crying. It was one big happy therapy session," Sasha chuckled.

"So what happened to him at Revival?"

Sasha took a massive inhale and loudly exhaled through her nostrils.

"It's fine," I said definitively. "We shouldn't be airing out business that's not our own."

Sasha said, "When her brother got back — Jeremy was his name, I think — it was almost like he didn't want to leave."

"You mean . . . he *liked* being there?" I asked dumbfoundedly.

"According to Sabrina, the smile on his face was so permanent the first week home that her parents were convinced it was never coming off. Apparently, the camp made him feel the most alive he had felt his whole life."

"I can't imagine how relieved his parents were."

"They were absolutely over the moon. They had all the proof they needed that all the cross-dressing and makeup was a phase and the camp showed him how to fill that void in his life."

"You *really* believe that place changed him for the better?"

"I never said I did, Ill," Sasha said, sounding slightly affronted. "I'm just the messenger here."

"I know, I know. I'm sorry, I feel bad putting you in the hot seat like this. It's not our business."

Sasha began shaking her head and said, "It's not that at all, it's just . . ."

"What is it?"

Sasha's eyes told me she was debating saying something she pushed deep down and had to decide quickly whether or not it should stay there.

But nonetheless, she said, "Sabrina never bought it for a *single* second. *Never.* She knew her brother and knew something was not right with him."

"Where is he today?" I asked.

"He goes to some state university in Oregon, I don't remember. But he deleted all his social media so that's all I can really say on the matter."

"Does Sabrina keep in contact with him?"

"Not sure. I haven't seen her in almost a year, and sadly, she deleted her socials as well."

I realized then that we had been so entranced in conversation, we hadn't realized our nail polish had dried completely and needed top coating.

Seven

AS OFTEN IS THE case in the epicenter of October, the sky was an ocean of bright blue unburdened by clouds which would otherwise be echoing the solemnity of Brent Cushman's funeral and burial. While most of the adults in Anthem were provided the day off work to attend, the students of Blount High were only provided a half day. While most students were outraged by what they perceived to be a sign of the administration's apathy, some small part of me understood the reasoning behind it. I suppose the structure and normalcy of school could act as some respite for students as well as faculty once they departed from Brent's "final resting place," as the clergy referred to it.

From what I gathered as I scanned the sea of people, for every tombstone in the cemetery there were at least two attendees. Mind you, that's not a completely gargantuan sight to behold given the population of the town as well as the cemetery. But suffice it to say you could feel the rusty and corroded gears that kept the town of Anthem in operation were brought to a complete halt as it dawned on the towns-people that one of the city's brightest would be laid to rest long before his prime.

If the youth of Anthem were bonded in any sort of way that hellish yet crisp morning in October, it would be from the sensation that we were in the middle of a final exam nobody spent a single second studying for. This was not the funeral and burial of our grandparent or our distant aunt or uncle. None of us understood grief. None of us understood finality in all its nightmarish glory. Hell, some of us were more concerned about running the upcoming mile in P.E. class the next morning or the midterm exam in government later that very day.

Sadly, when it came to the arena of grief, it was the adults who had us outmatched as well as outnumbered. But strangely enough, you would not be able to guess as much by their appearance and affect. The older attendees of the affair were surprisingly untroubled, if not mildly content. Parents of students and various business owners were slapping each other on the back, shaking hands, and discussing pedestrian goings-on as if they were at the Lion's Club's fish fry. Why? Had they skipped the first four stages of grief onto acceptance? Had they become so accustomed to funeral processions over the decades that they had no heart and soul to give anymore? Were they feigning cheerfulness for our sake? As some example for us to follow?

Suddenly, none other than Pastor Neary made his way to the front of the fold. Watching the pastor take any stage was not unlike watching the groundhog decide whether or not it's afraid of its shadow. The concern is absent from your mind 99 percent of the time until it happens again, and suddenly all eyes are focused on the affair with a burst of intensity. It wasn't until my eyes followed him to the front that I noticed Brent's mother and father dressed in black, consoling each other in one another's arms.

Pastor Neary spoke. "In John, chapter 14, Jesus tells us, 'My Father's house has many rooms; if that were not so, would I have told you that I am going there to prepare a place for you?' But those of us standing in the place where one of God's most devout soldiers will be buried, we *don't wish* for Brent Cushman to take a room with God. We want Brent *here*, continuing the Lord's work by spreading both His word and His glory. From this point in time, we will *begin* that journey of processing the pain of Brent's loss as well as the *confusion* regarding God's plan, His will, and His decision to leave a hole in our hearts only one person can fill who is no longer with us."

Once Pastor Neary's sermon came to a natural pause, the silence was informed by a wall of subdued sniffles and sobs. It was at this moment that the pastor withdrew a white handkerchief from his back pants pocket to blow his nose and wipe a cluster of tears away. Suddenly, the sound of sobs and sniffs was disrupted by the sound of footsteps approaching from behind. Before I could look, my hand was cusped into the firm grasp of another.

It was Sasha. She was dressed in a green Nuptse jacket over the black tube minidress she had planned on wearing to homecoming at the end of the month before it was canceled by the committee. I wouldn't argue with anyone who thought it mildly unseemly for a funeral, but more likely than not it was the only black formal attire she owned. After all, a teenage girl's closet is supposed to run deep for homecomings and proms, not funerals. Much less the funeral of a peer.

Pastor Neary continued his sermon. "Some of you may not know this, but —" His face braced itself for a plunge into the coarser part of his sermon. "Brent was a *mentee* of mine the past year. He sought my guidance this past summer while he was a counselor at Revival. Providing him mentorship this past year has been the single most rewarding stage of my career."

As a sudden breath of shock left my lungs, I heard Sasha gasp. It felt as if the huddled mass of grievers that surrounded us disappeared and the grounds of the cemetery housed only the two of us. It felt traitorous to allow our focus to stray from Brent and the Cushman family at that moment, but there was truly no helping the sensation. This was no news to either of us thanks to Rox, but the mere mention of Revival seemed to clench the both of us in a grip of awe and panic.

Neary continued, "The things we discussed in our sessions could fill 10 filing cabinets, but one thing I can tell you folks is this: Brent Cushman was a *healer* in every sense of the word. If there's one thing we discussed in infinite detail, it is the internal struggle felt and sacrifice made by a healer with every person they help. There are only a handful of professions in this world that understand what I mean by that, and Brent was suited to pursue any one of them he chose. But —"

Once again, Pastor Neary's face was coated in crimson red, and once again, he withdrew his handkerchief from his back pants pocket.

"But he will never . . . get to pursue . . . *any* of them." With each word, the struggle to keep his composure faltered worse and worse. Suddenly, the pastor broke down in ugly sobs.

Grueling sobs.

These were not just sobs of grief. These were sobs of deep, deep remorse. As is usually the case in such scenarios, this emotional breakdown acted as the breaching of a massive floodgate for fellow grievers. In other words, permission was granted.

Brent's mother suddenly withdrew herself from the arms of her husband with a violent flare and thrust her arms onto the brown copper steel casket which contained the only child she would ever have. This caused a cacophony of various gasps and bellows of shock from the crowd.

"DON'T PUT HIM DOWN THERE! IT'S NOT TIME. IT'S NOT TIME, GODDAMMIT!" Brent's mother shrieked with the tenor of a maimed animal.

It was at this exact moment Sasha clasped my right shoulder tightly between her biceps and began sobbing into my suit jacket. And it was also at this exact moment that I began sobbing too. I respected Brent and his family too much to put on that patronizing facade of grief with false tears the way some would. But this sadness was more a conglomerate of different feelings. This was physical and emotional exhaustion blending together. I felt no pause or embarrassment with these sobs, not just because men are entitled to any feeling they desire, but mostly because I was joining in a wider symphony of sobs and would go unnoticed.

Eventually, the chaos that erupted in seconds eventually came to a halt as Brent's mother returned to the arms of her husband, assumingly holding her in a *much* stronger grip. Pastor Neary excused himself from the role of emcee and opened up the dialogue for others to speak. A few of Brent's senior buddies spoke, wisely electing *not* to share any crazy partying stories. A considerate amount of Brent's teachers going all the way back to elementary school shared how much of a bright student Brent was and how considerate he was to his classmates, always sharing and going so far as to help his peers struggling in certain subjects understand criteria better.

Sadly, the vast number of speakers failed to hold my attention as I was still in the process of recollecting my emotions and regaining my composure. As my focus began floundering and I continued to be lost in the weeds of my own thoughts, my senses were instantly grounded by the sight of a lone figure high up in the tree line.

It was Rox. They were seated within the lap of a weeping willow stripped of half its golden foliage. And if you hadn't guessed it already, they were smoking. Appropriately enough they were dressed all in black, sporting black skinny jeans, a black men's dress shirt, and their usual black combat boots laced up. They had dyed their hair black since I had last seen them and had fashioned a quiff cut that swerved upward at the front with the sides buzzed. I was careful not to linger on them for too long lest I wanted to point the attention of others in their direction.

But as was usually the case, Rox was a sight to beat all.

I had finally managed to rein my focus back to the proceedings as more of Brent's classmates sang his dizzyingly long list of praises. Sasha seemed to have reined in her own focus as well, as she was laughing at jokes made by speakers and overall sounding more like herself. The proceedings unofficially came to a close around 11 a.m. as classes at Blount were scheduled to resume exactly at noon. Pastor Neary assured the crowd that the microphone would remain open to any and all speakers until sunset, if it came to that.

"Wanna grab lunch?" Sasha asked.

"Yes, please," I begged.

As the two of us made our way to my car parked a mile down the street, we were stopped in our tracks by the voice of Jordan, the Blount Panthers star running back whom I had not spoken to since our brief talk at the senior rager that cost Brent Cushman his life.

"Hey, Ilya! Wait up!" Jordan shouted.

Both Sasha and I turned our heads in his direction in perfect sync. He was dressed to the nines in a tailor-fit black suit, the collar of which seemed to sharpen his stubble-covered jawline fivefold. God help me.

"I was wondering if we could talk before school?" Jordan asked.

"What about?" I asked.

"Something private," Jordan said.

Sasha shot me a dissenting glance. "How *private*?" she asked.

Jordan's smile dropped as he assessed whether or not Sasha could be privy to whatever intel it was that he was anxious to share.

"It's about Brent," Jordan said finally.

"I think we owe it to his parents to at least wait until *after* they bury his casket before we speak ill of the dead, don't you?" Sasha said with arsenic in her voice.

"I'm sorry, but I'm not speaking ill of anyone. Well . . . not Brent, at least," Jordan said.

Sasha's sudden shift in body language made it more than clear she had no interest in debating.

"Give me the keys, I'll start the car," Sasha said, holding her hand out.

"Brent *drove* me to the party that night," Jordan said just softly enough for the two of us to hear. "He told me about Revival."

I felt my pupils dilate, as just outside of my peripheral vision, I saw Sasha's stretched-out hand fall to her side as her head pivoted in Jordan's direction. There was nothing in Jordan's expression that signified the usual excitement that preceded a juicy piece of small-town gossip being shared between teens. This was the rare type of intel that could jolt a young person from adolescence into adulthood with no abandon or forewarning. Once again, it felt like all other surrounding occupants of the cemetery, living or dead, dissipated into thin air in the blink of an eye.

"I call shotgun," Sasha said.

They say food going cold is the surefire sign of a great conversation. There are countless adjectives that could describe the conversation that had taken place in the past hour, but "great" was not one of them. Jordan had caught a rumor that the Blount administration was not even taking attendance for the half day scheduled following the funeral, which was much to our trio's collective relief.

"There's no way in hell Brent was the only one who saw all this happening," Sasha said.

"And you're sure there's nobody else he confessed this to?" I asked.

"I think so," Jordan said, shaking his head. "But I can't be sure."

"No girlfriend? No other buddies at school?" Sasha asked.

With this question, Jordan's headshaking came to a sudden halt. His distant stare came surging back and hurdled towards the two of us seated across from him.

"He mentioned that *priest*," Jordan said.

"You mean the pastor? Neary?" I asked.

"Today at the funeral, he said Brent was his mentee this summer, I assumed it was *through* Revival," Sasha said.

"And Rox told us as much the other day. What exactly did he say about Neary?" I asked.

Jordan's green eyes crept downward and gradually lost their zeal. "I let him down."

"No, Jordan, you *didn't*," Sasha replied. "None of us did. The Brent that made the decision that night wasn't the Brent —"

"No, I mean that's what he *said* about *Neary*," Jordan interrupted.

"That he let Neary *down*?" I asked. "How's that?"

"That's all he said. Well . . . not exactly *all* he said. For 40 straight minutes, he was just talking and *talking* like . . . there was a bomb underneath the car that would've gone off if he stopped."

There was at least 20 seconds of silence before Sasha asked, "Did he . . . did he give any impression he was feeling —"

"No," Jordan said, cutting her off. "To me, it just sounded like he had a weird, stressful summer and wanted to get it off his chest, is all. I was happy to listen, but —" Suddenly, Jordan gave an audible exhale through his lips and covered his face with his left palm. "I guess I should have listened *more*."

Sasha and I gave each other a sullen glance. It was then that Sasha gave me one of the biggest surprises of the day, strangely enough. She reached her left hand out to Jordan, who grasped it in his own as they locked eyes.

Sasha spoke. "That night, Brent was in pain. *Unthinkable* pain. What he needed on that night was a friend who would listen. And despite what has happened and will continue to happen, you provided him with exactly that. That was enough."

Jordan's eyes closed shut as it was obvious these were the exact set of words he needed to hear. It took all the energy and focus I could muster to not look completely dumbfounded at what had just played out and between which two individuals. But then again, bizarre and inexplicable events had been playing out left and right for two straight weeks, and small acts of decency usually prove to be the one oasis of principle in the middle of what can only be described as a complete shitshow.

"I don't get it," I said. "What horrible thing could Brent have done to 'let down' Neary?"

"There's only one person who can answer that question," Sasha said.

"Who?" Jordan asked.

"Pastor Neary," I answered.

"That's not exactly true," Jordan said. "What about your friend?"

"Who, Rox?" Sasha asked.

"You said they went there this summer."

Sasha and I both felt the conversation come to a palpable halt. Sasha was finally the one to break the silence. "Rox isn't exactly easy to reach these days."

Jordan nodded in understanding, but his eyes dropped to the floor. He mumbled out of the corner of his lip, "It's the same with Jozie."

"Jozie . . . your *cousin*?" Sasha asked.

"She went to Revival this summer too," I replied. "We talked about her going to Revival the night —"

My train of thought suddenly trailed off before I could find a suitable epithet for the night that changed the course of our lives irreversibly. The three of us sat in the painful silence that followed, opting to allow it the time and space it deserved.

Sasha finally broke the curse. "So what do we do now? *Confront* Neary?"

"And say what, exactly?" I asked. "If he's in Revival's pocket, he's just gonna be their puppet and deny any wrongdoing. We might as well drive to the camp itself and start demanding answers."

"I agree with Ilya," Jordan said. "Revival isn't exactly a thread you wanna tug on too tightly in this town."

Sasha audibly groaned and fumed. "When are we gonna stop treating this stupid camp like it's fucking *Voldemort*? Where we can't so much as *say* the damn name without being cursed for all eternity? Seriously, it's not helping any*one* or any*thing*."

"I get what you mean," Jordan said. "Treating it like it's taboo only feeds the mystery."

"What *mystery*?" Sasha sneered. "Are you even listening to yourself?"

Sasha's outburst was attracting the attention of nearby patrons as Jordan and I locked eyes, trying to map out how to further broach the subject or whether it was worth scrapping altogether.

Sasha fumed. "Have you ever stopped to consider that whatever was going on with Brent had *nothing* to do with Revival? Have you ever considered the possibility that this stupid town built him up with our own fucked-up dreams and expectations and it all finally came crashing down on him in the end?"

At this point, nearby patrons and restaurant staffers were frozen in place watching Sasha shoot off at the mouth. If only she could see it from anyone else's point of view, she could see how much of a sideshow she was making of herself. She looked around the room and realized how much attention she had garnered and began to blush beet red.

She sniffed. "I'll be outside." Suddenly she grabbed her coat and purse and dashed for the exit in one blurred motion.

"Let her cool off," Jordan insisted. "We're all hanging by a thread."

"What do you think we should do?" I asked.

"If the pastor and Revival truly are in cahoots, chances are he'll tip them off that people are getting suspicious and they'll nip it in the bud within the same hour. They have spin doctors on retainer whose job is to basically sit around until someone like you or me opens their mouth."

"Jordan," I said, "if it's okay my asking —"

"No, it's fine. What's up?"

"How do you *know* all of this?"

Jordan looked around to ensure our booth was no longer the epicenter of the room's focus. He then lowered his voice and leaned in.

"I've been doing some research the past month. Since the old camp dean was fired in '92 after the bombshell the *Tennessean* printed earlier that year, there hasn't been a single change in administration in that time."

"What's your point?"

"Since the firing, there have been stories from *eight* different papers across the state related to accusations surrounding Revival. *Eight.*"

"But no firings or resignations?"

"Nope, not at all."

"What does that mean, exactly?"

"Personally, I think the firing did more damage to their reputation than they could take. Families pulled their kids out, they lost donors, surrounding churches and congregations denounced them publicly."

"Their owning up to it was their confessing to it, right?"

"Yes, exactly."

I was one part impressed by Jordan's journalistic zeal and one part concerned by how clear it was that the deformed skeletons in Revival's closet taunted whatever free time he had for himself. And that was, of course, assuming it was *only* his time outside of school and football being used to map out a decades-long conspiracy. Images of red tape connecting cutout newspaper articles pinned to the wall flooded my mind.

I asked, "So all this negative press over the years didn't tip off a *single* cop? Not a *single* person from child protection?"

"It's not a matter of knowing and not knowing, it's what the people with authority are literally *capable* of doing about it. And since conversion therapy is legal in over 20 states still, you can guess what's gonna be done about it."

"Let me guess, jackshit?"

"You go after Revival, they'll make you out to be a threat to the church. And if you're a threat to the church, you're a threat to Anthem."

"So you're willing to bet there isn't a *single* Christian in Anthem who would be rightfully appalled if they found out what was really happening under their noses?"

"I'm not saying that at all, but my question is . . . who would be the ones telling them? Because it sure as hell isn't my little cousin, it isn't your friend, and it sure as shit wasn't Bre —"

"Don't," I said sharply. "I get it." This sobered Jordan up from his manic train of thought.

"I'm sorry, man," Jordan said. I could see in his eyes the apology was genuine.

I nodded to reassure him his apology was accepted, but neither of us had much left to say or ask. The blinding stream of sunlight beaming through the window and across our table reminded us just how much of the day was left. The day of Brent Cushman's funeral seemed to be taking the snail's pace, almost out of some comedic cruelty.

"Shit, Sasha's waiting for us outside," I said frantically.

"Let's bounce," Jordan replied, looking at his wristwatch. "My bio quiz just started."

Eight

NOTHING QUITE GAUGES THE spirit and the ethos of the nation's youth quite like the American high school cafeteria. What movies are the most quotable to us? Who kissed whom at whose party? Who is left to sit by themselves at an empty table and why? Is it their hair? Their piercings? Their sense of humor? Or does there ever have to be an ultimate reason why?

Carl Jung once said, "The world will ask you who you are, and if you do not know, the world will tell you." As a teen, this quote is exercised to its fullest potential since who sits with whom and at which table will inform how we see ourselves for possibly the better parts of our lives. Adults may not remember it later in life, but teenagers can't see the cafeteria as anything other than a no-man's-land where one's self-esteem is vulnerable to shock and awe each day. For example, Sasha is my closest friend next to Rox, but Sasha sits with her volleyball friends. And since Rox has been stacking up absences more than Ferris Bueller, I'm embarrassed to admit I've been having meals by my lonesome the past two months.

To anyone out there lucky to have never been in such a predicament, the only way I can describe the feeling is that your blood never stops moving. It shifts to your face, it shifts to your ears, and it shifts to your stomach to the point where you don't even bother trying to eat your weird, rectangular slice of pizza. Your blood is hot and cold all at once. It's just as unsure where to go as your eyes are, as your focus is in a constant state of fear of not knowing which direction will result in the minimum amount of embarrassment. You start to wonder what could have possibly gone differently during your first impression to your classmates that could have spared you the shame you were currently engulfed in. I can't even smell the aroma of a cafeteria without wondering how different life would be if I hadn't quote-unquote *come out* to my classmates in the fourth grade. I wondered if I would have had more friends to sit with if my coming out was something I could have waited to take the reins of at the time I wanted and deserved.

As I meandered towards the cafeteria down the hall, anticipating the usual wave of anxiety at the entrance, I felt a vibration in my right pocket. My first instinct was the hope that Sasha's friends were going off campus for lunch and she had used up her weekly allowance already, opting instead to sit and eat with me. But the contact name above the text did not read Sasha.

It read *Rox*.

I completely froze in my tracks as the handful of students behind me rammed into my back. This led to some verbal jeers and expletives from behind, but I was not privy to a single one of them.

Their text read but one word: *Reddish.*

Reddish Ford, as in Reddish Ford Bridge. As in *forty miles out of town* Reddish Ford Bridge. If I knew Rox like I thought I did, which was a luxury going out of style, this was all the context I'd be provided.

I repeated aloud to myself, "Reddish."

———

We were just over a week out of the funeral of Brent Cushman, but his absence had never felt more palpable in the halls of Blount High than it did during the weeks following his burial. Administration did its best to maintain regular attendance numbers but would eventually accept the fact that the building's morale was out of their hands. This being said, it was not an untypical sight during those couple of weeks to see half-empty classrooms and vacant spaces scattered across the school parking lot.

Deciding to capitalize on the trend for reasons outside Brent's memory did not sit well with me for the remainder of the day, but nonetheless, I was in my car bound for the Tennessee countryside under a completely overcast sky. The chilled rain was bitter but flirtatious as I never had my wipers on for more than two minutes. Weather like today was unkind to the golden and scarlet foliage that had overtaken the hillside as the brutal winds stripped the trees of their leaves, giving the overall impression that the season's days were numbered.

More likely than not, Rox's voyage into the deeper swells of the Ridge and Valley was braved either by means of bicycle or simply by foot. I loved Rox like a sibling but I know that if my mom rolled up to me in the middle of God's creation wearing nothing but a hoodie in weather like today's, she'd kick my ass.

Well . . . in a manner of speaking.

The grounds of the forest were shadowed, and the pavement was slick with rain and leftover dew. As I forged through the towering trees and the various inclines and declines of the road, I watched the temperature display on my rearview gradually drop every two minutes or so. I would be lying if I said a sudden surge of resentment wasn't building in my throat and fists with every mile I ventured further into the shadow and cold. What friend sends you on a perilous journey into the forest just for a brief chat? What absolutely *had* to be discussed within spitting distance of God knows how many buried bodies instead of a warm café? Or the cafeteria? With every gallon of gas lost to The Great Rox Voyage, I felt a keen sense of deep-seated frustration boiling over that had been building throughout the past three months every time I had to indulge Rox in their encrypted weirdness.

I deserved better. Sasha deserved better. Anyone who truly had Rox's best interests in their heart deserved *much* better.

As I made the final turn that immediately preceded Reddish Bridge, my headlights made out the perfect silhouette of Rox's short, stubby figure. Their hair was the same as it was at Brent's funeral, but this time they were dressed in green drawstring cargo pants ornamented with safety pins, a navy-blue faux-fur jacket, and the same laced-up black combat boots. But no Rox outfit could be complete without, you guessed it, a cigarette in hand.

I parked my car on the edge of the muddy lawn that lined the pavement and began the final leg of my pilgrimage to Rox, this time on foot. The time on my phone marked the beginning of dusk, but the location of the sun bore little importance to whatever creatures made their home this deep in the reaches of the Appalachia this time of year.

My march through the biting elements stopped directly in front of where Rox stood.

They looked me in the eye. They took a drag of their cigarette and were courteous enough to blow in the opposite direction over the rusty and graffitied guardrail that lined the bridge.

I felt the final embers of whatever patience I had left to indulge Rox in their antics begin to burn out. I sneered, "You know the expression *this could have been an email?*"

"Jordan Flores cornered me the other day . . . in the stairwell," Rox replied coldly.

There was no playing dumb with Rox, not if they knew you well enough to know the difference.

I mapped out 10 different avenues of how to proceed in my mind before I spoke again. "His little cousin went to Reviv —"

"I knew Jozie," they interrupted. "I don't need reminding of Jozie."

I glanced upward as I let out a deep exhale through my nose.

"You two talked then? About me?" Rox asked.

"Not exactly."

"And Sasha too? I saw the three of you walking together that morning of the funeral."

"Leave Sasha out of this."

"I don't like her. I never did."

"Oh really? You *completely* had me fooled, in that case."

Rox's nose scrunched up as they chucked the butt of their cigarette over the guardrail into the dark abyss seated underneath us.

I said, "And it wasn't about *you*. It was Brent. The night of the party —"

"You're really gonna throw the lifeless body of a dead kid under the bus to save face? Are you a sociopath?"

I felt those embers burn to blackened charcoal in that instant.

"Yes, Rox, *I'm* the sociopath. Not the one person here who ghosts their best friends for weeks at a time. Not the person who sends those same friends on goose chases into the fucking *Appalachian Mountains* when they want a little face time and attention. And sure as hell not the friend who makes a sport of alienating the only handful of people in this world who give a single shit about their well-being. Right. Not them. *Me*."

Rox's lips curled up into a pathetic pout. I was on the complete precipice of telling them to fuck off before storming off to my car to abandon them at that bridge. But I knew only two or three human beings, both in the state of Tennessee and on planet Earth, would be even mildly interested in driving them home and sadly, I was one of them. Full-bodied rage and a big heart are two of the worst neighbors to inhabit one's mind and body, and I could feel both of them wrestling one another in the mud and the muck.

"I'm sorry." Rox trembled, with tears streaming down their face.

Rox suddenly collapsed in on my torso, wrapping their small arms around it and resting their head on my sternum as the smell of cigarettes became much more prominent. Crucify me for saying this, but this display of emotion was the only gratifying part of the day thus far, since, largely speaking, this was the *only* display of emotion I had seen from Rox in nearly a year. The more they sobbed into the fabric of my green hoodie, the deeper and coarser the sounds of the sobs became. I grew more convinced by each second passing that Rox's remorse was genuine, and it wasn't long until I began to feel guilty for having prodded them to this point. But in the same breath, it then started to feel like this was the accumulation of countless different emotions felt over the past three months all consolidating at once into a vulgar, clamorous symphony.

I said, "It's okay. Hey, Rox. It's okay."

"It's *not*," Rox said through sniffles. "It's *not* okay." They withdrew from me and began wiping their tears (and snot) with the sleeve of their faux-fur coat. They took a few scatter-shot and hastened breaths in an attempt to recollect themself, but their hands were trembling and teeth were chattering.

Rox said, "I'm sorry I keep making you leave town. I'm sorry I'm a shitty friend. You deserve better and so does your mom and anyone else who actually —"

"Rox . . . you need to slow this all down," I said, spacing each word out.

They began nodding in agreement. "Can we hug again?"

I couldn't help but smile. "Yes, of course."

Rox closed in on my torso once again and wrapped their arms around it as tightly as they could. The smell of cigarettes was prominent too, but fortunately, the waterworks were absent. I rested my right cheek on the top of Rox's head as we embraced and felt a tear leave my right eye. The surroundings of the world vanished as they had at Brent's funeral but this time in a way that was purifying.

All the hours spent driving to and from the rendezvous with Rox weren't undone by any means, and I'm sure future moments of frustration waited for me past this point in time. A million complications had kept Rox and I separate the past three months in ways that tested our bond to the limit. But as often is the case with wayward friendships which were once full of color and life, the ties in each friend that are crying out to be bound once again can only find catharsis in one form: a hug.

A compact, tearful, cigarette-scented hug.

Suddenly, I heard Rox's voice and could feel the small sound waves vibrate into my chest from their cheek. "I never meant for this to happen."

"For *what* to happen?"

Rox withdrew from the hug. "Anthem has gone to absolute shit."

"In all fairness, that's not saying much."

Rox instantly shot me a glare that could melt granite.

"I'm sorry," I stuttered, "but I'm failing to understand what any of that has to do with you, Rox."

They began shaking their head as they stared off over the guardrail and towards the blackening tree line.

"Rox . . ." I asked, "are you talking about *Revival*?"

Their eyes dropped to the infinite abyss directly below us. I knew this exact question carved a crude fork in the road we would never travel back from.

"It's getting dark," Rox said.

"And *cold*," I replied.

"And cold."

"Why don't we continue this talk in the car?" I asked.

Rox pondered for about five or so seconds. "What about Shelly's?"

I smiled. "Only if I'm buying."

Shelly's was a 24-hour diner stationed discreetly off I-75. Families on vacation making their way to Watts Bar Lake for the week were more likely to stop at a fast-food store advertised on the exit sign. This meant Shelly's was *request by name* and the perfect stopover for cons on the lam and restless teens dodging curfew. Before this summer, Rox and I frequented Shelly's as many Saturday nights as we could to work on our various projects and compare notes. As far as the staffers of the diner were concerned, their service was keeping two teens out of trouble with brand loyalty to boot.

My poison was apple juice and Rox's was black coffee. Audrey, the wrinkled matriarch of the joint, would warn Rox with every refill that the coffee would stunt their growth. As much as we would dismiss the claim as an old wives' tale, Rox's stature wasn't exactly putting the myth to rest.

Rox and I picked our old booth in the corner of the diner next to the rusty cast-iron radiator we would occasionally burn the back of our elbows on when we weren't careful. We couldn't be too resentful since the radiator gave us the coziest and warmest booth in the entire diner, and on a night like tonight, it was like a warm blanket by the fire.

"What exactly did Jordan tell you?" Rox asked.

"Only that his little cousin went this summer and that they don't talk much these days."

"That's it?"

"Oh, he also *briefly* mentioned the decades-spanning conspiracy he mapped out with what I'm assuming was days' worth of research."

"What exactly did he find out?"

"He's convinced Revival has some influence on the media and the law that began in the '90s. It sounded like some four-hour YouTube documentary."

"That adds up," Rox said, "but I'm sure he only scratched the surface."

I leaned in as my eyebrows narrowed downward. "The *surface?*"

"There's a few message boards run by former counselors I've read up on who have their own opinions. As crazy as it sounds, from what I can tell, conspiracy theories have actually been the greatest asset to Revival. Conspiracies have become a dime a dozen and don't have the pizzazz that they used to. With each conspiracy that sprouts up, the further everyone gets from the *actual* truth."

"Have you *been* on social media lately?"

"I'm not talking about tinfoil hats on Facebook. I'm talking about the outside world where things have actual *weight* and consequences. You don't have to go down some journalistic rabbit hole to know the printing presses in the '90s were *greased* with scandals of Revival."

"So people got bored with the stories?"

"The rest of the country sure as hell didn't, but Tennessee did. Quickly. They didn't want the scandal to be resolved nearly as much as they wanted it to stop taking up space in their morning paper." Rox then took a sip of their black coffee, which gave me the much-needed recess to process.

I asked, "What do you think Neary would know?"

"The pastor? I can't be sure. I haven't quite cracked him."

"You and the rest of Anthem. Do you think he had some hand in Brent's death?"

Rox suddenly went quiet as the hiss of the radiator behind me filled the silence. I was absolutely certain I crossed the line and that the two of us would be making our way for the exit in five seconds.

"I'm sorry," I said. "Brent doesn't deserve to be —"

"Anytime I mentioned Neary, Brent's face went pale."

I pondered my next question very carefully. "Did it go pale any other —"

"Nope. He missed the day of orientation to meet with Neary at his home. When he came back that next day, he didn't seem like himself at all. Everyone thought so too."

Hearing this punched a hole in my stomach. Suddenly, things clicked brilliantly and cruelly into place. Brent telling Jordan he "let Neary down." The isolating from his best friends. The drinking. The *shame*.

I fumed. "He spoke at his fucking *memorial*."

"And funeral," Rox said.

"*And funeral*. So what are we gonna do?"

Rox replied calmly, "We're gonna tip and leave."

As we made our way back to Anthem through the pitch-black backstreets that occasionally grazed the Appalachian trees, there was an unspoken sense of both anger and resolve that flooded the car like a hotbox. If even an ounce of common sense was missing between the two of us, we would be making our way to the home of Pastor Erick Neary which lined the side of his chapel on Gillem Street. We would have no outlined plan or objective for the events that would play out once we got there, but strategy is a luxury that often leaves us when heads and hearts are hot enough.

I said, "If the town found out what really happened between them, they'd grab torches and pitchforks and —"

"Stop and think before you conjure up *that* image," Rox interrupted. "Besides, there's nothing we know for certain yet. No witnesses or evidence."

"With all due respect, there's a tombstone on the east side of town that I'd consider evidence enough."

"If that's really what you believe, you shouldn't be calling any shots."

My thirst for vengeance and Rox's rationale clashed like two freight trains going full speed. The bullshit enigma that Neary painted himself as came crumbling down in seconds, and Rox was still giving him the benefit of the doubt. Why?

I braced myself and said, "To me, it sounds like you're protecting him, and I cannot for the life of me figure out why."

"I get that you're upset, Ilya, but you're not using —"

"Upset? A kid was sent to his grave by an adult who is currently suffering zero repercussions and who still gets to preach the word of whatever God he worships to the whole town . . . and you think I'm *upset*? What the hell did that camp do to you that you're defending these scumbags?"

Rox twisted their head towards me so quickly it gave me whiplash just seeing it in my peripheral. I could feel their gaze burn a hole in the side of my temple, and I was immediately crushed under the weight of my words. My stupid, stupid words.

"Rox," I said, "I'm sorry. That was too far."

Rox said nothing, and I couldn't tell whether I should've been relieved or mortified. I could just make out the sound of their exhales becoming slightly heavier and prolonged. Nobody else would have noticed it but me, the friend who just snapped their best friend's trust in half like a twig. But still, Rox said nothing . . . and nothing said it all.

Once their silence ripped the proper portion of my organs out, Rox spoke. "There's a reason Jordan's cousin isn't talking, why I'm not talking, why Brent didn't talk until it was too late."

I didn't ask why. I didn't deserve the answer.

They continued, "You don't know what we stood to lose. You don't know the things they hung over our heads for the whole summer."

"No, Rox, I don't."

"I keep asking you to see me at these places because every second I spend at that fucking school is a reminder of Brent."

"Rox," I pleaded, "I love you, and I'm sorry I pretended even for a second I knew what this summer has been like for you."

Rox began nodding and said, "No, you *don't* know. But you will."

There was no sense of threat or anger in these words but rather a hopeful promise. The promise of a stronger trust growing from the soil given enough time. A promise given by a friend still invested in fostering said trust and giving it water and sunlight. Rox suddenly braced my right shoulder with their hand and squeezed it. Relieved beyond words, I grabbed their hand with my left as my right continued to steer and Rox rested their head alongside my right arm. All the resolve and furor that were raging inside me dissolved.

Rox repeated, "You will."

Nine

I TOOK MY USUAL seat in trig class in the back of the room. One of the unspoken joys of being an introvert is the ability to blend into the background so well, people don't even notice you walk in the room. You might consider this a sad or unfair observation, but personally, I reveled in it. I was the type of person who loved anonymity because it meant there was no bullying or judgment to live in fear of. Nine days out of 10, I was able to exist in an element that was entirely my own without the anxiety of prying eyes.

Today was not one of those nine days.

I noticed an immediate hush flood the room as soon as I walked in. If a pair of eyes wasn't cast downward towards the blue sky-colored tile floor, they were aimed at me. My throat went dry instantly, and my head felt light to the point where once I finally got to my desk, it felt more like I was grounding my body and senses rather than just taking my seat.

I looked towards our teacher Mr. Rannells' desk, but his chair was empty . . . and nobody was saying a word. An orchestra of slight motions in my stomach was warning me that something was wrong. Very, very wrong.

There was a small vibration in my right pocket, but before I could withdraw my phone, an announcement boomed through the speaker at the front of the room so suddenly it made the whole class jump.

"Could Ilya Burkhart and Sasha Dehwar come to the administration office, please?"

I knew it, I just *knew* it. I knew from that announcement that Rox was dead. Why else would they be calling down their two closest friends? Why else would the class have gone deadly silent once I walked in? Why else would Mr. Rannells be missing for none other than an all-hands meeting to discuss the second student death in less than a month?

If half of the classroom had their focus on me once I walked in, now it was every single student in the building. My backpack felt as if someone had put a cement block in it in the time since I had sat down, and I can only describe the feeling of walking down the lone hallway as a march to the electric chair.

I wanted to break down and cry. I wanted the entire town to hear *each* of my sobs as sirens to alert them that a child died because of their negligence, ignorance, and the sheer hatred in their hearts. I wanted to scream. I wanted to damage my larynx permanently if it meant not a soul in that stupid building would ever forget the bloodcurdling scream that could only come from a young person whose heart shattered too early in life and who had to spend the rest of his life mending it. My mind kept flashing back to the final conversation Rox and I had that night at Shelly's and our discussion of Jordan, his little cousin, and Pastor Erick Neary.

Erick. Fucking. Neary.

I wanted to kill him. I did. I wanted to put him in the ground. I wanted him to feel the pain he had caused all of us and the pain of countless other families and friends that lay at his door. I wanted vengeance for Rox. I wanted vengeance for all of the children who have to spend the rest of their lives unfucking their minds due to his cruelty and sickness.

I was only a few paces from the door of the administration office when I finally decided I would bring Neary and his evils to light. I would tell every single adult in that room what he'd done. If nobody would listen or if anyone was covering for him, I would threaten to take to social media and blow the lid off for the world to see. I would threaten to make the Anthem school district complicit in his evils if they didn't bring him to justice. I would threaten to end careers and ruin reputations.

The office door was propped open so I could just make out a handful of faculty and administration members seated at the conference table inside, including Principal Perdun, our fearless Superintendent Wolfhard, and our school police officer standing in the corner behind them. I marched directly inside and was about to launch into my bombshell testimony until something, or rather someone, broke my focus and train of thought entirely.

Pastor Erick Neary.

He was seated at the table across from the superintendent. He looked *directly* into my eyes. I was completely frozen in my tracks.

"Hi, Ilya," Neary said calmly. "I'd like for us to talk if that's okay."

Before I could reply, Sasha walked in directly behind me. "Ilya, don't you wanna sit?" she asked, before leading me to two empty chairs at the far end of the table. She gave the middle of my back a small, comforting rub with her hand as we took our seats.

"Thank you two for coming," the superintendent said. "I know it must've been scary hearing your names announced with everything that's happened recently."

"It's fine," Sasha said, "but why exactly did we get called down?"

The adults at the table shot each other looks of both concern and confusion as to how to proceed.

"Sasha," I mumbled, "Rox is —"

"How close are you two to Jordan Flores?" Pastor Neary interrupted.

This immediately snapped me out of my trance. Any relief I felt to realize Rox wasn't dead was usurped by complete confusion.

"What about Jordan?" Sasha asked.

Principal Perdun cleared his throat. "Jordan had a *visit* with Pastor Neary at his home last night."

"What visit?" I asked. "What the hell is going on?"

"Ilya, it's okay," Sasha said, clasping my left hand in both of hers.

"Jordan is fine," Pastor Neary said, "and he's getting some much-needed care as we speak."

"We believe Jordan is going through some *very* normal and natural feelings of loss due to Brent's passing, is all," Principal Perdun said.

"Is that what he said last night?" I sneered.

Principal Perdun and Pastor Neary shot each other a worried glance. I could feel myself losing patience for adults getting to call the shots on what kids could bear hearing and what had to be sugarcoated for our digestion. It felt like an episode of *Sesame Street*.

Pastor Neary let out a deep exhale. "I think Jordan would prefer he and I keep what we discussed last night between the two of us. But for now, it's extremely important for both of you to understand that he cares *very* deeply for you two and appreciates your friendship at this difficult time for us all."

I was not buying any of it. As the ancient maxim says, there's no bullshitting a bullshitter.

I fumed. "Did he mention his cousin Jozie? He cares about her more than anything else in the entire world. No mention of her then?"

"Ilya, *don't*," Sasha begged.

"I figured she'd sound familiar since she went to *your* camp this summer."

Suddenly, Neary's feigned smile dropped completely as the color left his cheeks.

"Ilya, *please*, I'm begging you, don't do this," Sasha pleaded.

Neary's eyes narrowed in on mine like a vicious carnivore lining up its prey. The look in his eye of a cornered beast desperate for a quick escape was all the evidence I needed, but whether or not I was the only one in the room seeing him for who he truly was, I was unsure.

Principal Perdun barked, "I understand you're upset, Mr. Burkhart, but that does *not* give you permission to disparage Pastor Neary or accuse him of any bullcrap. Not after he willingly gave up his morning to check on you and Sasha."

"That's alright, Mr. Perdun," Pastor Neary replied. "I understand. When young people try to make sense of these kinds of things, their imaginations tend to run wild. We can't blame them for a simple lack of life experience, don't you think?" The smile he shot me after this remark made my blood boil and my fists clench up. It was then he and I both knew there would be no trial, no due process, and no justice for Brent, Rox, or Jozie.

I could have filled his throat with teeth.

"Pastor, thank you for coming to check in on us," Sasha said. "Ilya and I really appreciate it, and we're sorry if we upset you or anyone at this table."

"That's quite alright, Miss Dehwar, and thank you for saying so," Principal Perdun replied.

Sitting next to Sasha had never made me feel lonelier in my life, which was saying a lot. The rage I felt towards Neary was suddenly snuffed out by feelings of disappointment and betrayal. All I wanted was to leave that room and those people who held the fate of the town in their hands and refused to see what was hiding in plain sight.

Pastor Neary said, "Now, Principal Perdun, if it's quite alright with you, I would love to speak with these two alone for some . . . *spiritual* counsel. Sounds like they need some."

"Yes, of course!" Principal Perdun beamed. The two other faculty members and the police officer sluggishly excused themselves from the room until it was just the three of us alone. Sasha and I shot each other a glance not of fear or panic, but rather dumb confusion.

The school police officer was the last one out and closed the door behind him with a firm grip. Sasha and I could do nothing but look on as the pastor collected his thoughts and formed his intended course of conversation. Suddenly, he brought his eyes back up in our direction with a stare that combined resolve and irritation.

He said, "If you two know what's best for you, you *will* let things play out." His voice had dropped an entire octave and sent waves of vibration through the room. "You really think you're the only ones piecing things together? You're not."

I sneered. "What did you do to Jordan?"

His facial expression didn't waver in the least. "Jordan's taken care of, don't worry. Now, if I were you two, I'd go back to your little teenage lives and stop asking questions. For *your* sake, and for the memory of Brent Cushman's sake."

"Don't say his fucking name," I said.

Neary wasn't fazed. He stared at me with the same cold, detached glare. "You think you know what's happening, I came here today to personally inform you . . . you *don't*."

I could feel my heartbeat stutter and a streak of chill course through my veins. We were in the presence of a true monster. We weren't watching someone be interviewed on *60 Minutes* or playing an actor in a television series. My only goal now was to escape the suffocating confines of that room and to never register on the sonar radar of Pastor Erick Neary ever again.

"Years from now," Neary said, "you'll look back and you'll be grateful we had this talk."

Neither Sasha nor I had any reply nor a semblance of a reply. All that was in our fleeting sense of power was to keep our heads down and avoid saying anything that could lead us into a worse situation than the one we were already in. We both jumped when Pastor Neary stood up from his swivel chair and made for the door. A shiver went down my spine as I tucked myself further under the table to make space for him to cross behind me. I could hear the door being opened behind me as the hustling and hectic sounds of students making their way to the exits let us know lunch period had started.

From a distance, I could hear Principal Perdun. "Thank you again for your time, Pastor. How are they holding up?"

"They're a little shaken up, sadly," Neary said, "but I have a good feeling they'll be better for it in the end."

Numb. My lunches were numb. My showers were numb. My drives in the car to and from school were numb. There was no justice coming. There was no trial coming. My quest to blow the lid off Revival and Pastor Neary was snuffed out long before it even began. All I could do now was bear witness each fall to empty chairs in classrooms, and spend the next two years questioning what potential for a happy life some kid had upheaved and decimated that summer. But the worst numb was the numb dinners with Mom. Anywhere else in this world, I could disappear into the ether unnoticed, but not with the one person whose entire world centered around me.

If you've never had to contain depression around your parents or parent, this is the time for you to thank your overwhelmingly lucky stars. I don't doubt the disadvantages that come with dealing with pain without the luxury of loved ones, but depression will make even the most privileged people feel like barren husks of who they once were, devoid of meaning or joy. A part of you thinks you are keeping this side of you under wraps from the people who care, but the wiser part of you knows you're not. They want to fix it all by wrapping you in their arms like when you were a child, but the lack of feeling in your system when they do will only pay compound interest on your pain and suffering.

"So . . . how was school?" Mom asked, serving herself mashed potatoes at the dinner table.

I could have broken down and cried but saw no point in it.

I mumbled, "School was . . . school."

My eyes were frozen on my plate and the bountiful meal that was getting colder by the minute. I couldn't bring myself to meet her eye, but I could hear the sigh of a person using all her might to keep it together.

She said, "I remember being your age, all I could think of was gradu —"

"Can I eat in my room?" I interrupted.

I looked her in the eye this time and saw a vague sense of hope that I had finally given her some sign of life, but it paled in comparison to the pain that flooded her eyes.

"Yes, of course!" she rejoiced painfully. I could feel my stomach turn to lead as she nodded. I kept my head down and took my plate down the hall to my bedroom. I didn't raise even the first pea to my mouth with a fork before I could hear soft sobs from the kitchen. I knew I had broken her heart a million times over. I knew I took a sledgehammer to her entire universe in one fell swoop. How a mother's heart can be resilient and fragile all at once, I will never know. I wanted my heart to shatter as well, but depression kept it frozen in nitrogen.

All I could do was lay in bed helplessly as the images of funerals and the sounds of bloodcurdling sobs filled my mind. I knew the next two years would be an ongoing lecture of just how coarse sobs and screams could become from bereaved parents who shipped their offspring off to a meat grinder hidden deep in the Appalachia. But in all fairness, maybe they deserved it. Maybe there was nothing about their kids that needed fixing. Maybe they should have listened or at the very least tried to understand in the first place. But then again, Brent wasn't shipped off against his will as much as he was groomed into it by the powers that be. Brent only wanted to *help*.

But then again . . . isn't that what every adult involved in Revival has convinced themselves of to some extent? Were they just following orders? Were they just as manipulated and brainwashed as the kids?

Before I could ponder any further, the darkness was cast out of my bedroom by a flood of white light beaming from my phone.

Sasha was calling.

It took me eight or so seconds, but I finally mustered enough energy to stretch my arm across the bed to answer.

Sasha said enthusiastically, *"Hey, bestie! So I wasn't sure if you're busy this Saturday, but my fam —"*

"Yes, I'll go," I said instantly.

"Ilya, I haven't even said —"

"Doesn't matter, I'm there."

"Ilya . . . is everything okay?"

If there were any three words that could slice through the fog of depression in an instant, it was those. I mumbled, "Yeah, of course."

"Well . . . anyway, my cousin is getting married in Nash-ville this Saturday, and my mom said I can bring a plus-one."

"Is it . . ."

"Is it a Muslim *wedding? Yes, Ilya. Believe it or not, I spent literally two hours last night looking at Mehndi designs on Pinterest. So much for studying for zoology."*

"And are —"

"Yes Ilya, they're alright with you coming. I assumed as much since Muslim teens aren't exactly a bumper crop in this town. I'm not sure who else they'd think I would invite."

I always hated the idea of leaving Mom alone in the house, but I knew in the back of my mind it was a reckoning on the horizon the closer we got to my leaving for college.

I replied, "Yeah, sure. I'd love to."

"Great! We should be back late Sunday, but pack for the weekend. Bring loafers so you can slide them off easily. You don't have foot odor, do you?"

There was a painful pause of silence for no fewer than five seconds.

Sasha said, *"I'm just kidding! Okay, I gotta run. Mom tasked me with taking my little cousins wedding shopping for the afternoon. The closest store that sells kaftans is in Chattanooga of all places. Remember the loafers! Love you!"*

Just like that, Sasha's voice dissipated, and I was alone in my dark room again. But for the first time in over two months, I was excited. I loved the idea of spending a weekend away with Sasha with road trips and hotel-room hijinks to boot. A weekend away from this hellhole and the population being slowly devoured into it was exactly what the doctor ordered. But even I wasn't blissful to the sheer irony that one institution of religion was acting as an oasis from another.

"Hey, Mom!" I shouted. I was startled by how quickly I heard the stampede of footsteps make their way down the hall. Suddenly the door swung open.

"Yes, Ilya?" Mom asked.

"Where are my black loafers? I need them for the weekend."

Mom couldn't hide her instant relief and joy. She beamed. "Hallway closet. Your loafers are in the hallway closet."

Ten

"SO *NO* ALCOHOL? AS in *zero* alcohol?" Sasha's teen cousin Aida asked from the backseat.

"Yes, Aida, as in zero alcohol. We went over this literally last week," Sasha replied from the front seat.

Sasha's mother Rida said from the driver seat, "Sasha, you won't learn until you're a mother that for Aida's age, it is in one ear and out the other. You were the same way."

"So no talking to boys and no alcohol. This is starting to feel less like a wedding and more like a funeral," Aida said.

"Don't let your Yumma hear you say that this weekend if you want her at *your* wedding," Rida snapped.

"I'm not *having* a Muslim wedding," Aida hissed.

Scenes of the Tennessean countryside streamed through our car windows as the four of us made our way to Nashville on I-40 West. The sky was a perfect marble of blue, but the chill of late October stripped the hills of its fall foliage, leaving the towering trees naked and charmless.

By this point, the four of us had bided the time singing along to two different Taylor Swift albums as well as an early

2000s throwback playlist including the likes of Black Eyed Peas and Kelly Clarkson. Our only holdup of the trip thus far was Aida's begging to the point of tears to stop for iced coffee when we were not even a half hour into the expedition.

"You know what your generation's problem is?" Rida asked.

"Ammi, *please* enlighten us. I know Ilya has been dying to know." Sasha sneered.

I stuttered, "I'm actually okay not —"

Rida interrupted, "Your Jadda taught us that the next generation would lead us into the future, but warned us of the dangers of giving you *too much* freedom. We've given your generation so much rope that you've strayed from the path your ancestors died on to pave."

"Thanks, Aunt Rida, *very* uplifting," Aida replied. "That should be your speech at the walima."

"You roll your eyes at tradition now, but you'll grow up and see how much it has anchored you and your family through troubled times," Rida said.

"Anchors weigh you *down*, Ammi," Sasha responded. "Some would say a little too much freedom is better than being tied down, and I'm willing to bet Ilya agrees."

I stuttered, "Well, personally I think we as humans —"

Rida interrupted, "You're not liberated, Sasha. You're *spoiled*. You and your cousins were all spoiled the minute we decided we could trust you with even a small crumb of intelligence."

Sasha's eyes fell to the floor as her lips curled into a pout.

Aida hissed, "Getting to think for ourselves is a luxury, and you know it."

"Can we all just be quiet, *please*?" Sasha pleaded.

"It was a *privilege* and you abused it." Rida sneered. "Your generation *thinks* it's open-minded, but it's complacent and ignorant. What trials have you undergone? What struggles have built your character?"

Aida said, "I mean . . . COVID was a lot, school shooting drills kinda sucked. The Forever Wars are doing quite a number on our homeland. Wasn't a big fan of the insurrection, either."

"And where did you see these things play out? On your little screens from the comfort of your beds. Those *things* in your pockets have you all convinced you know pain and hardship."

Sasha suddenly reached her hand towards me between her seat and the middle console centered between her and her mom. It wasn't until I grasped her hand in mine that I could tell how badly she was shaking.

Rida said, "You have all become *so* open-minded you have convinced yourself of just about anything those screens in your pockets try to tell you. That's exactly how your little friend at school got to be the way she is."

At this point, I had become completely dissociated from the debate, but this pulled me back in immediately.

"What *friend*?" I asked.

"Ilya, *please*," Sasha begged. "Please don't do this. I'm *begging* you."

Rida said, "The girl I see running around dressed as if she —"

"You're talking about Rox," I interrupted.

Sasha threw her face in both her palms.

"Is that her name this week or last week?" Rida asked.

"It's *them*," I shot back. "*Their* pronoun is *them* and *their* name is Rox." I managed to keep my voice soft and constrained, but there was a bell in desperate need of being unrung.

"Fine. Whatever." Rida sneered. "All I'm saying is I was relieved it wasn't them you asked to go with us. Your abbu and I were unsure whether to put them with the men or women. This saves us that headache."

I could do nothing but sit there stupidly with clenched toes and fists. For Sasha's sake, I wanted the conversation to be over and done with, but I was enraged it ended on the note it did. It felt like Sasha's mother had the final word on Rox in their absence, and it made me livid. But more than this, I was beyond disappointed in how willing Sasha was to roll over and let it go down the way it did. It was times like these I couldn't even be certain Sasha would defend me if I wasn't in the room.

"I'm sorry," Rida said finally. "Ilya, I'm sorry if I upset you."

"So Ilya gets an apology and we don't?" Aida sneered.

"Shut up! Everyone just shut up!" Sasha yelled so loudly it scraped my eardrums.

The car went completely quiet, but the silence was faintly punctured by the hum of the car engine. All I wanted to do at that moment was wrap my arms around Sash, but all I *could* do was sit there next to Aida, who by this point was aimlessly scrolling through her phone. I decided to follow suit and unstiffened myself just enough to grab my phone from my pocket. My morbid curiosity took me to my maps app where the calculations had us pulling into Nashville in just under three hours.

———————

Dusk was an inch away from breaking when we finally pulled into our hotel in Nashville after having tolerated an hour of complete silence. I was fortunate the Tennessean countryside provided just enough splendor to keep my mind from going off the deep end. Rida asked me to help with the luggage, just before Aida made a break for it as soon as we parked in the garage. Rida rushed off to meet with the band, caterer, photographer, decorator, and all other members of the army in charge of making her nephew's wedding a success. Sasha stuck around to lend me a hand.

"I'm sorry about that," Sasha said. "She's a bit . . . *conservative.*"

"A bit?" I chuckled. Sasha didn't laugh. Or smile. Or really show any sign she was in a joking mood in the slightest.

"She definitely had a lot to say about our friend," I said.

"What is that supposed to mean?"

"A little backup would have been nice . . . all I'm saying," I said as I reached to press the button to lower the trunk door of the SUV.

"You could not have chosen a worse time to discuss this than right now."

"Rox wasn't even here to defend themself, and you just sat by and let —"

"Ilya, who the *hell* made you Rox's defense attorney? Who the hell in this world is making you die on every single hill you can find for them? Who? Because it sure as hell isn't Rox."

I took a gulp trying not to show any embarrassment. I asked, "How do I know your mom wouldn't be saying the same thing about me if I wasn't here to defend myself?"

"I know you didn't just ask that." Sasha's eyes went from frustration to a mixture of sadness and deep disappointment.

"I'm serious, Sash. Does she even know I'm pan?"

"She doesn't know what —"

"Okay, fine. Queer. Gay. Whatever *she* would call it. It's not like she'd know the difference since it's all the same to her." I could hear the echoes of my words flood the floor of the parking garage.

Sasha demanded, "Don't talk about her like that."

"Like what?" I snapped. "Factually? Does she even know? Is the only reason I'm here because you decided to avoid the truth like every fucking adult in Anthem?"

My shouts were loud enough to reach the top floor of the garage. Sasha was on the verge of tears, but her stare did not leave my eye even for a split second. She was holding her ground completely.

"Ammi *loves* you, Ilya," Sasha said. "Really, *really* loves you. You're the son she never had, and if you *must* know, she really wanted one. We can all tell, even the cousins."

In an instant, my anger melted into shame. Deep shame. Sasha was being berated unfairly by a loved one for the second time that afternoon. I had merely swapped places with her mother.

Sasha continued to hold eye contact. "And she *knows*. She knows you're pan. Not because of the fucked-up notes they sent us home with and not because town gossip . . . but because I told her *myself* that same day in the fourth grade. I wanted to still be there for you. I wanted to stay your friend . . . but I didn't understand. I didn't know anything about . . . they never taught us. They never taught me or the cousins. But do you know what she told me?"

I was so overcome with shame, all I could respond with was a pathetic motioning of my head left and right.

Sasha continued, "She told me, 'What we do unto our neighbor, we do unto Allah.' That's all she said, and that's all she needed to say."

From the entrance of the garage, we heard Rida shout, "Kids! You make for lousy bellhops, did you know that?"

"We're coming, Ammi!" Sasha shouted. She grabbed two suitcases and was about to make her way to the garage entrance but turned to me with one final remark. "She loves you, Ilya. And so do I. There's so much more to religion than hate if you look hard enough. It's never too far away."

———

I was put in a hotel room connected to Sasha and Rida's. I had the television on mostly for necessity, lest I wanted the complete silence to drive me insane. Sasha would occasionally make her way down the hall to Aida's room to discuss details for the wedding and reception tomorrow, leaving me to my lonesome to steam in guilt and embarrassment. A big part of me started to think it was just her desperate escape from sharing a space with me after our dispute in the garage.

Maybe I deserved it.

While she was away, I would occasionally get texts from her discussing the finer details of tomorrow's proceedings, including when to remove my shoes and when not to talk to girls. There were no emojis or the usual sense of humor in her texts. Never had I felt more like an intruder in my life, and for a kid growing up queer in a town like Anthem, that's saying a lot. I debated requesting an Uber ride back home, but the hole it would make in my mom's checking account would be inexcusable regardless of how uncomfortable I was. My best bet was to be as courteous as possible for the next 48 hours while keeping my head down and not making any waves.

It didn't occur to me until the wedding that my support system throughout all my life had been predominantly women. I grew up without a dad. I had no brothers or male cousins, or cousins period for that matter. I never had male coaches to learn under.

With this being said, there was no understating how jarring an experience it was being physically separated from the female sex for an entire morning and afternoon. But with that being said too, the men I gathered with could not be more sociable and accommodating. They were relaxed, they cracked jokes, they talked sports, and they made me feel included completely. But if there was a man whose company I shared that made me feel looked out for more than anyone, it was none other than Sasha's father, Bilal. He wore a white mustache and was portly but tall, giving him a staggering build like a linebacker. He smiled the entire time he was with me, but it never came off as superficial or patronizing.

Once the wedding ceremony was complete (in remarkable time), Bilal offered to drive me to the wedding hall himself and even offered to grab me fast food if I didn't find the spread horribly appealing. But only a sociopath would turn down wedding sheermal. A part of me was sure it was half his natural generosity and half him running interference for Sasha and her mother after our squabble in the car and the garage.

During our drive to the venue for walima, I asked, "When did you decide it was time to leave Pakistan?"

Bilal replied, "It was not just a single moment, Ilya. First, the September attacks here, then the Indian parliament was attacked later that same December. We went into that new year knowing life was never going to be the same."

"But why America?"

Bilal took a brief second to ponder, then replied, "We saw what was happening in America. We were not blind to the changes being made in your security, for better or for worse. We knew an attack on soil would never happen here again."

"Well . . . now attacks happen here all the time. Just in movie theaters and schools, and most of the attackers look like me," I quipped.

Suddenly, Bilal's smile dropped, and he turned to look out the window.

"I'm sorry," I said. "It's not a joking matter."

"That's quite alright, Ilya."

"So why *Anthem*, then? If it's okay my asking."

"That's alright! Well, for the most part, it was actually Knoxville being one of the few cities that would offer me a salary that was close to the one I made back home. But the prices of houses in the city meant we would have to live below our means, and as a soon-to-be father and a husband, I knew this was unacceptable. I would accept for myself a dusty attic with roaches before I accepted for my family a house that was any less than they deserved. This is what a *man* does, Ilya."

"That's how you were raised, right?"

"Absolutely. My father was tough, but held himself to high standards for love. Was your father the same?"

I mumbled, "My father . . . wasn't really . . ."

"Ah, I am so sorry, my friend." At this moment, Bilal gripped my left shoulder with his right hand. It was the first physical affection I received from a man in my entire life.

"Can I tell you something, Ilya?" Bilal asked with a lowered tone of voice.

"Yes, of course."

"As you can imagine, Ilya, Anthem has been no picnic for us since we arrived. Our house is big, but we have few neighbors. All the money in the world cannot buy you trust from others. Do you understand my meaning?"

"Yes, I think so."

"It was not even the second week of Sasha's fourth-grade year that she was . . . bullied by her classmates. She came home crying, saying, 'Abbu, the boys yelled Allah! They yelled Allah! They chased me!' It wasn't until we met with the principal that we realized the boys were yelling 'Allahu Akbar' and chasing her through the halls." His voice began to quiver as the glisten of a single tear streaked down his cheek. "They treated her like a threat. She had *no idea* what they meant. We raised her to hear 'Allah' and feel sunlight, feel love . . . but these boys made her feel ashamed of herself."

I had never heard this story before. I was at a complete loss of words.

I stuttered, "I'm . . . so, so sorry, Mr. Dehwar. I cannot imagine what that was like."

More and more tears began streaming down from his eyes as he was desperate to keep his composure. "When I was your age during the Afghans' war with the Soviets, I could hear tanks just outside the village where I lived. My momma held me in her arms as tight as she could, but it could not stop the blasts rattling me to my core. But I would take those blasts every single day for the rest of my life if it meant I could forget the memory of Sasha's wailing and sobbing that day. It was the most painful day of my life watching the love of my life ask me why people feared her."

Bilal was drawing sizable exhales to keep his composure, but it was clear that this was more than a sore spot. This was a trauma that could not be rationalized and one I had no hope of comprehending.

I asked, "Why didn't you *leave?*"

"Sasha's mother asked the exact same question and continued to do so for the next month and the month after that. And I would have taken us back to our home that same night if it guaranteed we would never have to see our baby ashamed of who she was ever again."

"But you stayed."

"Yes, we did. Because despite what Sasha's mother and I both felt at that moment, we faced *immediate* protest when we suggested moving anywhere else."

"*Protest*? Who?"

"Sasha."

"*Sasha*?" I asked dumbfoundedly. "Didn't she wanna leave too? After what she experienced?"

Bilal replied, "She looked up at us, wiped her tears away and said, 'But Abbu, we cannot leave. I cannot leave my friend. I like my friend. I will not leave him. Leaving would make me and him sad. I will stay and you go.'"

"I think I know who that friend was."

"Yes, Ilya, you do," he said, smiling through his tears. "And leaving Anthem would have broken her heart, so we stayed. And we've stayed ever since. Do you know what she has taught both me and her mother ever since that day?"

"What?"

"Taking a stand only matters when it's somewhere no one like you has stood before."

The two of us sat in absolute silence for the next 15 minutes until we eventually arrived at the venue of the wedding reception. It was my mission in life at that moment to find Sasha as soon as I could.

———

Sasha's father and I made our way into the ballroom where the walima would take place and stumbled into nothing less than a fairy-tale wedding. The black ceiling was littered with white mini bulbs to recreate a night under the stars. Lush strands of flowers were suspended above the tables alongside a round silver chandelier the size of a MINI Cooper. Sasha's cousin and her newlywed husband were seated at the front of the ballroom atop a gold-plated velvet sofa. In all my life I had never been a part of anything more grand and luxurious than this. I felt like I was in the presence of royalty.

Bilal said, "Sasha is hiding here somewhere, see if you can't find her while I look for her momma."

I nodded before he took off, but this was the worst-case scenario for dealing with social anxiety. It felt like the lighthouse that was guiding you through a brutal storm suddenly went dark, leaving you to your lonesome. Not only this, but I had not seen Sasha, her cousin, or her mother the entire day and was unsure who was on speaking terms with whom. Nonetheless, I immediately scanned the ocean of tables for any familiar face until I found Rida.

Any port in the storm.

As I made my way towards her table while wading through the motioning tide of guests, I noticed she seemed to be in a much more cheerful mood than during our road trip. I wasn't sure if seeing me would do anything to change her affect for the worse, but I could handle being alone in a sea of strangers for only so long.

Rida smiled and said, "Assalamu alaikum, Ilya."

I smiled back and replied, "Walaikum Assalam, Mrs. Dehwar."

"*Rida* is fine. Why aren't you with Sasha?"

"I'm not sure where she is. I haven't seen her all day, actually."

Rida nodded but didn't break eye contact. She had a look of concern.

"Ilya" — she leaned in — "what happened yesterday was my fault. Not yours and not Sasha's."

"Oh, that's okay, it wasn't —"

"No, Ilya," she said with a tone that struck an eerie similarity to my own mother's. "Don't do that. Don't bail me out when I haven't earned it. And your friend deserved better than what I said about them. It was extremely uncalled for, and I am truly sorry. Sasha's abbu always tells me there's not a hill I won't die on. Maybe he's right."

"I think you were just concerned about how Sasha might —"

"Ilya," she interrupted again. "You are *kind*. In fact, your kindness is the only reason we have stayed in Anthem all of these years. But we have learned in that time that kindness, if used incorrectly, provides rope to people who will use it to hurt you again and again. Do you see what I mean?"

"You sound like my mom," I quipped involuntarily.

Rida smiled. "That just means your mom is extremely wise."

We both let out a belly laugh. "Yes, she is," I said. "She really is."

"I don't doubt it, look who she raised!" Rida grabbed my hand in hers, squeezed it. "Go find your friend, *bey-ta*. She needs you." Before I could ask what "bey-ta" meant, she signaled her head to the far side of the room where Sasha was standing around and joking with five other girls, including Aida. I gave Rida one final smile and found my anxiety had completely evaporated.

Much like with Rida, I was worried Sasha's cheerful mood might change once they had seen me coming her way. Aida was the first to see me and nudged Sasha to look my way. It was difficult to not be completely stunned by how gorgeous Sasha looked. Her blue kaftan and makeup made her look like a princess. She locked eyes with me. Her smile dampened, but it didn't disappear completely.

Sasha said, "I hope Baba didn't talk your ear —"

I instantly wrapped my arms around her before she could finish. It was maybe the tightest hug I had ever given her, or was at least a close second to the one we had during Brent Cushman's funeral. This had caught the attention of most if not all the girls she had been joking with, including Aida. I didn't care, and it wasn't until she hugged me back even tighter that I knew she didn't care either.

———

By the latter half of the evening, all of us under the age of 30 were crowded into one of Sasha's older cousin's hotel suite for lip-sync karaoke. The suite interconnected two separate rooms, giving enough space for what measured out to be no fewer than 15 kids including me, Sasha, and Aida. The guys were still in their formal attire, but most if not all of the girls had changed into hoodies, leggings, and/or sweatpants while still donning their hijabs. I had never been asked out to home-coming or prom and possibly never would, but I imagined this was what an afterparty felt like. A few of Sasha's little cousins were interrogating me on Christianity as if they were characters in a movie planning to break their friends out of prison, but I was the only one who had a mental blueprint of the joint.

"So . . . the kids get to drink too?" Sasha's nine-year-old cousin Samira asked.

I replied, "Just a little, but not until *after* their first communion."

"Isn't that when you drink someone's blood?"

"No, it's not blood. It's wine, but we just *say* it is. It's meant to be symbolic."

"What's sim-ball-ick?"

"It's like pretend."

"So you pretend it's blood? Why?" Maha, another little cousin of Sasha, asked.

"I'm not sure, really," I said. "My mom and I kind of bailed on the whole organized religion thing a while ago."

"Because you like boys, right? Which means they don't want you there," Samira said. Suddenly, Sasha whipped her head in our direction. "Samira, you're *not* supposed to ask about those sorts of things. It's disrespectful."

I was about to reassure Samira nothing was wrong but quickly remembered what Rida said about bailing people out too quickly. Maybe she needed the lesson.

"I'm sorry," Samira said with a small pout.

"It's okay," I said. "I'm not sure if the church wants me there, either."

Sasha snuck up behind Samira and wrapped her arms around her little shoulders, squeezing her in a bind she couldn't break out of, and gave her cheek a big smooch. "Ilya is the nicest friend I've ever had. If anyone belongs in a church, it's him. But the town we're from doesn't know actual kindness when it sees it."

"Baba says your town is bad," Samira said.

Sasha and I instantly shot each other a glance. Was she wrong?

Sasha replied, "People like Ilya and his ammi keep it from being *all* bad. They love people for who they are and ask for nothing in return. That's how it should be."

I smiled. "Sasha's family makes it easy to love them."

Sasha beamed and replied, "Our families are lucky to have found each other, I guess."

As the clock inched closer to midnight, more and more little cousins were being collected by their respective parents for bedtime. Aida gave the most protest as she felt 13 was old enough to stay up like her cousins, but her mother would hear none of it. Sasha and I must have just made the cutoff as once the younglings cleared out, Reza, the eldest cousin, announced it was time to head for the roof.

"The roof? As in the *roof* roof?" I asked Sasha.

"You don't have to if you don't want to," Sasha replied. "They mostly just smoke shisha and shoot the shit."

"But on the *rooftop*? With a *hookah*? Is that legal . . . or even *halal*?"

"Halal? Yes. Legal? Maybe not. Again, it's totally up to you if you want to join them. Personally, I was just gonna read and go to bed."

I had never smoked shisha before, or any drug, really. I was sure Rox had their plugs but just figured college was a better time to experiment. Still . . . it did feel a little cool hanging with an older crowd, especially those who were in college.

"I think it'd be fun," I said.

Sasha looked at me as if I had grown five noses at once. "Really, you? *Shisha? You?* The *roof? You?*"

I chuckled. "Yep, those were definitely all words relevant to the situation at hand."

"I mean . . . I'd be down. Just don't make a big deal out of it unless you wanna harsh everyone's mellow."

"Harsh their *what*?"

Sasha facepalmed. "I'll get my coat."

We had all gathered on the roof under the night sky using cement blocks and A/C vents as seats. The twinkling view of downtown Nashville at night was absolutely mesmerizing. We could hear a live band playing down the street on the strip, or the Honky Tonk Highway. I, as well as many others, was freezing cold as I had only packed a light jacket, but the elements only added to the thrill of staying up late with the older kids. I was not part of the hookah rotation, but they were nice enough to include me in the conversation, nonetheless.

Laila, Sasha's female older cousin in her early twenties, was holding court recounting her first experience on a lesbian date at college with a White girl. She was using the hookah mouthpiece as a sort-of conductor baton to emphasize her words. "So, I swear to God, the *first* thing this bitch asks me when I bring up being Muslim and gay is, 'Does that mean they'd cut your head off if you were back home?'"

The party instantly erupted in uproar, including multiple "Boos" and "What the fucks?!" I myself was slack-jawed.

"That honestly sounds about right," Reza said.

"So," I stuttered through chattering teeth, "is being Muslim different in college than high school?"

"Oh, *absolutely*," Laila replied, "except it's to the point where when some classmates see me walk in with my hijab, their eyes light up as if I'm their best friend already. It's like they earn some social justice points by just knowing me. It's so weird."

"Still, it must be nice getting to wear your hijab in class," Sasha said. There was more than a hint of resentment in her tone, but it was most likely envy.

Reza asked, "So, Ilya, is it true high school football teams dress up as the cheerleaders? I saw it on a TV show once."

I stuttered, "Oh . . . yeah, they do it for the homecoming pep rally, but as a joke."

"I'm curious how that happens in a state where drag is illegal. Will they all get bum-rushed by cops who did the exact same thing when they were all peaking in high school?"

I chuckled. "I'm not sure." My teeth continued to chatter.

Another one of Sasha's male cousins, Rayan, spoke up. "The most fucked-up thing of all is the beauty pageants in the South. Kids can't see a guy in makeup, but kids themselves can dress up like strippers and dance around? How are *those* parents not in jail?"

"Is the South basically some fever dream of a weird self-loathing priest?" Laila asked.

"I wish I could tell you," I said. Once again, I was acting as the de facto liaison for the Bible Belt. Strangely, despite being a queer teenager, I felt oddly qualified.

"Wait, holy shit!" Laila exclaimed. "Sash, isn't *this* the friend that came out to his fourth grade class via PowerPoint?" Despite the fact that my face was numb from the cold, I knew it was flooding red with embarrassment.

Sasha instantly intervened. "I don't think Ill wants to relive —"

"No, holy *shit*, when Sash told me about it, I remember thinking it was the most iconic shit I had ever heard. What even were the faces of the *teachers* like?"

"Uhh," I mumbled, "I don't really remember. It was like . . . three years before the pandemic shut school down."

"Can I just ask one question?" Laila said. "Did you at least do one of those PowerPoint transitions where the slide turns into a paper airplane and flies away, just to drive home the *gayness*?"

This landed a few laughs from the circle, but Sasha was noticeably withdrawn, maybe even irritated. But for me, it was weirdly comforting having the memory broken down with humor and encouragement. I had become so used to people back home treating it like the plague.

"What was the name of your town again?" Reza asked.

"Anthem," Sasha barked without looking up from her phone. It was clear she joined the group as a buffer for me but was not entirely interested in spending her night freezing on a rooftop stenched with shisha.

This caught Laila off guard as she froze in place before taking another drag. "Wait, *Anthem*?" she asked. "As in *conversion therapy concentration camp* Anthem?"

"That's an extreme and unnecessary exaggeration," Sasha replied.

"People in my dorm at Vanderbilt were talking about it one night," Laila said. "I remember the room got all quiet and serious. Apparently, my suitemate's best friend from high school got sent there when he was 13."

Even in the freezing cold, I felt my blood chill. I asked, "People at Vanderbilt know about Revival?"

Laila replied, "Anyone who had Tumblr in the early 2010s knows about Revival. It used to be you couldn't open your dash without seeing the most fucked-up stories you could imagine."

"Wait, shit, I know about this!" Rayan exclaimed, pointing his finger directly at me. "This was all over Reddit a few years back. Yeah, it was called Revival, and some guy who went there spoke up and it went viral. But he disappeared, and months later it turned out he —"

"Rayan, now's *not* the time. The same goes for you, Laila," Sasha demanded.

"Guys, let's switch up the subject, yeah?" Reza said. "It's a bit of a vibe-killer. And Laila, you get nightmares more than anyone here, so I know you're gonna shit your pants if you get too scared."

"Fuck you!" Laila said, laughing and lifting her middle finger.

I appreciated Reza's taking control of the conversation, but it wasn't enough. Once again, the mere mention of Revival twisted my insides into a tenfold knot.

"We should get out of here," Sasha said, putting her phone in her pocket.

This drew audible protest from the crowd.

"Oh c'mon, he hasn't had his first hit yet!" Rayan exclaimed.

"And for that I'm grateful, but we have to be up early tomorrow. You've given him enough excitement for one night. That *crap* would just mess with his mind even more."

Rayan sneered. "Alright, sheesh. Whatever you say, *Aunt Rida.*"

Sasha whipped her head back so fast I'm surprised I didn't hear an audible snap. She exclaimed, "Do NOT compare me to my fucking mother! Don't you ever fucking compare me to my mother, ever! Do you understand?"

The party went completely silent. The rotation stopped. Rayan looked like a scared child. All eyes were on Sasha.

"C'mon, Ill. We're done here," Sasha said, grabbing my hand and whisking me to the rooftop door propped open with a brick. She moved so quickly and her grip was so tight, it felt like my arm was about to get torn out of its socket. Before my senses could fully process, we were going down the emergency stairs as the hurried thumps of our shoes echoed down the stairwell.

"I fucking hate my cousins sometimes," Sasha said.

"I'm sorry about that," I said. "It wasn't cool."

"He knew what he was saying when he said what he said." Obviously, Sasha's rage transcended the finer points of grammar.

"He crossed a line, for sure," I said, still desperate to keep up with her as we barreled down the stairs. Suddenly, Sasha halted our descent once we got to one of the landings. In the same instant, she planted her face in both her palms.

"Sash, are you okay?" I asked softly.

Without making a sound, she began shaking her head with her face still in her palms.

I said, "Sash, I'm here for you."

Suddenly, the muffled sound of sobs echoed up and down the stairwell. In all my life, I had never seen Sasha cry outside of Brent's funeral. I had seen her annoyed with others and with herself. I had seen her pissed off at referees during volleyball games for unfair double-hit calls. God knows I've seen her frustrated with both Rox's bullshit and my tolerance for said bullshit. This was the sight of someone who had stayed too strong for too long. When she removed her hands from her face, her makeup was a jumbled mess and she was pouting like a child scolded by a parent.

"I'm sorry," she mumbled. "I'm so sorry."

"Sorry for what?"

Before I could let her answer, she wrapped me in a hug and began sobbing into my shoulder. One of the only times I can remember letting someone cry into my shoulder was when

Mom would do so the nights she missed Dad. She wouldn't stop doing so until I was around seven years old.

"It's okay, Sash. You did nothing wrong," I said.

"I did *everything* wrong," she sobbed. "I fucked up our friendship. I'm a shitty daughter. I'm a shitty friend to Rox. I'm a shitty ally. I got benched this year by coach for having too many outbursts on the court. I'm too scared to wear my hijab to school." Sasha's words continued to reverberate to the very bottom floor of the stairwell.

"Your baba told me about when you were a kid," I said.

"Every birthday and Eid my parents get me the most *beautiful* scarves and hijabs, and my baby cousins always make me little pins with tiny flowers that they made in arts and crafts to accessorize them with. And they all just sit in my closet and collect dust because fucking Anthem is full of fucking fascists and pigs. I'm just a shitty Muslim, a shitty daughter, and a shitty friend."

"Sash, that's not true. You're not shit. You're my *best friend*," I said.

"No, I'm not. Rox is your best friend. They understand you more than I do. They're a better friend than I am. You said yourself that I wouldn't defend you if you weren't in the room."

"I said that because I was *angry*. It's not true. I know you love me, Sash. You have a big heart."

Sasha withdrew from the hug and looked up at me with eyes red from tears. She wiped her nose with her hoodie sleeve. "Your heart's bigger."

I half smiled.

Sasha said, "I'm sorry they freaked you out up there, Ill. It was messed up."

"Do you think they're right?"

"I don't know and don't wanna know. Not after our meeting with the pastor when he quite *literally* struck the fear of God into us."

"Every time somebody mentions that place, I instantly shut down. I think of Rox. I think of Brent and Jordan's little cousin."

"I know you do, Ilya. You care about others more than you do yourself. You've always been that way even when we were little kids. But . . . this may not be your table anymore."

"What do you mean?"

Sasha's eyes darted towards the floor. She said, "I can't watch you take this on any more than you already have."

"What . . . *Revival?*"

"Yes, Ilya. Pastor Neary *came to our school* the instant he caught wind of us asking about it. He wasted no time snuffing us out like a flame."

"I don't need any reminding."

"I know you don't. But I need you to really consider if Anthem is *really* the place to take some giant stand against the status quo. Neary even said we were far from the first people to uncover what's really happening there."

"He could have been lying."

Sasha let out a deep exhale and gave me a desperate look. She began shaking her head. "If you knew what Momma and Baba went through trying to make Anthem a better place, you wouldn't even bother trying. You'd go back to living your life."

"What *life*? My best friend is a husk of the person they used to be. Kids are drinking themselves to death left and right, and no adult is doing shit about it. That's not life. That's torture."

"We don't know it's because of Revival, Ill. Brent wasn't gay . . . or anything else they'd see in need of changing."

"But he was *there*, Sash. He mentored under Neary. He saw with his own eyes what was happening."

"Maybe the pressure got to him. Maybe we all fucked up building Brent Cushman up *so high* that he looked down, lost his balance, and came crashing down."

"Maybe," I replied. "Maybe."

There was nothing much left to say. The two of us stood on that landing in the stairwell as the adrenaline of the day caught up to us. Religion. Revival. Anthem. It was all a monotonous blur in need of a conclusion.

"We should get to sleep, Ill. Ammi will worry. It's been a long day," Sasha said.

"That's the understatement of the year," I replied.

We both faintly chuckled. Before we made our descent down, Sash's mention of her mom reminded me of a pin I put in earlier in the night's proceedings.

"Hey, Sash, I need to ask something," I said.

"Yeah, Ill?"

"Earlier tonight I was talking to Rida and she called me bey-ta. What does that mean?"

Suddenly, a massive smile overtook Sasha's face. "*Beta.* It's Urdu for *son.*"

———

The hotel room was completely dark, but I was awake. Fully awake. I stared up at the blinking smoke detector on the ceiling and did the clearest thinking I had done in months. I thought about my future once I had finally put Anthem in my rearview. I thought about who I wanted to be and the things I wanted to embody. I imagined what it would feel like starting college like Sasha's cousins and the opportunity to turn a new leaf and be a new person. I no longer felt the tight talons of Revival Church Camp clenched around my waist. I felt like I could breathe. I felt free. Suddenly the time between now and being an upperclassman didn't feel so long. I could feel the positive effects this trip had promised taking their course. Taking a break from Anthem was exactly what I needed. I could feel my mind had been broadened.

Before I could make my full descent into a peaceful sleep, a bright white light flooded the room from my phone. I figured it was just a text from Mom asking about what my ETA for tomorrow was so she could know when to start making dinner. I turned to the nightstand and grabbed my phone, but it wasn't a text from Mom.

It was from Jordan.

Once I lowered the phone's brightness, I could make out what it read:

"*Call me when you can. It's about Jozie.*"

Eleven

I HAD NEVER MET Jordan's little cousin Jozie, but I had heard about her from others. Sadly, the conversations were never positive. She had an eccentric way of expressing herself, whether it be her fashion or her vocabulary. She was only a seventh grader, but Jordan always described her as an old soul regarding her taste in music and movies. It was not uncommon for him to drive her to an old art-deco movie theater out of town called The Royal for old cult classics like *Eraserhead* and *Monty Python and the Holy Grail*. Jordan was well aware Jozie's friend group was slim and always took any opportunity to make her feel sociable.

But since her stay at Revival, Jozie had been anything but sociable. Her Snap streak with Jordan fell off. She didn't seem interested in old movies, or any of her old interests for that matter. But her dissociation from life itself reached a breaking point that Saturday night Sasha and I were in Nashville, when she experienced a mental breakdown in the middle of the grocery store with her mother. Jozie's parents immediately called up Jordan as they knew damn well he was more of a Jozie Whisperer than they could ever hope to be.

Ready for the next twist? Once Jordan had made his way to her household, Jozie said she wanted to see me and Rox *personally*. She said we were the "only ones" who would understand what she was going through.

All I could envision was the Bat Signal beaming rainbow colors into the night sky.

As eager as I was to offer some assistance to Jozie, I knew Jordan well enough to know it broke his heart that his little cousin didn't need him. But then again, maybe Jordan deserved a tap-out after all the years of protecting her since the day she was born.

It was someone else's turn to help.

My second concern was recruiting Rox into the endeavor. This was the same person who would disappear from school for weeks on end with no explanation. How dependable would they be in a moment as critical as this? Jozie was obviously in an extremely vulnerable place, and neither me nor Jordan could afford Rox fumbling the bag by bailing the instant the inclination presented itself.

I texted Rox later the same night explaining the situation but received no reply. No surprise there. My coffee with Jozie would have to be a one-man show, but maybe it was for the best.

Jozie's second request apart from my and Rox's presence was the rendezvous point. She had asked if the three of us could meet at a coffee shop considerably far out of town called Common Grounds. She said the "culture" of the shop spoke to her and it was one of the few places in the world where she could truly feel like herself. Despite the cost of gas and travel, I was always willing to put Anthem in my rearview for whatever reason and for whatever amount of time.

Rox was still a phantom. They had not opened my two Snaps nor my five different text messages. You would think I'd be used to Rox's antics, but there was a unique type of sting that came along with it on this day of days given the circumstances. It was clear Jozie was having some mental health struggles and needed a little validation. Personally, I think we all deserve a bit of validation from time to time regardless of how high regard we hold ourselves in. But don't get the impression that I consider myself some makeshift counselor or psychiatrist by any means. My only offering to someone like Jozie was minimum attention and empathy.

But when someone is low enough, even the minimum makes a massive difference.

The coffee with me and Jozie was scheduled for two in the afternoon on Saturday. The trip to Common Grounds totaled up to just over 50 minutes, not quite an hour. It was considerably warm for the first Saturday of November. I had layered up for the bitter morning, and the afternoon sun punished me for it. It wasn't until I pulled onto the gravel lot that I realized the coffee shop was a converted church with brick walls adorned with a modest black steeple.

Once I had entered through the archway entrance, I instantly realized what Jozie had meant when she referred to the culture of the place. The first thing that caught my eye was the mile-long stretch of bookshelves that lined the walls from front to back. I noticed one or two cats strolling across the wooden floor, one black and one gray. The floor was overtaken by couches and chairs of various sizes and fabrics. I noticed a college-aged girl cuddled up on a blue accent chair reading a book with a cup of coffee resting on a white ceramic stand next to her. The stand looked like something out of an old museum.

"Hey, Ilya!" I heard from somewhere up ahead.

I scanned the room until I finally found Jozie . . . seated across from none other than Rox.

I was instantly flabbergasted. I could *not* believe they actually showed up. I had to hide my shock quickly as Jozie was immediately racing in my direction. She was wearing green corduroy pants, round spectacles, and an oversized sweater with a headshot of Sinéad O'Connor in the center.

I managed to throw on a smile mere seconds before she went in for a hug. I was caught off guard by just how personable the hug felt for someone who was, for all intents and purposes, a stranger. But nonetheless, Jozie hugged me as if we had known each other for years and this was our first reunion in half the time.

"It is so, *sooo* nice to finally meet you!" Jozie exclaimed mid-hug. "I've heard sooo much about you!"

"Oh?" I asked. "Good things?"

Jozie withdrew, or rather, *released* me from the hug. She looked up at me through her circular spectacles, and her eyes were wide with excitement. "Oh my God, of course! You're basically this queer icon of my class, and we always talk about your coming-out PowerPoint. It was *so* iconic!"

Her giddiness was off the charts. How much caffeine had she consumed in these last five minutes? I shot Rox a confused glance, and they returned it with a pair of raised eyebrows that seemed to say, *Yep, this has been my afternoon so far!*

Jozie begged, "Wanna sit down?"

I stuttered, "Uhhh yes, I do!"

She instantly took my left hand and led me to the couch where Rox waited for us. Jozie's manic energy was a cyclone I was whisked away into, whether I liked it or not.

Jozie took her seat. "Okay, so I just wanted to catch you up on what you've missed thus far. Rox and I have basically been discussing how *real* it was for Emily Dickinson to use her poems to protest the *heteronormative* standards of the times she lived in, but most *especially* given how Oscar Wilde was being *lit-er-a-lly* imprisoned for being gay around the same time. We literally *stan* until the end of time."

You could fill in the latter blank of the conversation with two words: *icon* and *literally*. It had become clear to the both of us that Jozie was a firecracker that spent most of the day staying boxed in, waiting to erupt in glorious fashion. Jordan was earning my respect with each second Rox and I spent sustaining his little cousin's bubbly, albeit relentless, energy.

And between you and me, seeing Jozie seated next to Rox felt like seeing double. It took all the energy I had not to burst out laughing at the sight of Rox sitting next to Mini-Rox.

"Also," Jozie said, taking a sizable exhale, "can we talk about all the fucked-up laws happening not just in this state, but the whole *country* too? It's honestly so scary, right?"

"Well," I said, "there's definitely a sentim —"

"And can we *please* talk about how fucked up it is that we have to do shooter drills at school in what's considered the freest country in the world? Doesn't that just make you guys wanna scream?"

"Yep," Rox said, anticipating disruption, "it's definitely hypocr —"

"But honestly," Jozie interrupted again, "I think it is so *awesome* for us Gen-Alpha kids to be really just stepping up to stand up for how we want to be treated and stuff, y'know? We are just so sick of the bullshit and the lies and evil stuff. What can you expect from a generation raised on *Hunger Games*, right?"

Neither I nor Rox replied. We figured she'd want to continue speaking, but an awkward silence began to pervade the conversation as a result.

I finally said, "*Hunger Games* definitely started the dystopian trend for YA —"

"OH MY GOD!" Jozie exclaimed. "We absolutely *need* to talk about how dystopia isn't really forewarning for the future but rather a *present* warning for things that are currently happening in society and the world overall. Isn't that *crazy*? How stories in far-off places like space or in fictional worlds like Middle Earth can still have stories that are so *universal* to us? Sorry, I don't mean to go on and on, but Jordan told me you guys like to write stories, so I figured it would be really cool to like . . . talk about that kind of stuff and maybe even bounce off some ideas and stuff. You guys are basically the two *biggest* icons in Anthem."

Jozie was blushing red and smiling so wide, I was worried she'd be stuck with a permanent smile for the rest of time. Rox and I made eye contact and had to stifle laughter from fear it would come off as insulting when in actuality, we had both met the coolest middle-schooler on the planet.

Exhausting in large doses? Probably.

Difficulty with social cues? No question.

But her wholesomeness and eagerness for basic conversation were too contagious to ignore. And beyond that, I had never seen Rox this lively in a long, long time. Could I box Jozie up into a PEZ dispenser Rox could carry around for when they need an instant hit of endorphins?

"Jozie," Rox said softly. Jozie *instantly* whipped her head in Rox's direction. "I'm sorry we spent all that time in Revival this summer and we never crossed paths." Jozie was drawing out a side of Rox I had never seen before.

"Oh my God, NO worries there!" Jozie exclaimed. "I was sooo busy as I'm sure you were too. The only real friend I had during that time was my bestie Rory. He and I hit it off really well during a hike and spent the whole summer getting close. He's my pen pal now! I was actually working on my next letter to him before leaving to meet you guys. Ugh, it was the best summer ever! Right, Rox?"

Rox and I locked eyes. I could swear we were hive-minded to each other sometimes.

Rox asked softly, "You mean . . . *Revival*?"

"Yes! Personally, I was totally *not* down to go at first, like . . . *at all.* I had heard stories about it being some scary cult place *deep* in the woods, but not the fun kind. I don't know, there's definitely some . . . *reputation* it's had the past couple years that freaked me out. I figured I would just keep my head down and maybe meet some friends. Speaking of which, what *genius* decided to make boys bunk with boys and girls bunk with girls?"

"Sounds like wishful thinking on their part," I quipped.

Jozie instantly threw her head back in maniacal laughter, but Rox shot me a glance of disappointment. It felt as if they were caught off guard by my making light of things. I reciprocated the glare with instant remorse. It was never my intention to make it a joking matter.

"Okay, that is literal *facts*! Kinda conceited of them, right?" Jozie said.

"Jozie," Rox said, "it sounds like you . . . *enjoyed* the camp?"

Jozie nodded frantically. "I'd say so! The counselors are honestly *so* nice and wanna help you succeed so badly. I always went to bed each night feeling like I learned *so much* about myself and what I'm capable of! I always fell asleep with a smile on my face."

"But Jozie," Rox said, "Jordan says you've not been feeling like yourself lately."

"Oh," Jozie replied, her excitement retreating. "Yeah . . . it's been a weird two months, I guess." Suddenly, Jozie's spark went from a blinding white spotlight to a faint flicker. "But after all . . . they said that was normal."

"Normal?" Rox asked. "Who did?"

Jozie's face scrunched up in confusion. She said, "The counselors did . . . didn't they tell you too?" Rox's face instantly went pale as they locked eyes with me. I tried to mask my worry as best as I could.

Jozie said, "My counselor said the adjustment phase the first few months would feel a little weird, that there would be some depression and even some confusion. I guess the rush of the camp eventually wears off once you're back in school. Sorta like when you come home from an awesome vacation, y'know? In fact, Rory is going through it *much* worse than me, according to his most recent letter. But my camp coun-selor promised that it was all perfectly normal and actually, if anything, expected for someone my age. They didn't tell you the same thing?"

I knew Rox well enough to recognize when their affect had nowhere to go but south. Eyes fixed on the ground. Inhales happening with less and less time in between each one. It was all culminating at once. I knew we had to change course.

"I'm sorry," Jozie said. "Did I say something wrong?"

"No," I replied instantly. "Not at all, Jozie. Rox is just trying to remem —"

"I said something stupid, didn't I? I'm such an idiot. I'm so sorry. I do it all the time. I really do try to get better at conversation stuff like this."

Rox began shaking their head. "You did nothing wrong, sweetheart. Nothing at all." It was then that Rox put a hand on Jozie's back as a sign of comfort.

"Are you sure?" Jozie asked, with the utmost need for reassurance.

"Yes, of course. Nothing wrong at all," I said.

Suddenly, Jozie was visibly choked up as her lips curled into a pout and her eyes scrunched inward. "Thank you guys for meeting with me," she said, with audible quivers in her voice. "You guys are *literally* the coolest people to me, and I bet you had, like, *30* cooler things you could have done with your Saturday."

"Jozie," Rox said, "there is no place I would rather be in this world than in this creepy, converted church with you."

Jozie laughed as she wiped a single tear away.

Rox smiled then looked at me. "Ill is cool too, I guess."

I smiled too, though not wholeheartedly.

———————

The conversation between the three of us clocked in at just over three hours and proved just as sporadic as Jozie herself. We leaped from topic to topic including but not limited to our favorite member of *Queer Eye*, David Lynch movies, Kurt Vonnegut novels, and Oscar Wilde. There was a subconscious understanding between the three of us to not broach the subject of Revival for a second time, although the topic burned a hole in my brain the entire time.

After Jozie said her goodbyes via two tight hugs that averaged about 20 seconds long, Rox asked for a lift home as they had followed the creek to the coffee shop that morning. I knew the conversation we would have during the car ride home would split the mystery of Revival in two.

"I thought that would never end," I said while driving.

Rox said nothing, content to look out the window.

"Rox?"

They still said nothing.

My mind kept flashing back to the morning Pastor Neary paid a visit to Blount High to scare the hell out of me and Sasha. And for what? What was our cause? Was this just a mountain out of a molehill? Was Neary the one to blame for Brent's death this entire time? Was this stupid summer camp just a red herring that *he* put in place to throw us off? Suddenly, I could feel the blood rush to my ears and cheeks. My jaw became clenched so quickly, I accidentally bit the tip of my tongue, which only made me angrier.

I was through with the cloak and dagger.

"Rox . . . any idea why the Revival you went to and the Revival that Jozie went to this summer are completely different things?" I asked.

I could just make out Rox twisting their head in my direction out of my peripheral vision.

"What the hell is that supposed to mean?" Rox demanded.

I began shaking my head. "I should have known you were playing us for chumps."

"Playing *who* exactly?" Rox asked.

"Me and Sasha, for starters. Jordan. My mom. Our entire fucking school. Pastor Erick fucking Neary."

Rox was stunned for five straight seconds before asking, "What *about* Pastor Neary?"

"Jordan went to his house for God knows what reason. I don't know what the hell happened, but the next morning the pastor showed up to school to talk with me and Sasha in private. It was terrifying."

"But why you two?"

"Jordan must have told him about our lunch. Then he took it on himself to nip this all in the bud by scaring the shit out of me and Sasha at fucking *school*, no less."

Rox went silent. Meanwhile, my heart was racing, and my breath was becoming shorter and shorter as the argument went on.

I said, "I really thought I could take you seriously for once. But all this mystique and cryptic bullshit was nothing more than a game to you. A cry for help, maybe? I don't know and honestly, I really don't want to. You've gotten all the help the people who love you can possibly give, but obviously, it'll never be enough."

Rox stayed silent.

As was usually the case, anger proved to be nothing more than the warm-up act that preceded a flow of tears. My sense of self-righteousness in berating my best friend melted into shame. I've noticed that when you go too far in an argument with someone you love, your body is the first to take notice. Your chest becomes hollowed out, almost as if your mind was trying to locate a heart and was failing to do so. How could someone who inflicts cruelty on a friend or family member own a heart?

"Stop the car," Rox demanded. "Let me out, now."

"Rox," I begged, "I'm didn't mean —"

"Fucking let me out, now, Ilya. I swear to fucking God."

I instantly pulled over to the gravel side of the highway and threw my hazards on. It wasn't until I looked over that I noticed a streak of tears flowing from Rox's eyes down their cheeks. A million arguments can never evoke even a fraction of the shame that comes from making a loved one cry. Take it from me. Rox climbed out but didn't slam the door. They hated the sound of slamming doors more than anything in this world.

———

As I continued the drive home, I had only a small amount of time to be completely alone with my thoughts. But it turned out to be just enough time for my self-pity to morph into resolve. It wasn't even suppertime, and yet that day had given me full incentive to put this headache surrounding Revival to rest. Up until that point, I was merely a transcriber of the events and members of Revival itself. Hearsay, conspiracy, and conflicting testimonies were the only brushes I had to paint a full picture. It wasn't nearly enough. For the past 90 days, this stupid camp in Appalachia was a tick in my scalp that gnawed at me and tormented me at infrequent times. Just when I thought I had a grasp on it strong enough to cast it out, it burrowed itself even deeper into my subconscious and fortified itself using the unwillingness of others to discuss it in detail. The tick's sustenance was mystique. The more time I spent avoiding its presence, the sharper its bite became. I was so desperate to rid myself of its torture, I was on the brink of ripping off my scalp in one swift motion.

By the time I had made it to my driveway, my mind was made up. It was time for Revival to be demystified. It was time for the counselors and directors to have faces and voices. It was time to rid myself of the agony of the tick by any measure possible.

The scalp was coming off, in shreds or in whole.

Twelve

ACCORDING TO THE REVIVAL website, the camp still ran through the fall but in limited capacity with campers and staffers returning home on the weekends. Campus tours were held each Tuesday and Thursday at 9 a.m. with limited staff. I spent the whole Monday morning at school that following week racking my brain for a believable excuse to ditch school. The typical cock-and-bull story of a doctor appointment was less likely to fly in a town like Anthem where schoolteachers and doctors lived only a couple doors down from each other and gossiped like it was going out of style.

My next concern was whether or not to tour Revival alone. An unaccompanied minor strolling into a camp asking questions would certainly raise some eyebrows, but I could not guarantee the safety of the adults nor the structural integrity of the building should my mother join me on the visit. Speaking of which, I knew damn well my mother's awareness and approval of the trip was a nonstarter. She would rather send me to juvy than allow me to come within a hundred feet of Revival. The challenge then became coming up with an excuse that would pass the bullshit detector of both Blount High and Carol Burkhart.

As I made my way down the hallway for zoology during passing period, I got a poke on my left shoulder. I turned around and found Sasha.

"Hey," she said somberly. "How was Jordan's cousin?"

"Oh. It was . . . a lot of fun."

Sasha instantly gave me a peeved look. "Someone should remind that to your face."

"I mean . . . it was a lot of things."

"I know what you mean. I met Jozie during the volleyball clinic at the middle school this April. She was definitely . . ."

"Energetic?"

Sasha giggled. "To say the least. But still, it went fine, then? It wasn't awkward that it was just the two of you?"

"Don't tip over after hearing this if you can help it, but Rox actually showed up."

Sasha's jaw dropped. "No *freaking* way. Are you serious?"

"Yep!"

"They're still full of surprises, I guess."

I feigned a smile, but a disturbing question presented itself, one I couldn't turn away.

"Hey Sash, can I ask you something?" I said.

"Of course!"

The question rewrote itself millions of times until it was finally rushed out. "What if Rox is playing us?"

Sasha's smile dropped instantly. She asked, "Ilya . . . why would you ask that?"

I stuttered. "Jozie filled us in on her experience at Revival at the coffee shop. She had nothing but positive things to say, calling it the best summer ever. Apparently, she even made a friend who she pen pals with today."

Sasha's eyes scrunched inward in deep thought. She said finally, "But . . . but Jordan said she's been struggling really bad mentally. Didn't you say she had some kind of breakdown?"

"Rox brought that up exactly. But Jozie said the counselors warned them of an 'adjustment phase' that would happen once they were back in school. They made it sound like depression and anxiety were some kind of . . ."

"Ritual."

"Yes, exactly."

Sasha began shaking her head as her eyes darted back and forth.

"You think Rox is going through something similar?" she asked.

"I don't know, they stormed out of my car."

"What? Why?"

"I was a complete idiot. Jozie made the camp out to be the happiest place on Earth so convincingly, I was sure Rox was dragging us along. I accused them of playing us."

Sasha's eyebrows narrowed downward in disappointment. "That's not what a *friend* does, Ill. What the hell were you thinking?"

"Don't make me feel worse than I already do, please."

"So what are you gonna do now?" Sasha asked.

I scanned the hall to make sure nobody was within earshot, and noticed how vacant it had become the closer we got to the bell.

I leaned in and lowered my voice. "I'm thinking of *visiting*."

"*Visiting*?" Sasha asked dumbfoundedly. "Visiting *who*, exactly?"

The word itself felt cursed. I tried to let my eyes provide the answer.

Sasha's eyes widened with realization. "You *cannot* be fucking serious."

"I am, Sash. It's the only way."

"The only way to *what*? Land in a room alone with Pastor Neary again? You didn't think once was enough?"

"He doesn't have to know."

"Bullshit! I thought *you* were the one who said the two of them were colluding. Who do you think would be the *first* call they made once we left?"

"Visiting for a scheduled tour is *not* a crime."

"Oh yeah, you're absolutely right, Ilya. It's *not* a crime at all. It's just the best way to guarantee that we get suspended for skipping school for going to the *last place* any adult in this building wants the two of us to go, let alone Neary. Do you want me kicked off volleyball? Because a suspension and enough time spent in that office is a great way to make it happen."

"No, Sash," I retreated. "Of course I don't want that for you. I never said I was roping you or anyone else into this at all. I don't want anyone else punished. If anyone is going down for it, it's gonna be me."

"How do you even plan on skipping school, first and foremost?"

"That part I'm not quite sure on yet. I've been mulling it over."

Sasha's eyes lowered in deep thought for five or so seconds. She said, "I could always say it's a Muslim feast day. That usually works."

"Wait, what?"

"Yeah, last year I had tickets to see Feeble Little Horse and told them it was an Islamic feast day. It worked like a charm."

I let out an abrupt laugh. "No *way* did that actually work."

Sasha smiled. "No questions asked!"

I pondered the option for a second then asked, "But how does that get *me* off school?"

"I'll just say my nanni doesn't have much longer, and I want her last memory of me involving having found a boy."

I laughed again. "That's messed up for so many reasons."

Sasha giggled. "That's *Anthem*!"

"Wait . . . so does this mean you *are* coming with me?"

Sasha shrugged. "Ilya, it sounds like this is what it's gonna take to put this to rest for you. It's all you've talked about the past two months."

"Yeah . . . I guess it's been on my mind a lot."

"You've been obsessed, Ilya. Like, *seriously* obsessed. And it *kills* me watching you be tormented by some stupid church camp. If us going there and putting a face to the name finally gives you peace . . . I'm gonna be by your side for it."

I instantly felt a ton of bricks lifted off my shoulders. For the first time in months, I felt like I truly wasn't alone.

"So . . . " Sasha asked, "whose car are we taking tomorrow?"

Thirteen

I WOKE UP AROUND six in the morning, an hour earlier than usual. I had to meet Sasha at our rendezvous point for the trip, but beyond that, I couldn't stand to have breakfast with Mom knowing what my plans for the day were. Lying to Mom to stay out late with Rox or Sasha usually made me sick enough as it was. But skipping school to willingly attend a tour at Revival Church Camp was just plain loathsome. Sasha and I met and left her car in a Dollar Store parking lot outside of town around 7:30 a.m. Only an hour and 15 minutes stood between us and Revival.

"So remind me *one* more time, it's a tour of the whole campus?" Sasha asked from the passenger seat.

"Yep. The website said it clocks in just under two hours."

"So other families are gonna join us?"

"I would think so, yes."

We had been driving for just over 40 minutes. Sasha stared out the car window and said nothing for 10 or so seconds.

I asked, "And you're sure the volleyball team won't kick you out or anything?"

"I never said that, I just said I would love to see them find another spiker with a 21-inch vertical." Sasha gave me a smirk. I would have smiled back but was too damn anxious. Sasha picked up on this instantly and grasped my forearm with her left hand.

"You okay, Ill?" she asked softly.

I let out a hurried exhale. "It just occurred to me that we're gonna be spending our morning with horrible parents and the queer and trans kiddos they're holding hostage."

"I mean . . . you may not be wrong. But then again, we don't know these parents' mindsets or end goals, either."

"What do you mean?"

"Maybe some of the parents *are* approving of their kids whether they're gay or bi or trans or whatever . . . and they just want to introduce them to Christian values. Maybe their kids are struggling to make friends *because* they're queer and this is a great opportunity for them to socialize and kind of vibe with their tribe, y'know?"

"You mean like Jozie?"

"Yes, exactly! Didn't you say she even has a pen pal that she met at camp?"

"Yeah . . . and apparently they became best friends almost instantly upon meeting."

"See? Maybe the rumors are just that, *rumors*. Maybe some bored kids had nothing better to do so they just made up some ghost stories to keep conversations interesting."

A tide started to turn in me. I actually started to feel the smallest sliver of reassurance. I said, "I wonder if the scandal in the '90s caused them to clean house and actually work on their image. Maybe they really did change."

"Maybe!" Sasha said. "But we'll have to see for ourselves."

"Then maybe I can actually start sleeping again."

Sasha's smile dampened into a faint grin. She said, "You've definitely shouldered this in a big way, haven't you?"

I nodded. "I did a little bit, but then Brent's death changed everything. It sent it all into overdrive. I couldn't think about Revival without thinking of Rox's funeral and Jozie's funeral. The only lens I could see the world through were the funerals of kids. It was horrible."

Sasha nodded in agreement but remained silent.

I said, "Then I really started to wonder . . . if Brent didn't die because of Revival or Pastor Neary . . . what or *who* did he die because of?"

Sasha remained silent. The words hung in the air for what felt like five minutes when in reality it couldn't have been more than 20 seconds.

Sasha finally broke the silence. "Maybe we didn't know and will never know the *person* who made the decision he made."

"The decision to *die*, you mean?"

"Yes. Maybe it was a Brent that was hidden from us all, even his family and buddies. Maybe we all have that secret person inside us that nobody else knows about."

"Do you have that person inside *you*?" I asked.

Sasha looked at me and smiled. "Sometimes. And so do you, Ill. But what matters is making sure we do right by each other to give that hidden person their best shot at being seen and heard."

I suddenly realized I wasn't hearing Sasha, I was hearing the wisdom and resilience of the parents who raised her combined into one. The Sasha that was bullied as a child but still chose to be kind to others. The Sasha that sought out the loner kid and gave him a friend. The Sasha that stood by the loner kid's side when he sliced his slim chances of being accepted in half when he unintentionally came out to all his classmates in the fourth grade.

Do you know the feeling of driving under an overpass during a thunderstorm and enjoying those two brief seconds of calm silence? Sasha was what every best friend *should* be: the calm silence in the storm.

We spent five or so minutes driving through the towering eastern white pines of the Appalachian forest that blocked out the sun. Streaks of sunlight would occasionally make their way through the branches and blind me for a brief second or two. A thick fog coated the forest floor. The further we ventured into the shadow and the mist, the more I felt we were leaving civilization behind. A chilling realization dawned on me as the Maps app notified us of our approach: nobody knew where we were. No adult could account for us as we made our descent deeper and deeper under the cover of fog and shadow. I felt untethered and naked. It felt like an umbilical cord keeping me connected to the Earth was cut by a pair of scissors, and the deafening sound of the cut was heard by no one.

We were alone.

A wooden sign made its way out of the fog and stood to greet us, reading:

REVIVAL WELCOMES ALL! "LET THE CHILDREN COME TO ME AND DO NOT STOP THEM, FOR THE KINGDOM OF GOD BELONGS TO SUCH AS THESE." LUKE 18:16

I couldn't help but feel like Sasha and I had become intruders the second we drove past the wooden sign and the bible verse inscribed onto the front.

Suddenly, out of the fog materialized a two-story building with an exterior of tall and brown wood panels standing side by side. The first and second floors were separated by a gray asphalt awning, the same color and shingle as the main roof. A line of parents and teens wrapped around the left corner of the building to the entrance door. A rectangular sign carved from tree bark was seated in the center of the front lawn that read:

REVIVAL YOUTH est: 1977

Yard signs driven into the lawn directed us to the parking lot on the left side of the building. The reality of our decision was starting to dawn on us in whole. But the thought of going back to Anthem and continuing the cycle of paranoia, depression, and anxiety proved incentive enough to steady on. I had to face my fears head-on to finally put them to rest. It was time for a textbook case of exposure therapy.

I would have just preferred it not to be so far removed from civilization.

Sasha and I were greeted by a tall woman not quite broaching her middle-aged years. She met us with an intense smile and reached out to shake our hands while her other hand held a clipboard.

"Hello! Welcome to Revival Youth, my name is Robin, and I'm the outreach coordinator! Did you register for the tour online or call ahead?"

I muttered, "Uh . . . we —"

"We called ahead, but it got dropped," Sasha interrupted.

"Oh, rats!" Robin said. "We apologize for that. The reception out here can be a bit dodgy. But regardless, you two made it here, and we're so excited to have you! Can I get your names down?"

I froze in place. We couldn't afford either of our names being immortalized in this place for a number of reasons.

"My name's Meredith and his is Derek," Sasha said finally.

"Okay, fantastic! So Meredith . . . and . . . Derek . . . you two are in!" Robin said as she scribbled our names on the register. "We're gonna be starting our tour in just a short second, but go ahead and mingle with the other tour members! They might just be your bunk buddies next summer!"

A chill shot down my spine. The place that had haunted my dreams was stretching out a hand with the sole intent of lunging me forward into its jaw.

Sasha leaned in and asked, "What exactly is our plan here?"

It wasn't until then that I realized I truly had no plan. None whatsoever. Now that we were standing in the lion's mouth itself, there was nothing left to demystify. I knew nothing could potentially happen during the tour that would hint towards foul play. My mental outline of the day halted at the entrance of the building and ventured no further.

"Uh . . . take the tour," I stuttered, like an idiot.

"Ilya, please do *not* tell me we ditched school and drove over creation to take a fucking tour of the woods," Sasha snapped under her breath.

"There might be a clue that —"

"A *clue*?" Sasha hissed. "A *fucking* clue? Are we preschoolers watching a fucking kid's show on TV? Seriously, Ill? A *clue*?"

"I had to come here, Sash. I had to."

Sasha let out a large exhale through her nose and replied, "I know you did, Ilya. I know."

"I didn't ask you to come," I said, regaining my resolve.

"I know *that* too, believe me. I just figured there was some game plan . . . like in volleyball. Some kind of play, a *strategy*. You don't want this to be a waste of time, do you?"

"No, absolutely not. You said a *strategy*?"

"Yeah, like in volleyball, one strategy is to either play the ball long or short, depending on the other team's spiker. If the spiker is tall enough to have the advantage, you play it long to keep it out of their hands."

"Playing the ball long gives you more options, right?"

"Yes, exactly. It's tedious as hell, but you learn patience and discipline. That's usually what wins the game."

I said, "So, we look around the camp . . . and play the ball long . . . but we need to find the *spiker* of the camp . . . and make sure their height —"

"Ill, I know you're a writer and whatnot, but maybe leave the volleyball metaphors to me."

"Okay, folks!" Robin belted. "You've waited long enough, and we know you gave up your mornings of work and school to be here. We truly appreciate the sacrifice and we promise you won't leave disappointed. We always start the tour by saying, 'Take a look at where you're standing, because your journey at Revival starts *here*!'"

Sasha took my right hand in her left, and we paced onward.

My mind recalled Samwise the Brave, "If I take one more step, I'll be the farthest away from home I've ever been."

The mass of us 30 or so tour members were led into what looked like an old school gymnasium well past its prime, with the squeaky wooden floors and cement-block walls that have haunted many an American childhood. There was a steel countertop along the wall with paper cups containing drinks of various bright colors. Gatorade, maybe? But no old-school gymnasium would be complete without the overwhelming humidity and stickiness of the air. It felt like we were being led into an oversized oven. I developed pit stains in my shirt not two minutes after walking inside. Parents began using their handout pamphlets to fan themselves.

"Is the A/C in this place broken or something? Sweet Lord have mercy!" an elderly gentleman sneered. Possibly a grandfather.

"We do express our deepest apology for the temperature, folks," Robin said. "As you locals know, humidity reached a staggering *56 percent* this summer. Our amenities may have good bones, but they're *old* bones too, quite frankly. We've spent the last two summers having our gym A/C bug out. And with the winter coming, we've decided to minimize A/C use until we can get it replaced."

"It's November out there!" a woman sneered. "Just open a damn door, why dontcha?"

This drew an audible chuckle of agreement from the crowd.

Robin feigned a smile and replied, "We sincerely apologize for the discomfort, folks, but frankly speaking, where you're standing is nothing short of the *heart and soul* of Revival, and no tour would be complete without it."

An adult man in the crowd barked, "Don't tell me our *kids* are gonna be sweltering in this oven next summer! I won't have any of it! You'll have a lawsuit on your hands, I'll tell you that!"

The crowd became even more restless and the murmurs became louder.

Robin pleaded, "Folks, we would *never* put your children at risk when we have countless measures in place to guarantee their comfort and safety. Not only do we have six different industrial fans on hand should the A/C fail, but our campers are offered cooling refreshments that keep them physically adept to the heat, should it be inevitable during the service."

"The service?" the same mother from before asked.

Suddenly, Robin sprouted a massive smile and replied, "Remember when I said this gym was the heart and soul of Revival? Many of our campers and alum would agree with me, and there's one simple reason why. We have a weekly service scheduled for every Saturday afternoon in *this* gymnasium led by our dean of the camp, Reverend Pine. Many of our alum have reported these very services to be the highlight of their summers, and given the activities we offer from hiking to archery to kayaking, this is *very* high praise!"

"But it is *not* my praise to claim, but His and His alone!" a deep voice from behind us belted. The entire herd of tourists snapped their heads back in unison and found a stout man dressed in a black suit, blue tie, and small gold crucifix necklace. Judging from sight alone, the man fell just short of elderly status and clocked in at no younger than mid-50s. But his smile and eyes beamed with such joyous intensity that he seemed to de-age himself at least a decade.

"No reason we can't hear about it from the man himself, please give a round of applause for our very own Reverend Pine!" Robin exclaimed.

An obligatory but sturdy applause swept over the crowd of us tourists.

All of us but Sasha.

"That'll do, pig! That'll do!" the reverend said. This drew an audible laughter from the crowd. It was glaringly obvious Pine put his hours into working the huddled masses.

He said, "But all joking aside, words cannot express how grateful we all are to have you spend your morning with us, folks. I'm sure our fantastic outreach coordinator Robin here expressed our deepest regret for the goshdarn heat! From the outside looking in, you'd think we were a clump of no-good sinners not knowing they wandered into a church!" This drew an even bigger laugh from the crowd. Sasha and I immediately locked eyes and gave anxious smiles.

Reverend Pine continued, "But what we do here is no laughing matter, folks. When kids first come to Revival at the start of each summer, they're scared, they're angry, but above all . . . they're *lost*. Maybe they don't see it for themselves, but their parents or their grandparents do. But if it's anyone who sees it more clearly than all of creation . . . it's *Him*!" Pine lifted his index finger to the ceiling. Various shouts of "Amen!" and "Yessir!" were murmured in agreement.

Pine said, "So what is it we do in this very room? Well, I'll tell you what it is we *don't* do . . . we don't *preach*. We don't *shame*." Suddenly, Pine made direct and startling eye contact with me. "We *listen*. We *understand*. And above all, we *heal*."

Nearly every single face in the crowd wore massive smiles and determined eyes. As painfully routine as the sermon sounded, Pine had the crowd where I'm sure he was used to having them: the palm of his hand.

"That's all good and fun, Reverend," a young man from the crowd said, "but from what I've heard, this place reeks of bigotry and hate, and the youth of this state are worse for it. How do you call that healing, exactly?"

The crowd instantly became flustered with agitation and uproar, but Pine was completely unphased. He simply smiled and replied, "That's alright, folks. To tell you the truth, I don't hear a hint of malice in this young man's words . . . brash though they may be. It *is* true that those who once led services in this very room called themselves servants of God but were anything but. They were proven to be nothing short of *monsters* and . . . *hideous blots* on the fabric of our divine work. They had no business calling themselves worshippers of God, and rest assured that each one was met with *His* wrath and *His* retribution. End of story."

I couldn't help but wonder . . . why did "His retribution" take its sweet time while children suffered?

Pine said, "Now I'm sure y'all wanna get out of this brick oven as much as I do, so I'll keep it short and sweet. This gymnasium may not be winnin' any beauty contest in the near future, but believe you me when I tell you nothing short of divine intervention takes place in *these* very walls. Year after year, summer after summer, these young souls share in the *euphoric* experience of a presence . . . *His* presence. It is an *unforgettable* experience, folks. The accumulative joy felt between young people in this room during any given service can last a man five lifetimes. They take that wisdom with them after they leave . . . that *anyone* can sit beside God himself, no matter their age or background."

Nearly every face in the crowd was beaming with excitement and intrigue, some even with tears in their eyes. All but Sasha and me.

"Reverend," the same young man said, "I'm just gonna ask you plainly and simply: where does Revival stand on gay and trans kids?"

The elation of the room was snuffed out completely. Audible groans swept the crowd.

Pine let out an annoyed chuckle. "Son, there is a time and a place for a conversation like this, but if you insist, there's no reason I can't air this out for you nice folks here today. Revival is not ignorant to the changes in our world, nor are we ignorant to the rumors that have plagued us since our change in mission *and* leadership some decades ago. We at Revival believe the love and grace of our Lord is accessible to *all* souls of the world: young and old, rich and poor, straight and gay, whatever the . . . LGTBQRS . . . however many darn letters y'all got these days, I can't keep 'em straight anymore!"

The crowd erupted in laughter and verbal agreement. All but Sasha and me.

Pine said, "But jokes aside, young man, Revival does *not* commit itself to converting or even persuading a *single* soul that walks through our front door. The only thing we can do is humbly offer a nonjudgmental space, a listening ear, and a helping hand. And I'm beyond privileged to say . . . that nearly *every single soul* that graduates at the end of the summer doesn't wanna leave. Wild horses and all that."

I instantly flashed back to coffee with Jozie. I couldn't help but hear Pine's words as a near-perfect echo of Jozie's description of her summer here.

"Now I don't know about y'all," Pine said, "but I'm swelterin' like a hog in heat in this suit. How 'bout we get some fresh air?"

An uproar of endorsement sung from the crowd. Robin commanded, "You heard the reverend, let's take in some Appalachia!"

Robin led the sweat-ridden tour group to the back door of the gym. Sasha leaned in and mumbled, "Remember when you said you didn't want this trip to be a waste of time? That window is closing fast, just so y'know."

"I know. I'm thinking we break off while we're in the woods and come back here to look around."

"Ilya, that is *not* a strategy. That is complete lunacy."

"I'm playing short ball. We're the spikers now."

"No. We are *not* spikers. We are not even *players*. We are sociopaths burning down the fucking net with a flamethrower while the players and their families made for the exits. You don't think they'll notice two unaccompanied minors are missing from the group?"

"Then maybe one of us breaks off and the other says they had to make a phone call and had to hang back. Remember she said the cell reception is shoddy?"

We were only a few paces from the back door that led us outside. This transition was the best opportunity to duck out without being noticed, but the window for the opportunity was shutting fast.

Sasha said, "I'll tell them you have to check in with your mom every hour and that you had to use their landline. And grab me one of those drinks on the counter, I'm about to pass out."

"Okay . . . that works. I promise this won't be a waste of —"

"I hope you know what you're doing, Ill," Sasha interrupted and walked ahead. She was the last group member to exit, and the sound of the door shutting behind her echoed through the gymnasium.

Suddenly, there was silence. Eerie and dreadful silence. The silence after glass shattering in a crowded restaurant. I turned around and saw the room was completely empty. I was alone. I saw the countertop with Gatorade in paper cups and remembered Sasha's request. I was surprised there weren't more of them missing given the grievances surrounding the heat. I would be sure to grab one for myself too, as I had become overwhelmingly parched in just the five minutes spent listening to Pine's sermon. Hopefully, they wouldn't notice one or two missing.

As I reached both hands out to grab the drinks, a voice startled me from behind. "You're certainly makin' yourself at home, son!"

It was Pine.

I gasped so loudly that I nearly lost my balance. I fell back on the counter and managed to knock over a handful of the paper cups, creating a massive spill. Pine began lightly jogging to the kitchen door. "Don't you worry, son! I'll get some paper towels."

All I could do was stand there like an idiot and gawk at the spill helplessly. Pine emerged from the kitchen with a roll of paper towels and began cleaning up my mess. In all fairness, he was the one who startled me in the first place. I had a feeling it was a bit of sport for him.

"That's okay, kiddo. It happens to the best of us," Pine said.

"I was actually just gonna grab a few for me and my friend. That's why I stayed."

Pine began to shake his head as he wiped. "These are all probably stale and warm by now. Let's getcha some nice, cold water bottles from the counselor lounge for you and your lady. Whaddya say?"

"She's not my lady," I sneered, "she's my best friend and has been since we were little. And her name is Sasha, for your information."

"Sasha . . . Sasha . . ." Pine pondered.

"What about her?"

"Sorry, son, but I don't remember a Sasha on the tour registry. Is that her nickname or something?"

Shit. Shit. Double shit. Triple shit.

"Uh . . . yeah. Her nickname," I stuttered.

Pine nodded. "What's her real name, then? Just curious."

Fuck. I couldn't remember what she had put down. Mary? Madalyn? Madison?

Pine let out a laugh and slapped the side of my left arm. "I'm just teasin' ya, son! Now c'mon, let's getcha some water and get outta this caboose."

Pine handed me two cold bottled waters as I sat on the edge of a leather chair. The counselor lounge was infinitely cooler than the gymnasium, and the furnishings were surprisingly lush for a place that couldn't afford a new A/C.

"So tell me, son, what excuse did you give your teachers? Stomach flu? Leprosy?" Pine asked.

I said nothing. I couldn't think of a response that wouldn't incriminate me and Sasha.

Pine said, "Lemme guess, you used the trip here as your *initial* excuse to do something *more* fun, but then you got boxed in by your principal and didn't want them to catch on?"

Again, I said nothing.

"Good gracious, kid. I've done a lotta pullin' teeth in my line of work, but you'd give the guards at Fort Knox a run for their money! Can ya at least tell me *somethin'* about yourself? Your *real name*, perhaps?"

I stared up at Pine as he crossed his arms and gave me a shrewd glare.

"Ilya. My name is Ilya."

"Nobody knows you're here, do they, Ilya? Not your folks . . . and not your teachers."

"No, they don't," I mumbled.

Pine looked down at his shoes and slowly nodded. He grabbed a metal chair from underneath the lounge table and seated it and himself across from me.

"Ilya, you would not believe how many kids have been in your shoes. Comin' here without their folks and teachers bein' any the wiser. The sad reality is . . . the world is losing its tolerance for what it is we do here. We get angry phone calls, death threats, bomb threats . . . we've actually received feces in our mail if you can believe that."

I can, Reverend. I really can.

"We have and continue to work *tirelessly* to purge our image from our demons of the past, but it's obvious people will never be satisfied. So what happens now? Kids come to us in secret, under the cover of night. They show up to our doorstep needing respite from this crazy world and the pressure it puts on them. Do you see what I mean, Ilya?"

"Yeah," I muttered. "I think so. I think at this age it's hard to decide between what you want for you and what the world wants for you."

Pine clapped his hands together, pointed directly at me. "Young man, you are *right* on the money! That is exactly what I mean, and I'll tell ya what, son . . . it's only gotten worse."

As bizarre as the ongoing scenario was on an infinite amount of levels, I did feel as if Pine and I were on some similar page. I had never really been able to express my convictions this way to an adult before. I felt like I was actually being taken seriously, like I was being heard.

"Ilya, can I ask you something?" Pine said.

"Yeah, I guess so."

Pine leaned in, and suddenly, his eyes were filled with worry and unease. He lowered the tone and volume of his voice. "Does your *school* make you feel this way?"

School? What's school? Who goes to school? I've never heard of school. School doesn't need to know I was here. Can we please axe school from the conversation, please?

"No," I stuttered, "definitely not. School's fine. No worries there."

Pine nodded to himself. "Ilya, I want you to know that Revival is more than a summer camp. It's also an oasis — a *refuge,* rather — for so many kids, whether it be from school, from society, or, more often than not . . . their homes."

It was in that instant I knew where this was headed. I had to double back now.

I stuttered, "Oh . . . no . . . my home life is fine, really."

"Ilya, this is a safe space. You'd be surprised how far we extend our care for the welfare of our —"

"I don't need you to extend anything. There's nothing wrong with my home."

Pine nodded not in agreement or understanding, but in retreat. "Son, I am so sorry for intruding. I've obviously overstepped the line and I sincerely apologize. I guess it's an occupational hazard. I hope you can understand. So often we get kids whose parents have ideas in mind for them that they cannot possibly understand and we . . . well . . . anyway, let's forget about the whole ordeal. You oughta catch back up with your tour group."

I instantly stood up from the leather lounge chair and made my way to the door.

"Ilya, stop!" Pine shouted from behind.

I halted in my tracks, and my arm froze just short of the door handle. Suddenly, I remembered whose arena I was in. Footsteps started to make their way towards me from behind. I debated making a break for it but didn't want to cause a scene that could make its way back to Blount High, Mom, and Pastor Neary.

The footsteps stopped just behind me. I slowly turned and found two arms stretched out with water bottles in each hand. "You almost forgot you and Sasha's waters!"

The wave of relief was so intense I nearly tipped over. I let out a shivering laugh and took the cold bottles, nearly dropping them due in equal parts to the slipperiness of the bottles and my trembling hands.

"Thanks," I stuttered.

Pine rested his right hand on my right shoulder. He smiled widely and looked me in the eye before saying, "You are so welcome, son. I am so happy we could talk. I can already tell you are a bright and intelligent young man wise beyond his years. Your father must be extremely proud."

"Um . . ." I mumbled, "I actually don't . . . my dad left when I was a baby."

Pine let out a massive exhale, and his eyes welled up with deep devastation. "I am so, so sorry to hear that, Ilya. I try my best not to be a judging man, I leave that part to the big man . . . but all I *will* say is that man made the biggest mistake of his life walking out on you. You are gonna go far in this world, son. I promise."

The left side of my lip scrunched up in a half smile, and I said, "Thanks for saying that. Reverend, can I ask you something?"

"By all means, son. Shoot!"

"Did you know Brent Cushman?"

Pine's eyes lowered in pain. "Yes, son. I sure did. Now that kid was the true pencil in God's hand if ever there was one. It's damned tragic what happened. *Damned* tragic."

"Yeah, tragic. Do you know anything about his relationship with Pastor Erick Neary?"

Suddenly, Pine's eyes filled with shock. "What *relationship* with *Pastor Erick Neary?*"

"He mentored Brent over the summer. He tutored him very closely, from what I've heard."

"Son, you better not be pulling my leg. This is no laughing matter."

"I promise, I'm not."

Pine pouted. "I knew nothing about this, son. But promise me if that man ever comes near you or gives you the heebie-jeebies, you'll tell me straight away. Promise?"

"Yeah, of course. I promise."

Pine smiled and gave my shoulder two firm pats before saying, "Now go catch up with the tour or Robin's gonna beat my behind!"

After an hour or so of walking through some of the hiking trails and the archery range, the group made its way back to the main building where the tour began. We were taken through the dormitory hallways. It was eerie walking past all the vacant rooms with sheetless bunk beds and empty bulletin boards on the walls. It felt like the campers mysteriously vanished the night before and we were all there to investigate. My conversation with Reverend Pine reverberated through my mind the entire time.

The tour officially concluded directly at the spot where it began at the entrance door with Robin just before noon. I could tell Sasha was anxious for a status report on what exactly happened after our split-up, but I was at a loss for words. I was unsure of what we were there for in the first place, or how it was I would proceed. The visit seemed to spur more questions than answers. Even in the car ride home, I sat in a stupor.

"So, what happened? Did you find anything?" Sasha asked.

"I talked with the reverend guy," I mumbled.

"Okay . . . and? What did he say? Did you ask about Brent or Rox or Jozie? Did you ask about Neary?"

"Sasha, what if I was wrong?"

"*Wrong?*"

"This place, these people, what if it's a red herring?"

"A red *what?*"

"A red herring, it's something in a story that distracts the characters."

"Oh. Well . . . what would it be distracting us from?"

I pondered for a minute then replied, "I think it's time we go all in on Neary. Find out what his deal is. Maybe Jordan can —"

"No," Sasha said, or rather, demanded.

"No?"

"I knew this was a mistake. I knew it from the beginning."

"What was a *mistake?*"

"I'm so fucking stupid. We're gonna get found out, I'm getting kicked off volleyball, my parents are gonna ground me —"

"We are *not* getting found out, Sash. This was just a stepping stone so —"

"Ilya, STOP!" Sasha shouted.

I slammed on the brakes, and we both jolted forward. Sasha hung her head low with her eyes closed.

"Sash?" I asked pathetically. "What's wrong?"

Sasha was silent for a brief moment before whispering, "I just want you *back*, Ill."

"What do you mean?"

Sasha lifted her head and stared me square in the eye. I had never seen her more scared in my life. She said, "Ill, do you remember when we'd take hikes in the summer as little kids and we'd recreate your stories?"

"Yes, Sash, of course I do. We would pretend we were being chased by ghosts. You would pretend to fall, and when I would look back to save you, you would say, 'Run! I'm done for! They're gonna make me a ghost too! Save yourself!' You said it was because heroes always tell other characters to keep running."

Sasha smiled, but the tears that fell from her eyes were not joyful. She looked at me like I was an impersonator, something masquerading as a person they're not.

She asked, "Why can't I have that Ilya back? The Ilya that would spend hours telling me about the worlds he was building and the new languages he was making up? The Ilya that told eight-year-old me she didn't have to be scared about being so far away from Pakistan because 'heroes always start their journey far away from their home'? The Ilya that made me feel like I was actually in charge of my own story? What happened to *him*?"

All I could do was sit and stare back at her helplessly. I remembered every single story she shared, though it had been years since I last recalled most of them. I wanted so painfully to give her the friend she wanted. But that friend was gone. That friend was far, far away from that car in the middle of the woods.

Sasha said, "You're killing yourself, Ill. All of this . . . whatever *this* is . . . it's destroying you. Carol sees it too."

"Mom?"

"She called me last night. She was completely breaking down crying. She said she didn't even recognize you anymore. She said you don't talk during dinners like you used to. She said her heart breaks every night again and again. She wanted to know if I knew anything about what was going on with you. She said she wasn't mad at anyone, she just wanted her son back."

I had never seen Sasha look more fearful in our entire friendship. Since we were little, she was always the bravest person I knew. But the look in her eye reminded me that even if I had no issue walking into the gates of hell for a friend, the people standing by my side would be joining me. I felt like I had been violently shaken from some deep trance by a hypnotist.

"I'm sorry," I said. "I never meant for you or Mom to be hurt."

"We just want you to be okay, Ill. I know you love Rox and I know you want answers for why we lost Brent, but there may not be any to find."

I reflected on this. "Maybe you're right. Coming here was a mistake. Putting you at risk of getting kicked off volleyball was a mistake."

"Ilya, it's fucking *volleyball*. You're my best friend. And I don't think coming here was a mistake at all. If it helped put your mind at ease in any way, it was worth it for me."

I smirked a pathetic half smile. I was so indebted to Sasha at that moment I could have broken down and cried. Suddenly, she took my right hand in hers and gently said, "Let's go *home*, Ill."

Fourteen

I STARED UP AT the ceiling from my bed for hours. Sasha's words echoed through my mind the entire time. I never wanted anyone else to get hurt. It had never occurred to me until then that I was scaring the people who loved me most. All I wanted was to better understand what Rox was going through. I couldn't just take a crowbar to them and force the answers out, despite how much I wanted to at times.

Maybe all I could do from this point on was be there for Rox in any way I could. Maybe I should go back to caring about school. Maybe I should try out for theater like I've always wanted to. Maybe I should put Revival and even Pastor Neary in my rearview. Maybe Sasha was right; maybe we built Brent Cushman up so high he lost his balance and fell hard.

Before I could ponder any further, I felt a vibration from the left side of my bed. It was a phone call . . . a phone call from Jordan.

I answered, "Jordan?"

"*Ilya, we gotta talk. I've got some serious news.*" His voice sounded manic.

"What news?"

"I tracked down some alumni message boards online recently, and one of the alumns reached out to me personally and said he's willing to meet in person."

"So let me get this straight, an *anonymous* person from an *anonymous* message board *anonymously* expressed interest in meeting you in person, site unseen?"

"That would be correct, yes."

"Terrific. Next question, were you planning on purchasing oil at a hardware store in case this guy needs to lubricate his chainsaw before chopping you up into bits in his shed?"

"I know it's a little shady, Ill —"

"A *little?*"

"But it's about time we really start to dig even deeper than before. For Jozie's sake, for Rox's sake, for Brent's sake, for the sake of every kid who was —"

"Jordan," I interrupted, "we can't keep doing this."

"Doing what? Uncovering the truth? Blowing the lid off Revival and putting those pieces of shit behind bars where they belong?"

"Let's just say this guy you meet up with talks and gives you the bombshell testimony of the century. What then?"

"We share his story for the world to hear. We finally hold that cult accountable."

"Did he even mention how long ago he was a camper? What if it was before the '90s? Before the change in leadership? It would all be old news."

"Ilya, I'm not sure why you're grilling me on this. If memory serves, you were more hell-bent on nailing these assholes than anyone else."

He wasn't wrong.

"I was, until I realized how much I was hurting the people who care about me. I know you're worried about Jozie, but maybe all we can do is be there for —"

"There is no being there for Jozie anymore. Jozie doesn't talk to me. You don't think I've tried to be there for her this entire time? Every single day I text her and call her. No answer. There is nothing in this world I want more than to be there for her. But she's built a wall around herself and blocked everyone else out. And it kills me. It absolutely fucking crushes me not being able to just talk to her about anything. Anything at all. The weird movies she likes. The old bands she obsesses over. I don't care."

I could hear Jordan getting choked up the longer he spoke. *"If you've made peace with those scumbags and what they've done to our friends and family, I won't take that away from you, Ill. I'm happy for you. Truly. But I love that kid more than anything in this world, and if there's even a chance somebody hurt her, they're gonna deal with me. End of fucking story."*

Jordan was TFG. Too far gone. I knew from experience that there was no changing a manic person's mind once it was made up.

"His name is Nathaniel. We're meeting at Shelly's tomorrow at four. Either you're coming or you're not."

Beep beep.

Jordan hung up. I let the phone slip out of my grip as I stared at the ceiling. I was feeling the suffocating grip of Revival finally starting to loosen. But now I was hurled back into the same crossroads from earlier in the day in the car with Sasha. How legit was Jordan's source? Was it a ruse? What if it was some plant from Revival to catch us asking questions? What if Jordan was walking into a trap? I knew I would only drive myself even crazier than I had already felt if I kept asking myself questions, so I decided to throw my phone on the charger and make an attempt to sleep.

But for the next two hours, I laid in bed with my eyes closed and pictured my walk through Revival. The hallways, the humid gym, the trees, the dorm rooms. I wondered if the Deep Throat that Jordan was meeting tomorrow had walked those very hallways and slept in those bunk beds. I wondered if he was gay, or bi, or pan, or ace. Maybe he wasn't even queer at all. Maybe he was just misunderstood at the wrong time and in the wrong place. I wondered what he looked like and how old he was. I wondered what his favorite bands were at the time. I wondered if he had ever been in love. I wondered what his goals and dreams were before he was driven up to that front door, the same one Sasha and I walked through just hours ago.

Before I finally and miraculously drifted off into sleep, I had made up my mind. Maybe it had to be made up in order for sleep to come.

———————

"So what exactly's the lowdown on this guy?" I asked.

"All I know is he was a camper in the '80s when it was Wetmore's reign. Trust me, he's been in the shit," Jordan said.

The two of us were seated at a table in the center of Shelly's Diner. One lone metallic chair sat across from us, meant to seat Jordan's message-board herald. He was running 20 minutes late.

"What's a *Wetmore*?" I asked as I peered out the diner windows.

"Pastor Martin Wetmore. Revival was *his* brainchild. He opened it in the '70s after Harvey Milk started what he deemed the 'devil's ongoing doctrine threatening the Christian family's stake in the US.'"

I could tell from his inflection that Jordan had this quote memorized. It could only mean his knowledge of the history of Revival was broaching encyclopedic. It made me uneasy.

"Any idea what he looks like?" I asked.

Before Jordan could answer, the entrance of the diner swung open and the bells atop the threshold chimed throughout the room. Jordan and I lifted our heads in perfect sync, but we only found a wrinkled elderly man in jean overalls, a trucker hat, glasses, and a white mustache. A stock image of Farmer Brown couldn't do better justice.

"Hello, Audrey dear!" the old man said. "How's the hip?"

"Oh, just fine, Nate, thank you for asking!" Audrey replied with a bright smile as she poured coffee behind the bar.

Jordan and I both sighed and looked out the window.

"He's 20 minutes late, Jordan. What are the chances he got cold feet?"

"He'll be here. Just be patient."

"The longer we wait, the longer this feels like a giant mistake. What exact questions were you planning on asking?"

"Don't overthink this, Ill. You're stressing me out, and I'm really not appreciating it."

"It's not overthinking for me to ask what your game plan is. I mean, Jordan, you're asking a complete stranger to spill his guts on probably the most fucked-up experience of his life to a couple of kids. It would bode well for you to —"

"What would *bode well* for me is if you quit running your damn mouth while I try to think. I didn't put a gun to your head and make you —"

"Excuse me, are you Jordan?" Jordan and I instantly glanced upward in the voice's direction and saw the old farmer looking down at us with wide eyes through large square spectacles.

"Yes, do I know you?" Jordan asked. "We're kind of waiting on someone and —"

"Nathan," the old man said. "Nathan Holtmeyer. We spoke . . . well . . . we spoke on the net."

The wrinkled gentleman was Nathaniel. The old farmer in overalls was Deep Throat. Jordan and I continued to stare up at him but said nothing.

"Mind if I sit?" Nathan asked gently. "I got a bad leg."

Still, Jordan and I said nothing.

Nathan barked, "You fellas are makin' me nervous. I don't like feelin' a nuisance much."

"We're sorry," I said. "Of course you can sit."

Nathan withdrew the metallic chair from under the table, and the sound startled Jordan and I both out of our trance. He took his seat, crossed his arms, and stared back at both of us. I gave Jordan's leg a small kick.

"Um, what's your name?" Jordan mumbled like an idiot.

"My *name*? Well damn, son, you got a short-term memory? I ain't said my full name but five bleedin' seconds ago. You sayin' you already forgotten it since I sat down?"

"Oh, right. Um, sorry. Right. Nathaniel. Your name." Jordan was flailing in the wind. I could have passed out from the sheer cringe.

Nathan instantly got restless and did a strange shuffle in his chair. "The good Lord and his heavenly angels were short on brains when they pieced you Rhodes Scholars together."

"Our friends and family went to Revival," I said finally.

Nathan shot me a glance. "Well, ain't that somethin'? They do any canoein'?"

It was painfully clear we were wasting precious time, but Jordan wasn't exactly putting on a clinic with his gift of gab.

"You went to Revival, though. Right?" Jordan asked.

Nathan kept his sights on me. "Yes, son. I did go to Revival." There was something distrustful in his eyes. It was the look of someone who spends their day on guard with no rest.

"Well . . . we were just wondering what that was like for you," Jordan said.

A part of me wanted to stuff Jordan's mouth with a muffin from the display case to shut him up. It was becoming more and more clear by the syllable that he was brutally unprepared.

Nathan's wrinkled lips curled up into an odd pout, and he stared down at his boots. "Hmm, what was *Revival* . . . like . . . for *me*?" Nathan asked with a bitter and condescending tone. He continued to look down at the floor and appeared to be deep in thought, but it was more likely he was dragging us over the coals.

He said, "Welp, I'll tell ya one thing, it wasn't no fuckin' Fourth of July jamb-o-ree. No stargazin' at night and s'mores around the fire, no siree."

"If it's okay my asking, what year did you go and how old were you?" I asked.

Nathan shot me the same wary glance as before. "That'd be 'bout 1981, and I figured I was no north or south of . . . 15 years old. Reagan had been inaugurated that same January."

"What happened?" Jordan asked. This was the least tactful way of going about things, yet it was the smartest thing Jordan had asked since Nathan took his seat.

Nathan stared Jordan down for five or so seconds before lowering his yellow, jaundiced eyes to the floor. Slowly but surely, his eyes became glazed over in thought for what felt like 20 straight seconds. Jordan and I could only sit and watch his thousand-yard stare.

I panicked. "I'm sorry, we're sure it was a —"

"You fellas know 'bout the *Greyhuff Review*?" Nathan asked.

"The gray what?" Jordan asked.

"*Greyhuff Review*, son. It was an old magazine from, hell, probably long before either of your mommas were born. This may come as a shock to you two brainiacs, but we didn't have phones and internet when I was your age. We had newspapers and magazines. That's all."

"What kind of magazine?" I asked, though I had a strong suspicion.

Nathan went silent as his eyes became fraught with unease.

He said, "My paw found it under my bed one night, and he beat me purple. Momma threw herself between me and him and ended up gettin' a shiner herself in the process. Well, a *new* shiner that is. Paw was a hard man. He had expectations for us. *Good* expectations. That's what Momma always said, at least. Still, I always blamed myself when she got purple too. She joined the almighty back in '02 and, hell . . . I still blame myself."

Jordan and I said nothing, but we both nodded.

"Paw yelled, 'I'd sooner tip over with Grammy's necrosis before I let a sod sleep under my roof and share a dinner table with my wife.' Soon after, he heard tell about a facility that deals with young boys goin' sideways. Hell, he woulda shipped me off then and there with a big red bow on my head if he had a mind to."

The more Nathan talked, the quicker the words came to him. I could see in his eyes the events playing out before him in real time. He was almost witnessing them for the first time along with us.

Nathan said, "First thing they do with us boys after we get dropped off by our folks was file us into this big ole gymnasium. Hotter than a blister bug, I remember. Suddenly, a man in a white suit and white pants come out onto the stage they had with a microphone in his hand."

"Pastor Martin Wetmore?" Jordan interrupted.

Nathan closed his eyes shut with a wince of pain. Suddenly, his exhales became slightly louder and more prolonged. "He was a loud gentleman, big boomin' voice that scared us boys half to death. He launches into some spiel about our souls and damnation, somethin' involving a lake of fire. I remember his face was beet red and drenched in sweat, a 'whore in church,' my grammy would say. You could hear a pin drop when he'd stop to catch his breath. He tells us that the devil took many forms and that he could be inside any of us, plotting and scheming. All of a sudden, he —"

During this pause, I noticed Nathan's hands were trembling. His lips shivered. "He stretched his arm out and pointed to a gentleman to my left. His name . . . Lance . . . Lambert, come from Temple, Texas. Well, he points his finger directly at poor Lance and he says into that microphone, 'The devil may exist in any of you young boys, it could even be that boy standin' there!' I'll never forget the look in poor Lance's eyes, that boy was scared shitless. Suddenly, that man in white comes down from the stage . . . makes his way towards Lance and stations himself right in front of the two of us boys. He held the mic up to poor Lance and asks him his name. I hadn't said much to Lance at that point, but I could tell he was a bit shy. Well, once poor Lance says his name, the man tells us that the devil may well live inside Lance and that he needed casting out. No, not casting out . . . *beaten* out. *Beaten out.*"

Nathan's yellow eyes were fraught with dread and looked as if they were on the cusp of tears. "'Gentlemen,' he says, 'we are each of us soldiers in God's battle against wickedness. We are enlisted in his fight against Satan and his perversions.

We must not only rise to face the devil where he stands, we must also save your brother Lance from his grasp.' Suddenly, the man THREW" — Nathan banged his fists on the metallic table, startling nearby customers and knocking over the saltshaker — "THREW his hands on Lance's shoulders and began to shake him stupid, as he ranted and raved about the devil and his trickery. Then, he gave Lance a big shove into the other fellas, and the boy he landed on gave him a big heave from behind with both his hands."

Suddenly, tears began to dart down Nathan's cheeks, his nostrils flared, and he pouted like an angry child. "Before he even realized it, a boy struck him straight in his jaw during the commotion, and down goes Lance onto that wooden floor. I bent down to help him up off the floor, but the rest of the boys . . . started . . ."

Nathan's eyes shut closed. His mustache was wet with tears and a little snot.

"*Kickin'*," Nathan whispered. "Them boys started *kickin'* poor Lance while he laid there on the floor like a stump in the grass. He started to wail and holler like a little boy, but the kicks kept comin'. The man with the microphone kept wailin' on about the devil and his tricks as those boys beat Lance silly. It wasn't long until . . . lil drips of blood began to leap and jump out from under us like jumpin' beans. Lance kept on wailin' and sobbin' like a bleeding newborn baby."

Nathan went silent. Tears continued to stream down his wrinkled face, but his sobs were suppressed. He continued to tremble like a leaf. Jordan and I sat in complete and utter silence, neither of us moving a singular muscle.

"I'm sorry," I mumbled, "I'm so sorry you went through that."

Nathan said, "I cried myself to sleep that night, right in that bunk bed. I had spent my whole childhood watching my daddy beat my momma, and I swore to myself I'd never hurt no one in the world ever. But I stood there and let them bastards beat poor Lance within an inch of his life for no goddamn reason. Each sermon after that day, the man would pick on another poor son-of-a-bitch and sic us on him like dogs. Bloody shoe prints would —"

In that instant, Nathan broke into soft sobs. Gentle sobs.

"It's okay. You don't have to relive it anymore. We're sorry," Jordan said.

"They taught us to hate each other and to hate ourselves, and I ain't never been properly loved since. Not by my paw or momma. Not by a man or a woman. Spend most nights alone in bed starin' at the ceiling fan and wonder what we boys did to deserve those beatings. If we didn't have the devil beaten out of us that summer, we sure as shitfire got beaten *into* devils by the time we packed up and went back home."

"We're sorry they convinced you you can't be loved. It's not true," I said.

Nathan's brow scrunched, and his eyes filled with anger. "Why the hell did I come here? Why did you damn kids make me remember that shit? Are you sick in your heads?"

"We just want to make sure no kid ever feels the way you did," Jordan said. "We want to blow the lid off Revival and put those scumbags like the pastor behind —"

"Pastor?" Nathan asked. "What *pastor?*"

"His name's Neary, he's —"

"Erick Neary?" Nathan asked.

Jordan and I instantly locked eyes. "Yes," Jordan said dumbfoundedly. "Do you know him? Did he hurt you?"

Nathan's eyes darted between me and Jordan with an unsettling intensity. "I don't want no part of this anymore. I knew this was a damned mistake. I don't wanna hear any damn Erick Neary ever again. Don't you say his fuckin' name again, understand?"

Suddenly, Nathan stood up so quickly that his metallic chair tipped over behind him. The crashing sound stunned the entire diner into silence, which was then broken by the sound of the bells chiming as Nathan thrust the front door open and stormed outside.

"What in the Sam Hill did you boys do to poor Nate?" Audrey shouted from the kitchen. "That poor soul's gotta cross to bear none of y'all can even imagine. Shame on y'all!"

"We're sorry, Audrey," I mumbled.

"Sorry ain't gonna cut it, you two best get your behinds out this diner before I call the cops. We treat elders with *respect* in here, dammit."

Jordan and I threw a handful of dollars on the table for our sodas and headed for the exit.

"Those fucking animals, they belong *under* the jail for what they did to him and his friends. They fucked them all upside their heads and got away with it," Jordan barked as he crossed the street to his car.

"Jordan, why did you go to Neary's house?" I shouted in his direction.

He froze in the middle of the crosswalk. He turned around and marched back to the sidewalk where I stood. "How the hell did you —"

"Sasha and I got ordered to the principal's office the other week, and *he* was waiting for us. He emptied the room and threatened us into silence."

"What do you mean *threatened*?"

"Jordan, what the hell were you thinking going to his house?"

"I just wanted to know if anything happened to Jozie. All I asked about was Jozie. I was so fucking scared and I just couldn't go back home. I just couldn't, Ill."

"What did Neary do?"

Jordan shrugged. "He told me he wasn't at Revival this summer and had no idea about Jozie. I couldn't tell if he was bullshitting or not. But what do you mean he *threatened*? Like, threatened to hurt you two?"

"He told us to let things play out if we knew what was best for us."

"You mean the horror story we just heard in there? He wants us to let *that* continue to play out? Like fucking hell we will."

"Jordan, that was over 40 years ago. That was a decade before the scandal and before they cleaned house. Everyone who oversaw what happened is probably dead by now. What are we supposed to do?"

"I'll go back on the message boards. I'll find someone who went there more recently and get them to agree —"

"Jordan, you *need* to stop this. *All* of this. Do you even know what you're saying?"

"Y'know what, Ilya? I guess not. I guess I made a mistake thinking Brent's life mattered as much to you as it does to me."

I snapped, "This has *nothing* to do with Brent, Jordan."

"Fine, what about your friend Rox? What about Jozie? Are you just gonna give up on them too?"

"No, I'm not. Because no matter what we find out on the internet or whichever old bastard we fish out of the woodwork and make relive a waking nightmare, there's no changing what happened to them. We're not even sure Revival is to blame for Brent's death."

"What the hell makes you say that?"

I paused for a brief second. "Sasha and I went to Revival yesterday. We took a tour."

"You *what*?"

"You really think you're the only one losing sleep because of this? I've been numb the past three fucking weeks thinking about Brent, Rox, and Jozie nonstop."

Jordan's anger melted into suspicion. "What happened?"

"I met with the reverend, we talked in his office. He asked a few questions, but, Jordan, what are the chances Revival has just been blown out of proportion this entire time? What if Brent just had too much to drink at a stupid party? What if Jozie is just lonely and needs a friend? What if this whole goddamn conspiracy theory is just a rabbit hole we both fell down?"

Jordan simply stared at me and said nothing.

I said, "I'm sorry, Jordan. I blame myself for letting things go this far. I mean, what the fuck business did we have making some lonely old man relive something so unspeakably terrible?"

"No, it's not your fault, Ill. It's my fault. I should have listened to Brent more that night of the party. I feel like if I would have just stayed in the car with him, he —" Jordan's eyes suddenly welled up with tears. "It's my fault he's dead."

"No, Jordan. It's not."

"I never should have gotten out of that fucking car. I should have let him keep talking and talking the whole night if it meant he never went into that house."

"Jordan, you *did* listen to him. You were exactly the friend he needed that night."

"But he's gone, Ilya. He was my best friend in the entire world and right now he's in the fucking ground. We were supposed to be roommates at U of M and rush together. Now I'm on some . . . *pathetic* crusade trying to avenge him because I don't know what the hell else to do with my life. And Jozie won't even —" In that instant, Jordan burst into tears in the middle of the sidewalk. Before I had time to process, he wrapped his arms around my shoulders and began sobbing. I never would have imagined an alpha type like Jordan crying and hugging another dude in broad daylight.

I hugged back. "Brent didn't die because of you, and Jozie has you, me, and Rox now. She knows we love her to death, and we're gonna continue to love her through this chapter of her life *together*."

Jordan continued to cry into my left shoulder. "I'm so fucking tired of being scared. I'm so fucking tired of being tired."

"I know, so am I. But we have to push through this *together*. None of us can do it alone."

"You're right. I'm sorry. I'm so sorry, Ilya."

"Don't be sorry. I'm here for you."

Jordan's sobs began to simmer down. He eventually withdrew from the hug and began to recollect himself. "I wanna go home."

I nodded. "So do I."

"Oh, one more thing. I know this is awkward timing and all, but Jozie's birthday is this Saturday. You and I both know she doesn't have a lot of friends, but she's still throwing a party for herself. I don't think you know how much it would mean to her if you and Rox showed up even for a minute."

I replied, "If Jozie wants us at her party, we're gonna be at her party."

Jordan smiled. "The party theme is *X-Files*."

Fifteen

"THE THEME IS X *what*?" Sasha asked.

"*X-Files*," I said. "It was an old TV show back in the '90s. Jordan says it's the theme Jozie wanted."

Sasha was struggling to find an outfit in her closet that would be fitting for a sci-fi show involving aliens and the FBI. I was fortunate to make do with a regular black suit and tie.

"Y'know, I remember girls in middle school opting for horses or boy bands for their birthday themes," Sasha said as she tried on her baba's old brown blazer.

"Jozie's a bit of an old soul."

"Who's all coming, then? I really *don't* feel like being on babysitter duty while all the parents get drunk."

"I don't think kids in seventh grade require babysitting. Plus, I wouldn't worry about that. I don't think she has a lot of friends."

"*Please* don't say that," Sasha said with a pout. "That actually breaks my heart."

"I know, mine too. But I remember that age and how badly nobody wanted to stand out, combine that with living in Anthem."

"Yep. Standing out from the crowd has to be social suicide before it can be cool for some stupid reason. Now you know why I never wear my hijab." Hearing this stopped me in my tracks. Suddenly, I had a flashback to my talk with Sasha's baba and the story of her getting bullied.

"Have you ever considered wearing one to school one day?" I asked.

"What? A *hijab*? Are you serious?"

"I mean, what better way to show people you can't be deterred in your faith? What if it was your way of taking a stand?"

"Ill, that's *not* how hijabs work. I don't wear them to make others uncomfortable or to piss others off. It's a symbol of my *faith*. It's not something I wear to shove in people's faces."

"But you still think people will be upset by you wearing one?"

"Ilya, you're still missing the point. I'm not basing my choice on the criteria of what idiots at school think. I couldn't care less. It's more than just appearance. It's about *control* too."

"Control of when and where you choose to wear one?"

"Yes, exactly. It's an autonomy thing, I guess."

I noticed it was getting close to time for the party. "Maybe I can get you one of those athletic hijabs for when you start playing in college."

"You mean *volleyball*?" Sasha asked.

"Well, yeah. Aren't you gonna play in college?"

"I don't even know if I'm gonna be playing next year."

"What? Why?"

Sasha gave a slight half frown. "I just don't know if it's me anymore. I see memories on Snap of me playing freshman year, and I wonder where all that heart went. But training camp has felt like I'm just going through the motions. I can't really explain it."

"Do you still get along with the girls?"

"I mean, we still have inside jokes and hang out. But there have been sleepovers where I lay in the middle of the room and I just feel . . . *surrounded* by people who don't even know me. Sometimes I wonder how they talk about me behind my back."

"I'm sure it's never anything negative."

"I'm not sure, Ill. I mean, everyone knows I can have a temper on the court. I promised Coach I would work on it this season."

"Since when was playing with your heart on your sleeve a bad thing?"

"Since it resulted in me drawing *four* different miscon-ducts in a single season."

"Oof, that'll do it."

"And sometimes I really do sit and wonder if any of these girls would give me the time of day if it weren't for the fact that I was a great spiker. What would we even have in common?"

It upset me to hear Sasha talk about herself in this way. Anyone who couldn't or didn't want to appreciate how strong, funny, and kind of a friend she was didn't deserve her.

She said, "The worst was last year when we had a game during Ramadan. I was fasting and kept having to preserve my energy during the game. A lot of the girls were mad that I was choosing fasting over my team. They said I wasn't being a team player."

"That's complete bullshit, Sash. You're a bigger team player than any of them."

"But it was obvious they preferred Volleyball Sasha over Muslim Sasha. None of them were even trying to understand the position I was in. It felt like . . . they weren't seeing me for the whole person that I am."

"Well, if they don't see it by now, they don't deserve to have it."

"Ilya," Sasha said, "this doesn't have to be a therapy session. You don't have to rescue me with affirmations and nice words."

"I'm sorry," I mumbled, "that wasn't my —"

"And you don't have to be sorry every single time, either. You're literally fine. But sometimes it'd be nice to just sit here with you and talk about these things and have it just be that. You don't have to have the perfect thing to say to each of my problems. Sometimes I just wanna vent."

"Okay, I understand. I guess I just hate seeing you be down on yourself like this."

"But maybe it's okay that I am. Maybe I deserve to feel a little lost or confused."

"Yeah, I guess." The truth is, I wasn't exactly sure what Sasha meant by saying she deserved to feel this way. Was she saying these feelings were some kind of punishment or atonement? Or were the feelings something she was entitled to feel?

"We should go, it's about that time," Sasha said, having settled on her baba's black blazer from his adolescence. She had the stature and build to fill it surprisingly well.

———

"YOU CAME! YOU ACTUALLY CAME!" Jozie shrieked as she darted straight for us from the couch in the living room. While I was trapped in Jozie's ironclad hug, I noticed Rox was seated on the same couch with a Nintendo 64 controller in their hand. Our entrance had disrupted what was surely a fierce duel of *Mario Kart*.

Rox and I had on matching outfits.

"Oh my God, you came as Mulder too! Absolute slay!" Jozie said, bouncing up and down with glee. I would have been heartbroken by the glaring lack of seventh graders if Jozie's happiness wasn't exhaustingly contagious. "And you must be Sasha! I've *literally* been obsessed with you since forever! I think it's so awesome that you're Muslim! Did you know that an Islamic university deemed gender reassignment surgery to be acceptable under Islamic law in the '80s? Isn't that awesome? I guess Muslims are the *real* trailblazers!"

Sasha's eyes widened, and she said, "I did *not* know that! I guess you learn something new every day." Sasha and I both made eye contact and had to stifle laughter.

Jozie said, "So Ilya, let me go ahead and catch you up on what's been going down while we graciously awaited your arrival. Basically, Rox thinks Alison Bechdel should have won the MacArthur award for *Dykes to Watch Out For* instead of *Fun Home*, but personally I think her capturing family dysfunction during the '70s and tying it to her coming to terms with her sexuality was basically iconic. Don't you agree?"

I said, "Well, I definitely —"

"Also, Rox and I had a *heated* debate on Cher's best era. Personally, I think *Believe* was her best comeback era, but Rox thinks her starring in *Moonstruck* encapsulated how dynamic of a performer she was. What do you think, Sasha?"

Sasha replied, "I actually don't know a lot of —"

"Oh my GOD! You guys are gonna LOVE the karaoke contest later tonight! We have everyone from Bonnie Tyler to Tori Amos, so get your vocal chops ready!"

"I'm down!" Sasha said enthusiastically.

"Yay! This is gonna be the best birthday ever! Just me and my besties singing and telling hilarious stories. This is all I ever wanted."

I could have cried. Why couldn't I have been this easily content when I was her age?

"Hey, where's Jordan?" Sasha asked.

"Oh. He said he was feeling sick so he's staying home. Such a loser, right?" Jozie chuckled. "I'm just kidding, he's literally the best big cousin ever! But we'll have to just have fun without him. Do you guys want any Fanta?"

After an impassioned game of *X-Files*-themed charades and karaoke, Jozie had worn the three of us out in remarkable time. Whether it was the incessant leaping from pop culture trivia to debates on which Lady Gaga album was the most divisive amongst fans, it was clear she didn't regularly have many sociable moments to shine and was getting the biggest bang for her buck tonight. But little to my surprise, all of us were game for just about anything thrown our way.

"So Jozie," Sasha said, "are you ready for high school?"

"Yes, absolutely!" Jozie replied emphatically. "I plan on getting super involved and I wanna make a lot of friends and make memories."

"That's great!" I said. "What were you planning on joining? Theater? Choir?"

"Oh, I won't be joining anything! Here's how I have it all pictured: I'm gonna march *straight* to the principal's office the first day of my freshman year, and I'm gonna create Blount High's first-ever LGBTQIA+ social club for students! I have all sorts of amazing ideas and I don't plan on taking no for an answer!"

Rox and I made eye contact instantly. I could tell we were both having the exact same internal experience.

"Wow, that's amazing, Jozie!" Sasha said. Her enthusiasm was genuine, but she was no doubt covering for the joint silence from me and Rox.

"Right?! Basically, I have this grand plan of me storming the bigoted and colorless gates of the high school, leading a rainbow-colored parade, and marching Blount forward into the future."

"That *really* is amazing, Jozie," Rox said. "Have you told your parents about this?"

"Oh . . . no, not really. I don't think they'd like the idea," Jozie said, her tone flattening.

"Why wouldn't they?" Sasha asked.

"They think my being bi is some kind of phase. They say it's just like any other trend like when they were both young, and that I'm gonna look back one day and regret it."

Rox said, "My dad said the same thing when I told him I was nonbinary."

"Really?"

"Yep. He asked me if I was having a manic episode and considered driving me to the hospital."

"Rox, if it's okay my asking . . ."

"Of course, dearie, what's up?"

"When did you *know* you were nonbinary?"

Rox smiled and stared directly at me. I smiled back.

"Beast Boy." I said.

"Beast Boy?" Jozie asked. "Like from *Teen Titans*?"

Rox said, "Beast Boy was a shapeshifter. He could manipulate how others saw him on a whim. When I was little, I would sit in class and think about what I would shift into if I had that power."

Jozie replied, "But you didn't have the power. Nobody does, sadly."

"But that's not exactly true, Jozie. What I learned was even though I couldn't morph into a T-rex or a jaguar, I had the power to *express* myself. I realized that if it didn't feel right how others perceived me, I could always change how I was *perceived*. I remember one day when I was your age, I ditched school and went thrifting with my dad's credit card and got all the crazy and wacky clothes I could get my hands on. Some days I felt like wearing boy polos, other days I wore skirts and flared bell-bottoms. I wrote shapeshifter characters all the time in my stories too. And the more I did, the more power I realized I actually had."

"That's so *amazing*, Rox," Jozie said. "You're honestly such an icon for that. I wish I had a cool backstory with being bi instead of my parents sending me to some camp to fix me."

Rox, Sasha, and I exchanged glances. We knew we had to proceed with caution but didn't want to treat the issue like a taboo.

"What did the camp have to say about it? Your bi-ness?" Rox asked.

Jozie said, "Well, you could really tell they didn't want us making choices that weren't true to ourselves. They never came out and *bashed* being gay or anything like that. I just remember them telling us to stay true to ourselves, and not to 'give in to the crowd,' whatever that means."

"So . . . they never made you feel *guilty* or *ashamed*?" Sasha asked.

Jozie took a brief moment to ponder the question, then began shaking her head and replied, "I guess not. I don't remember them specifically calling it out or anything."

"You mentioned you had a pen pal at our coffee date," I said.

"You mean Rory?" Jozie asked.

"Yes, Rory. What was his experience?"

"We only really saw each other during recreation and service. He liked archery the most, but sometimes he'd be absent for counseling."

"Counseling?" I asked.

"Well, yeah. Rox, you were there too. Didn't you do counseling?" Jozie asked.

Rox could only look on with an expression of complete and utter confusion.

"Well, I guess they only had so many counselors for us," Jozie said.

"How would Rory feel after his *counseling*?" Rox asked.

"I wouldn't usually catch up with him again until service that same night. But by then, he usually seemed like himself. Weren't the services *amazing*, Rox? They were probably my favorite part of the whole summer."

Rox's eyes were turning from confusion to panic. I knew we were heading for calamity and had to steer the conversation in a different direction completely. *Quickly.*

"I think the LGBTQIA+ club is an amazing idea, Jozie," Sasha said. "I think you're gonna help a ton of kids feel proud of themselves."

"Thank you for saying that! I really, really hope so. I want so badly to make other kids feel the way you guys make me feel."

Rox's eyes were darting back and forth, deep in thought. Too deep for me or anyone present to intervene. But I didn't want Jozie taking on any blame or feeling she was responsible.

"Jozie," I said, "can I ask you something about Revival?"

Jozie's eyes lit up. "Yes, of course!"

"How often did you interact with Pastor Erick Neary?"

Sasha and Rox both shot me confused looks.

"Oh, the church guy? Not a lot. I mean . . . Rory said he saw him drop Brent off in his car one time."

"Brent Cushman?" I asked.

"Yeah. It's really terrible what happened to him. He was seriously the nicest guy I've ever met in my life. He always had a smile on his face. I never would have figured he'd . . . well . . ."

"How often did you *see* Brent?" I asked. Sasha and Rox continued to stare me down as their confusion turned into suspicion.

"I just remember he was around a lot more in the first half of the summer. After July, he fell off the face of the Earth. Nobody knew why. But I do remember Rory saying that whenever Brent would get dropped off by Neary, he would look like a scared little kid."

Rox anxiously shot up from their seat. "Ill, you forgot your story journal in my car last week. Wanna go out and grab it?"

I never took my story journal out of my room. Rox was lying so we could have a sidebar, but why?

"Oh, right. Good thinking," I said sheepishly before getting off the couch to head for the front door.

———

I followed Rox to their father's truck parked across from the house. The sun had gone down around 5 p.m., and I could see our breath in the cold air as we crossed the street. Rox suddenly whipped themself around and stared daggers at me. "What the *hell* was that?"

"What do you mean?" I asked.

"Don't act stupid, Ill. It's that girl's fucking birthday party, and you're turning it into a courtroom drama. What the hell are you thinking asking about Revival and Neary?"

"I had to make sure stories were lining up."

"Stories lining up?"

I instantly froze. Rox didn't know about our trip to Revival or my and Jordan's botched meeting with Nathaniel.

I mumbled, "Yeah, your story and —"

"No," Rox interrupted, "you said *stories*. Whose stories are you referring to?"

I said nothing.

"Ilya, tell me now, or I swear to God I am never talking to you ever again." Rox's voice began to shake.

"Sasha and I went to Revival this week."

"You *what*?"

"And yesterday, Jordan and I met with an alumnus of Revival who went there in the '80s."

Disappointment. Deep, deep disappointment filled Rox's eyes. I wanted so desperately for them to give any reply to spare me from the shame I felt, but no reply came.

I said, "I can't sleep, Rox. I can't focus on anything. Not school. Not writing. Not books. Nothing. I've been worried sick for you the past three months, but you've been so distant and cold and vague . . . I couldn't take it anymore. I couldn't stand the idea of one of my best friends suffering in silence. I never meant to hurt you or anyone, all I wanted was to better understand what you were going through. Please don't hate me, Rox. Please."

Rox said nothing but continued to stare up at me with eyes full of disappointment and sadness. Finally, they said, "I never, *ever* wanted to be some social case for you and Sash to rescue. I never wanted for you to go on some crusade to avenge me or Brent or Jozie. I wanted one thing. One, simple thing. I wanted you to understand. I wanted you to just try to understand why I can't relive this summer. Because I'm fucking horrified that if I start to relive it, I don't know if I'll ever stop."

I felt the red-hot shame inside of me burn hotter with each passing second.

I mumbled stupidly, "Rox, I'm so sorry."

"That's all you are, Ill. You're *sorry*. You're always *sorry*. So sorry that you went behind my back and disobeyed my one singular instruction."

"I just wanted to help you."

"You really wanna help me? Go home. Be with your mom. She's worried sick about you and she doesn't deserve to be. Why don't you rescue *her* instead?" Rox turned to their dad's truck and opened the driver-side door. Before I knew it, the truck was roaring as it peeled off and drove through the dark neighborhood streets, leaving me to stand stupidly in a cloud of exhaust.

"Ill? What happened?" Sasha shouted from the front lawn behind me. I turned and saw both Sash and Jozie standing in the cold.

"Did I say something wrong?" Jozie asked.

"Ill, we're gonna catch our deaths out here. Why don't you come back inside and we can keep the party going?" Sasha shouted.

I wiped away a few tears with my suit-jacket sleeve and made my way back to the house.

"You did nothing wrong, Jozie. I promise," I said. "Rox remembered they have a midterm tomorrow and had to take off to study. They're really sorry, Jozie."

"Oh, well . . . that's okay!" Jozie said. "I understand. I bet high school is a *lot* harder than middle school, huh?"

"Yep," Sasha said earnestly, "much, *much* harder."

Sixteen

MOM MADE BEEF STEW as it was tradition to do so on the first evening of fall when the temperature dropped below forty. It was also tradition for me to grab Thanksgiving decorations from the basement while she cooked. But tonight, I stayed in bed . . . or rather, I felt *bolted* into bed. I was at a complete crossroads. Between the shotgun visit to Revival and the emotional upheaval of a disheveled old man living out his final years in solitude, I had dug myself too deep a hole to simply climb out of and walk away from. But who I had unknowingly brought into the hole with me the entire time? Sasha. My mom. Rox. Jordan. The people in this world who love me the most. What did I owe them as opposed to what I felt like I owed myself by seeing this thing to its natural end?

"Stew's almost done, hon!" Mom shouted from down the hall. Despite night after night of my closing myself off from the world and locking myself away in my room, my mom still had hope in her voice that *this time* I'd finally emerge from my dark chambers and give her her old son back. She refused to give up on me . . . and it was more than I deserved as a son. I thought back to what Rox said about rescuing Mom. I decided then and there that Revival couldn't break me. Pastor Erick Neary couldn't break me.

Anthem, Tennessee, couldn't break me.

"Coming, Mom!" I shouted before jolting out of bed. Suddenly, I was overtaken by a gush of energy and life as I marched down the hall. Once I made it to the kitchen, I saw Mom frozen in place as if she had been petrified by some supernatural force. She stared at me as if I had been resurrected from the dead.

"Ilya?" she begged. "What's wrong?"

"Nothing's wrong, Mom. I'm just starving and I've had a long day, and I know your beef stew is gonna make my day so much better." The look in Mom's eye shifted from shock to relief. The relief you've spent what felt like an eternity begging for. The kind of relief it physically pains you to finally welcome in your arms.

"I'll fix you a bowl," Mom said. The glimmer of tears began to take shape in her eyes before she turned back to the crockpot.

It was time to be Ilya again. It was time for Carol Burkhart to have her son back.

"Do you remember when you'd stage your stories for me in the backyard?" Mom asked as she reached across the table for bread.

"Yes, I do! Sometimes I'd have to break the fourth wall by asking you to participate."

Mom snorted and replied, "And I was a *horrible* actress!"

"Don't say that, Mom. You did your best, I'm sure!"

"You were always my little storyteller. Every day you would wake me up with a new idea you had come up with in bed the night before. You would yank me out of bed, make me popcorn, take me out to the backyard, and pull me into your crazy, amazing world. Even when it was sweltering hot or freezing cold, it was the best joy of my life seeing you come alive. You were this little . . . *firecracker* of imagination."

The conversation was only broaching half an hour, yet it felt like the longest talk we had both had in years. It was the most joyful I had seen Mom in a long time, and I wanted to do everything I could to keep the feeling going.

"But sometimes . . . I worried . . ." Mom said.

"Worried? About what?"

"Worried that all your stories were some kind of . . ."

"Escape?" I asked.

"Yes, Ilya. Do you remember what all your main characters had in common?"

I was drawing a blank. I knew they were usually courageous, optimistic, and self-sacrificing, but what did any of those have to do with escape?

"Ilya, they were *orphans*," Mom said finally. "Every single one was an orphan. And a part of me really started to wonder if it was some . . . subconscious . . ."

"Mom, no. Absolutely not. I mean . . . Harry Potter was an orphan. Luke Skywalker was an orphan . . . well, in principle. Batman was an orphan. It just makes for good built-in internal struggle, that's all. Kids' stuff."

"*Kids' stuff* . . ." Mom began to ponder. Ponder *what* exactly, I couldn't say.

But before I could further reassure her, there was a loud *KNOCK-KNOCK-KNOCK* from the front door that startled us both.

"Oh, that's probably Mindy," Mom said. "I called and asked to borrow onions." Mindy was our neighbor from across the street. Mom made her way to the front door as I continued to eat my stew as I noticed it was beginning to cool.

"Ma'am, is this the Burkhart residence?" a low, sturdy male voice said from down the hall. I glanced up and saw a man and woman standing on the porch, both dressed in suits.

"Um . . . yes, yes it is," Mom mumbled. "Is something wrong? Who are you?"

"Is Ilya Burkhart here, ma'am?" the woman asked.

"Mom?" I asked. "Who is it?"

My mom worriedly asked, "Is Ilya in trouble? I'm sure this is a misund —"

"Ma'am," the gentlemen ordered, "we've received some concerning news surrounding the safety of one Ilya Burkhart. If it's alright, we'd like to step in for a brief second and ensure things —"

Mom interrupted, "Wait just a goddamn second, what *news* are you referring to? You can't just show up to a house and order your way in with fucking weasel words like 'concerning news.' I wanna know who the hell you two are and why the hell you're interrupting my dinner with my son."

My blood went cold, and I began to feel faint. I stood up from the table, but my legs nearly gave out. In an instant, the gentleman and woman in suits were inside our living room and staring directly at *me*.

"Son, are you Ilya Burkhart?" the man asked.

"Y-yes, yes I am," I stuttered.

"And son, did you and a friend of yours pay a visit to Revival? I think her name was . . . Sasha?"

Suddenly, my mouth dried up like cotton. My throat ached with soreness.

"Let's just make sure we're all on the same page, and we'll be out of your hair and you folks can get back to your dinner," the woman said.

I couldn't meet Mom's eye. She spent the last six years shielding me from Revival.

The man said, "Son, is it true you met with one Nathanial Holtmeyer at a Shelly's Diner outside of town with one Jordan Flores?"

"Yes," I said. The word tore through my dry throat like sandpaper.

"Ilya," Mom pleaded, "please tell me what's going on right goddamn now."

The woman said, "Ma'am, we're gonna have to ask you to lower the sound of —"

"Don't fucking tell me to lower the sound of my voice like I'm one of your goddamn basket cases. So what if my son went to Revival with a friend? What right does that give you to storm into my home and accuse —"

"Ma'am," the woman said calmly. "We have it on good authority to believe your son expressed feelings of being coerced and pressured into unwanted lifestyle choices, but specifically said it wasn't his teachers or his peers."

"I don't know what those freaks at that fucking cult in the woods told you, but just know when I sue their asses six ways to Sunday, you two are gonna be standing there right alongside them."

"We've also been informed that your son has engaged in conversations *relating* to sex with his classmates when he was only seven years old. When the administration met with you to discuss recourse, they reported you as acting *combative* and, quite frankly, *hostile*. You can understand why this didn't instill confidence in the adults assigned to your son's welfare and safety."

Mom stammered, "My son didn't need *any* recourse —"

The man asked, "Is it also true your son skipped an entire day of school when he visited Revival? Were you aware of this, or did he elect to hide this knowledge from you as well?"

"Mom, don't listen to them," I begged. "I only went to —"

"Son," the man said. "You don't have to —"

"I'm not your fucking son," I shouted. "There's nothing wrong with me and there's nothing wrong with my mom. I don't know what you heard or what you think you heard, but I don't really give a shit. My mom's a better parent than either of you assholes ever will be, and right now you should be a lot more concerned with *your* welfare than mine."

As the man and woman stared at me, I could see in their eyes some epiphany dawn on them. "We're gonna take off," the woman said. "Ilya, let's talk just the three of us sometime, yeah?"

"Get out of my fucking house," Mom said with enough venom to kill an elephant.

The man and woman nodded with a smile and exited through the front door, followed swiftly by Mom shutting the door behind them. With her hand still gripping the doorknob, she stood in place with her face to the door and her back towards me.

"Mom?" I mumbled, on the verge of tears. But Mom gave no reply and continued to stand facing the door.

"Mom, I'm so, so sorry. Please say something."

Suddenly, Mom whispered, "Foobar."

"What?"

"FUBAR. Fucked Up Beyond All Recognition. That's what your grandmother said to me when your father left when you were a baby. She said a single nurse has no business raising a boy without a man in the house. She said you couldn't become a man without a father. She had no advice to give me. No advice or even the slightest bit of reassurance for her own fucking daughter raising her *only* grandchild. I've spent the last 16 years looking at myself in the mirror convincing myself *over* and *over* again that I'm worthy of being your mother. Do you have any idea what that's like?"

"Mom, I didn't know they —"

"I've dealt with those *people* before. I see how they *talk* to the shitty, strung-out mothers coming to pick up their OD'ing kids from the hospital on a daily fucking basis. *That* is exactly how they *talked* to me. *That* is exactly how they *looked* at me. Like a neglectful, brain-dead, basket-case mother who can fill an entire fucking warehouse with what they don't know about decent parenting."

"You *are* a good mom. They don't know —"

"Ilya, you are gonna tell me right now. Is it true you went to that place?"

". . . Yes."

"But *why?* Have I not spent the last eight years warning you how fucked up, corrupt, and sick that cult is?"

"Rox went there. Jordan's little cousin went there. Brent Cushman went there. I hated not knowing what they went through and why. It made me sick to my stomach every waking second."

"Oh baby," Mom said, "why couldn't you just *tell* me?"

My eyes became wet with tears as I ran to embrace her. "I've been so scared. So scared every single day. I go days at a time without hearing from Rox, thinking the worst. Thinking they died or killed themself. Scared the pastor is gonna come to school again and threaten us into —"

"What? The *pastor?*"

"Erick Neary. He came to our school. He found out we were asking questions. He scared the living shit out of me and Sasha."

Mom withdrew from the hug and looked at me, completely dumbfounded. "Baby, what does *he* have to do with Revival? Erick Neary is a good man."

"No, Mom, he's not. He mentored Brent this summer. He's the reason Brent stopped showing up to camp. He's the reason Brent broke down that night of the party. And we met someone who went to Revival *decades* ago, and even they knew who he was. They freaked out on us and ran out of Shelly's."

"And he threatened you?"

"Yes, Mom. He told me and Sasha to leave Revival alone and to stop asking questions, or else he would come back. Mom, what if Revival isn't to blame? What if Neary takes these kids under his wing and messes them up somehow? What if this is all because of him and he's using Revival as a diversion?"

"Ilya, I've told you time and time again what that place did to my —"

"But Mom, that was *30* years ago. What if they changed? What if they're just good people trying to prove to the world that God loves gay and trans kids exactly as they are? Would that be such a bad thing?"

Mom took a brief second to ponder this before replying, "If Neary shows up to your school to confront you and your friends again, I want you to call me immediately. Do you understand?"

"Yes, of course."

"Good. Now before I go to bed, there's one last understanding we need to have. I know you're scared for your friends, and I know you want to get to the bottom of what happened with Brent Cushman. But I've lived here all my life, and I am going to tell you from experience that things only play out in this town exactly as they should. I've seen countless people try to prod this town's fat, hairy underbelly, and 99 percent of the time, they get run out on a rail. I don't want to scare you, honey, but I just want you to see this from my perspective. After 16 long years, I *finally* have my schedule and my pay exactly where I've needed them since your father left. If you want to go to a semi-decent college, we cannot afford to leave and we cannot afford to start over. Do you understand?"

"You want me to just *let things play out*? Like Pastor Neary?"

"I just want you to recognize that there are more ways to skin a cat. If you want to prove to your friends that you care, you should be there for them. You should offer to help them and love them in any way they need. But running around and asking questions like Perry Mason is just gonna piss off the wrong people, as you so *obviously* saw tonight. Sweet Lord, when I saw those ungodly badges, I nearly fainted."

"What were they gonna do?"

"I wasn't gonna let them lay a single finger on you. But I've seen families torn apart for the most asinine of reasons the past couple years. You can blame Clinton for that. More kids in the system means more kickbacks for the state."

"Kickbacks?"

"*Money*. Bonuses for adopted kids. Don't forget, I'm a nurse, I know every crossed t and dotted i in the state's budget."

"Mom, I'm sorry they —"

"Hush, kid. Wild horses aren't taking me away from you. Now let's sit back down, the stew is getting cold."

Seventeen

ISOSCELES TRIANGLE. I SAT in class and shaded in the space of an isosceles triangle for 15 straight minutes. I was so transfixed in thought that I had become completely unaware of the time and my surroundings. I thought about Pastor Neary. I wondered how word got back to him that Jordan and I had met with Nathaniel. I wondered if he had been following us. I wondered if he would follow me after I left school today. I kept envisioning the police storming my house in the middle of the night and taking me away because I didn't act fast enough to can Neary.

I thought about Rox. I wondered if I would ever see them at school again. I routinely glanced up at my classmates and wondered how many threads there were between them tying back to Revival and Pastor Neary. I wondered how many of their siblings or cousins would be another victim of the town they had the misfortune of growing up in.

Before I could ponder any deeper, the school intercom clicked on in its abrupt and crude fashion. A message sang through the box speaker:

CAN JORDAN FLORES, ILYA BURKHART, SASHA DEHWAR, AND ROXANNE SWAIN PLEASE COME TO THE ADMINISTRATION OFFICE IMMEDIATELY?

Once again, all eyes were on me. I was filled with the exact same sensation of dread and panic as last time, but worse. I knew Neary would be waiting for us once again, but this time he was equipped with evidence of our skipping school and lying to the principal. I stood from my desk, and once again, my backpack felt as if it were filled with cement.

As I trudged down the hallway, the worst anxieties flooded my mind. Would Sasha be expelled from the volleyball team? Would we all be expelled from school? What conspiracy was Neary weaving in the room while we were all walking into his trap?

When I finally made it to the office, Jordan, Sasha, and Rox were all waiting for me with Principal Perdun and two police officers. The officers were one man and one woman, but different from the ones who paid Mom and me a visit last night. No Neary, either.

"Mr. Burkhart," Principal Perdun said with a grin. "So happy you could fit us into your busy schedule. Take a seat, please."

I sat at the end of the table between Jordan and the female officer.

Perdun said, "Now that we're all gathered, let's —"

"Before you kick Sasha off volleyball and expel us all," I interrupted, "I just wanted to say this was all my idea. The trip to Revival. Jordan's going to Neary's house. Jordan and I meeting with the Nathaniel guy. It was all my idea and all my fault. I should be the one punished, not anybody else."

All heads at the table were turned in my direction except Rox's. Perdun began nodding and smirked, "Alright, well . . . thank you, Mr. Burkhart, for that *awe-inspiring* display of selflessness. How very honorable. Let's get you a medal when all this is said and done. But if you can hold on until then, I just want to get to the very bottom of why Officers Callahan and Garrity here are so keen on seeing you four individuals in particular. Now, since Mr. Burkhart spent all his elocution ability in his speech, I'll save the privilege of filling me in on why my lunch has to be postponed an hour to one of you three."

Rox, Jordan, and Sasha all remained silent.

"Y'all forgot to get a story straight, didn't cha? That's fine, do either Officer Callahan or Officer Garrity wanna save me the suspense before I pass out from anticipation and malnutrition?"

The male officer asked, "Which of you are Jordan and Ilya?"

Jordan and I begrudgingly lifted our hands. I felt like a middle schooler getting called on the carpet for passing notes in class.

"Gentlemen, do you know a Nathaniel Holtmeyer?" the female officer asked.

I felt an instant surge of déjà vu.

"But you already asked this," I said, almost involuntarily.

"What was that?" Perdun barked.

"Last night . . . in my house . . . you people asked me the exact same question. Was storming my house during dinner and accusing my mom not good enough for you? Now you have to come to school and interrogate —"

"Mr. Burkhart," Perdun interrupted, "I suggest you choose your next words carefully if you wanna graduate in this lifetime. Now could you enlighten us all as to what in the Sam Hill you are talking about?" Both officers stared at me completely dumbfounded.

"Last night . . . two cops came to my house and asked about Nathaniel," I said.

The male officer shook his head and asked, "Son, what were their names?"

"I . . . I don't remember. But they were from Anthem Police Department, I saw it on their badges." The two officers continued to gawk at me in complete astonishment.

The male officer leaned in, narrowed his eyes into mine. "Son, our report on you boys and that geezer didn't hit my desk until earlier this morning. I recommend you better start making some sense soon before I consider this little lapse in memory an obstruction of justice."

"You better do what the man says, Mr. Burkhart," Perdun said. "You may not like me, but I'm the only thing standing between you and your friends in handcuffs."

"Handcuffs?" Sasha asked. "Why the hell would we need *handcuffs*?"

The female officer said, "Nathaniel Holtmeyer is a ward of the state. He's unfit to live without guardianship due to his mental condition, and last night one of our officers conducted a welfare check on him at his home. According to his guardian, he had suffered a nervous breakdown due to triggered post-traumatic stress related to his youth.”

Oh *fuck*.

She said, “Mr. Holtmeyer landed in the hospital and is currently under surveillance to monitor his mood swings. When doctors probed him on his breakdown, he referenced a conversation with two gentlemen . . . one of whom was named Jordan. Now, as for Mr. Holtmeyer’s family, all of whom we met this morning and who are understandably shaken up, are considering suing those responsible for infliction of emotional damage.”

“But we didn’t do anything!” Jordan shouted. “He flipped out when I mentioned Neary’s name and he —”

“Mr. Flores, I advise you shut your mouth right now,” Perdun barked.

“Neary?” the male officer asked, puzzled. “The *pastor*?”

“When I mentioned Neary, the Nathan guy completely flipped his lid. That’s what caused him to storm off. It was like a trigger for him.”

Mr. Perdun became flustered. “Officers, please find it in your hearts to excuse Mr. Flores’ completely baseless and hysterical accusations. As you know already, we here at Blount suffered a terrible loss with the passing of —”

“Mr. Flores,” the female officer interrupted, “Nathaniel Holtmeyer attended Revival over *40 years ago* at a time before Pastor Neary was even born. What exactly are you implying?”

“He’s implying nothing, Officer Garrity,” Perdun said. “You’ll have to excuse his imagination and how far off the reservation it appears to have run. Believe me when I tell you that Pastor Erick Neary is a good, *decent* Christian man who would sooner cast himself into the pits of hell before causing hurt to another soul. Why . . . it wasn't three weeks ago in this very room he personally gave spiritual counsel to Mr. Burkhart and Ms. Dehwar in their time of grief. Isn't that right, Miss Dehwar?"

All eyes were cast on Sasha, who was visibly stunned by the question. She shot me a glance wrought with panic. I could see in her eyes the same sense of fear we both shared that day Neary threatened us behind the very door that currently stood between us and the free world.

"Miss Dehwar?" Perdun asked.

"He didn't counsel anyone," I said finally. "He didn't *comfort* anyone."

Perdun's face twisted into sheer stupefaction. "How's that?"

"He told us to let things play out and stop asking questions," Sasha said. "He didn't mention our grieving Brent once."

"But he *was* Brent's mentor before he died," Jordan said. "The night he died, he told me he let Neary down."

Rox remained silent.

The two officers were glued onto every last word uttered on the kids' side of the table. There was no hint of cynicism in their facial expressions.

"How did Pastor Neary make you *feel* that day in this office?" the male officer asked.

Sasha and I made eye contact once again. The fear in her eyes told me she was reliving it just as vividly as I was.

But neither of us spoke, though our breaths were becoming shorter.

"Officers," Perdun said, "let's table this discussion until after lunch. It's obvious emotions are running a bit high, and I don't think any of us want those emotions to dictate how a legal proceeding takes shape."

The two officers nodded in agreement but didn't take their eyes away from us kids.

"Let's meet back at one, sound good?" the female officer asked.

"Just peachy," Perdun said tonelessly.

The two officers stood up, packed up their papers and files, and excused themselves from the room. Perdun sat completely still in his chair, deep in thought. The tension in the room was so palpable, it felt as if we'd all be crushed under it if somebody didn't break the silence soon.

Perdun took off his glasses and spoke softly. "My mamaw had an expression growing up. She'd say, 'Peter, if God brought you *to* it, he'll bring you *through* it.' Those simple words brought me immeasurable comfort as a boy at times when I sorely needed it. God rest her soul, she knew how to bring comfort to people in their worst times. I grew up thinkin' there was no struggle in this lifetime God hadn't prepared me for in some way. That was . . . until I woke up on a beautiful Saturday morning to the news that Brent Cushman left his Earth."

Suddenly, Principal Perdun turned red in the face as his eyes welled up with tears. "I spent the whole rest of that Saturday wonderin' how God could remove one of his brightest students from this Earth so long before his time. I looked back on my own life and started to look *real* close for a time that prepared me to lose him so goddamn soon, and couldn't find anything. But before the day was out, I began to stop feelin' sorry for myself . . . and startin' feelin' sorry for y'all. You kids —"

Perdun began hiccupping in sobs as he reached for a box of tissues on a filing cabinet behind him. "In this whole big stinkin' mess, you kids were the most unprepared out of all of us in Anthem. And I started to wonder . . . when and where did God prepare you *kids* to lose your classmate? And then I started to wonder . . . what *purpose* did God have in springing that pop quiz on y'all so early in life?" The bass in his voice was fading and growing weaker with each syllable. "This might come as a shock, and try to hide your disbelief . . . but I remember perfectly what it was like being your age. I know that . . . because this is the *oldest* and the most *mature* y'all have ever been in your lives, you think y'all are grown. But I want you all to know from the bottom of my heart . . . that you're not. You are all . . . still . . . *children*. And you were each given a battle you were *astronomically* ill-equipped to handle, and I could live to be a thousand years old and still not know why. I respect y'all too much to sit here and pretend to know what y'all are goin' through, so here's what I'll say instead. If there is ever anything y'all need in this lifetime, I'm here to listen and help in any way I can. And that includes if anybody in this town is making you feel unsafe or unsure of yourself. Do you understand?"

Sasha, Jordan, and I nodded. Rox stayed still and silent.

"Good. I'm gonna talk to the officers about those charges. I'm happy we could have this talk. But now, I'm afraid we have to move on to less pleasant fare. Miss Dehwar, on the supposed day you and Mr. Burkhart visited Revival, you assured me it was a celebratory day in the Islamic faith. Do you remember this?"

Sasha mumbled, "Yes, I do."

"Do you remember what this celebratory day in your faith was titled?"

"The Feast of Hala Al Turk."

"That's correct, Miss Dehwar. Outstanding memory! Now, being the considerate and open-minded principal I am, I went ahead and took the liberty of educating myself on this fine feast day of the Islamic faith."

Suddenly, a small smirk appeared on Sasha's face.

"I have just one question, Miss Dehwar . . . was Miss Al Turk rewarded with a feast day of her own before or after she appeared on *Arabs Got Talent*?"

Sasha suddenly let out a burst of laughter. Slowly but surely, the rest of us kids joined her in what went from faint giggles to belly laughs.

"Y'all are cruisin' for a bruisin'." Perdun sneered. "Get outta my damn office and let me enjoy my tuna melt in peace."

Eighteen

"THAT STILL WOULDN'T EXPLAIN how Nathaniel knew the pastor," Rox said.

Rox, Sasha, Jordan, and I were out to lunch, but all the food on the table had gone cold.

"Maybe Neary's father was a pastor too," Sasha said. "Maybe he followed in his father's footsteps."

Jordan said, "Nope. Neither of us said the name Erick. We said Neary . . . the old man was the one who said the name in full."

"Anthem is home to well over eight thousand people," Rox said, "I'm hard-pressed to think of a name better known to the general public than that of the town pastor."

The table went quiet in thought, as it had well over a handful of times the past hour.

"Rox," I said, "the mere *mention* of Neary's name landed the old man in a hospital bed. Surely there's a little more than just small-town familiarity there."

"You two shouldn't have been talking with him in the first place," Rox sneered. "What the hell were you thinking? Was there a single brain cell between the two of you?"

"They just wanted answers, Rox," Sasha said.

"What answers were those, exactly?" Rox hissed. "How to make a lonely, sad old man relive a waking nightmare from his childhood? How to end up in jail for elder abuse against a ward of the state?"

After 15 or so seconds of silence, Jordan said, "Six months ago, my little cousin got sent to Revival. But the little girl that I knew never came back. You refused to tell us what happened there, so we had to improvise. Not that you haven't been given countless opportunities to talk."

Sasha said, "Jordan, shut *up*."

Rox had no anger or fear in their eyes. Maybe slight curiosity.

Jordan said, "Your best friends . . . your *only* friends in this whole world have been worried sick this entire time for you. They've hunted you down in the woods, they've driven hours and hours just to talk . . . I don't even know why the hell I'm wasting time telling you what you already know."

Sasha said, "Jordan, you need to shut the fuck up *now*."

Jordan said, "And what, Roxanne Swain, have you given those worried friends in return? Nothing. You don't talk. You don't care. You don't give any impression that you give a damn about their well-beings. Even while we're sitting right in front of you, trying to solve a fucking conspiracy theory decades in the making, you don't say a damn word. Not a damn fucking word. You just *sit* there like a sad, pathetic creep and pout that sad . . . fucking puppy-dog pout while the people around you work themselves to death to —"

SMACK!

Sasha slapped Jordan. In the face. *Hard.* She reached across the table of the booth and open-palm *smacked* him in his face, clear as day. Every single jaw dropped to the floor. The restaurant went deadly silent. If something other than smashed glass can shut a room up in record time, a slap can. Jordan held his right hand to the part of his cheek, perfectly imprinted with four of Sasha's fingers. His eyes were filled with a mixture of astonishment and fear.

Sasha stared in Jordan's direction with her eyes wide open. It was clear she was processing what the hell had just happened as much as the three of us were.

Suddenly, Sasha stuttered, "Oh my God . . . Jordan . . ." Before she could finish, Jordan reached for his pocket, withdrew a $20 bill, and threw it on the table before running off.

"Please tell me I didn't just do that," Sasha quaked.

"It happened, Dehwar," Rox said, "you grew some balls."

"I told Coach I was working on my temper," Sasha said. "If she finds out —"

"She's not gonna find out," Rox said. "Jordan won't snitch."

"How do you know that?" Sasha asked.

"I smoke behind the fieldhouse of the football field sometimes; I know the team laundry schedules. If Jordan runs his stupid mouth, we'll see how easily he can run with Icy Hot in his jockstrap."

Sasha let out a laugh that startled both of us. Rox had a particular skill in lightening even the most nerve-wracking situations with one line.

After her laugh winded down, Sasha said, "Rox, don't listen to him. We want you to share whatever you're comfortable with, *whenever* you're comfortable."

"Thanks," Rox said with a slight smile. "That means a lot. But it pains me to say nothing I saw or experienced ties back to the pastor. Maybe he isn't tied to Revival at all."

"But the night Brent died, he told Jordan he let Neary down," I said. "And more importantly, Jozie said Brent would look like a scared little kid when Neary would drop him off after 'mentoring' him. Combine that with me and Jordan setting off the old man with Neary's name and his coming to school to personally scare the shit out of me and Sash, and Neary has stood at the end of *every* corner we've turned. Why? Why would he care so much to show up to our school?"

"Maybe he was *warning* us," Sasha said. "Maybe he knew more than he let on."

"Then he'd be complicit and abetting," Rox said, "which is just as bad."

"Are you suggesting they're all in cahoots?" I asked.

"Birds of a feather," Sasha said. Those four words echoed in my mind. *Birds of a feather*. Suddenly, as is often the case with epiphanies, the scattered puzzle pieces locked together like a symphony.

"Today at the meeting . . . those cops said they had no idea what I was talking about when I mentioned their showing up to my house last night," I said.

"Yeah, speaking of which . . . what *were* you talking about, Ill?" Sasha asked. "They said the report didn't come down until earlier this morning. Why would they be at your home *last night*? It doesn't make sense."

"Last night, they mentioned the meeting with Nathan but didn't mention the hospital or the charges."

"Then how would they know it happened?" Sasha asked.

"It wasn't just about the old man, Sash. They knew about our trip to Revival too."

"They *what*?" Sasha trembled.

"They knew we skipped school to go to Revival. They knew about everything."

Sasha stared at me with a look of utter confusion. Even Rox couldn't hide their puzzlement.

"He's following us?" Sasha said in a small, quivering voice.

"He could be watching us right now," I said. A sharp shiver trickled down my back as my skin turned to gooseflesh.

"What if the cops showing up to my door was his shot across the bow? What if he wanted me to know . . . wanted *us* to know he was onto us?"

"You're saying he tipped them off?" Sasha asked.

"I don't know, but they started talking about me coming out to my class . . . and suddenly it felt like a court hearing."

"What do you mean?" Sasha asked.

"It felt like . . . it *sounded* like . . . they were making Mom out to be . . ." My words trailed off.

"What . . . like they were gonna take you away from Carol?" Sasha asked.

I knew if I kept expounding on the events of last night, I'd become a mess.

"Carol is literally the best mom in Anthem, Ill," Rox said. "Anyone who wants to take her away from you is gonna have a fucking problem with me."

"And me," Sasha said.

"Thanks, guys," I mumbled. "I was so fucking scared. I never saw Mom look the way she looked. I never had to watch her . . . *defend* herself like that."

"You think Neary sent child services to scare you?" Sasha asked.

"I don't know," I said. "Maybe."

"It's possible," Rox said. "If Neary made some case that you were groomed into being queer, they could rule abuse. It's Tennessee, after all."

I thought back to my talk with Mom last night. *Kickbacks.*

"That's so fucked up," Sasha said. The table went quiet for a full minute. The tension which had been building for the past hour had reached an apex. I knew if I pursued the hypotheticals any further, I'd be plunged into full-fledged paranoia and anxiety.

Sasha finally broke the silence. "What do you guys think other Blount kids are talking about right now?"

"What do you mean?" Rox asked.

"I mean, we're out to lunch talking about conspiracies and police and conversion therapy and religion. What do you think other kids from our school talked about during their lunches?"

I faintly chuckled. "I don't know, movies? Bands? What kind of insurance they're gonna be selling 20 years from now after they peaked in high school? Why?"

"I don't know about you guys, but if I have to hear about Revival or Pastor Neary or Brent Cushman, I might actually go ballistic. Call me crazy . . . but what if tonight we actually *tried* being normal teenagers having a normal night? Doing what teens do, talking about what teens talk about. No church camps. No death. No conspiracy theories," Sasha said.

"If knowing what normal teens in normal towns do *requires* being a normal teen in a normal town . . . I'm afraid Ilya and I are out of our depths," Rox quipped.

"There's a new bowling place up by Johnson City," I said.

"*Bowling*?" Rox hissed. "And I thought good writers avoided clichés."

"It's perfectly cliché and perfectly *teenager* behavior," I said.

"Touché," Rox said.

"So . . . bowling . . . tonight? Yeah?" Sasha asked.

"If there aren't nachos involved, I'm not going," Rox said.

The three of us left our tips and headed for the exit.

———

"It's nights like tonight that make me wish Blount had a bowling team," Rox said after bowling their seventh strike in a row.

"Sign me up," Sasha said, grabbing a handful of fries from her tray.

We were the only teens at the bowling alley. Hell, we were the only customers with the exception of a few old geezers.

"What's wrong? Volleyball not boring enough?" Rox asked.

"I'm just sick of the drama," Sasha pleaded. "So much backstabbing and shit-disturbing. All the while, we pretend to all be on the same team. It's such bullshit."

"Sash," Rox said before they slurped their soda, "there are *two* invaluable commodities in the world of Blount High: beauty and athletic prowess. And you won the lottery in both respects. Surely it's not as bad as all that."

"I'd be happy to switch places, Rox. Just let me know when."

"Right, because being a nonbinary hobbit with a nicotine addiction is surely gonna be a step up."

"How come you don't quit smoking?"

Rox grabbed their orange bowling ball from the rack and lined themself up with the lane. They asked, "How come you don't quit volleyball?"

"Not the same thing, Rox."

"You put your body on the line on that volleyball court for an adrenaline rush every other night. You're gonna tell me that rush doesn't become addictive? Like something you absolutely need in order to figure your shit out?"

"Volleyball isn't slowly killing me, Rox."

"Clearly," Rox said before bowling.

"And you're sure you don't wanna play in college?" I asked. "At least then there won't be any more teen drama."

"In all honesty, I'm starting to think teen drama lasts well into adulthood. It seems like more and more each day, I see full-grown adults acting like teens. You're up, Ill," Sasha said, pointing up to the TV.

As I stood up to bowl, I asked, "So you won't play in college?"

Sasha replied, "I don't even know if college immediately after graduation is the move."

"You mean you're taking a gap year?" Rox asked.

"What I mean is this is the youngest any of us will ever be for the rest of our lives. Our youth is gonna come and go just like that. Why does it have to be spent in school?"

"Where would you rather it be?" I asked.

"Traveling, learning new languages, trying new foods, going all the places I learned about in a classroom. Why can't that be my education? You learn so much more outside of a classroom anyway."

"A lot of schools offer studying abroad," I said before bowling. I had never bowled without bumpers before.

"But you still have to go to class and do homework," Sasha said. "They still control where you live and what you study. Where's the independence? Where's the rush of going to sleep not knowing what country your bed will be in the next night?"

"Would you go to Pakistan?" I asked after knocking down six pins.

"My parents would never let me," Sasha said, "but they won't say why. The weird part is Pakistan is *much* safer today than it used to be."

Rox said, "Maybe they have some guilt about leaving and taking you away."

"Yeah," Sasha said. "Maybe."

"So how come you don't wear your hijab?" Rox asked.

"You know why, Rox," I said.

"I'm not asking you," Rox said. "I'm asking *her*."

Sasha shot Rox a glare of reproach before her eyes became downcast. She said, "My parents have been looking for reasons to move since we got here. There have been so many times where we nearly did until I talked them out of it. If my faith and my devotion spark even the smallest outcry, that would be the final straw."

"I thought you said it was your choice," I said.

"It is. But our choices always have consequences, and a lot of times they involve the people we love most. So you're right, Ill, it *is* my choice. It's my choice to keep me and my family safe and to keep us all together by not giving my parents another reason to leave Anthem. Don't you understand?"

"Let me ask you something, Sash," Rox said. "What about Anthem scares you?"

"*Scares* me?" Sasha snapped. "I'm not *scared* of anything."

The television notified us it was time for Sasha to bowl, but the alert went unnoticed.

"Yes you are, Sash. You're scared the same way I was scared in middle school. I hear you rationalizing things to yourself in the same bullshit manner I did to myself for years."

"Excuse me?"

I said, "Rox, now's really not the time —"

"You think I dress like this because it's fun?" Rox asked. "Because it's *amusing*? You think I like being the leper of Blount High?"

Sasha said, "You always say to dress unapologetically you."

"Yes, and I do, but it's more than just building up the smoldering pile of ash that is my self-esteem. It's about counter-friction."

"Counter *what*?" Sasha asked.

"It's from Thoreau's *Civil Disobedience*. Counter-friction to stop the machine."

"So Anthem is the machine, then?" I asked.

"Yes, exactly. And something as simple as an outfit can be enough to fight back against the system that condemns it. It's a form of protest."

"It must be nice," Sasha said.

"I never said it was nice, Sash," Rox replied. "It's absolute hell feeling like the foil of something. Like you're some kind of glitch. But as long as the people who make Anthem the way it is are content and comfortable, you can't expect change. Why *would* you want to keep peace with people like Pine and Neary?"

"Taking a stand where nobody else like you has stood before," I said to myself.

"What was that?" Sasha said.

"Nothing," I said. "Just something I heard once."

"Look, I'm happy you two can wear whatever you want whenever you want," Sasha said. "Truly, I am. But the one thing . . . the *only* thing that brings me peace in my life is also the thing that I have to hide. Do you have *any* idea what that feels like?"

"I used to," Rox said, "but I don't anymore, you know why?"

"Enlighten me," Sasha said.

"Because I learned that other people's peace was a byproduct of my own suffering. And I refused to accept that. And all I want is for you to refuse to accept it too."

"It's not that simple, Rox," Sasha said.

"I know, and I don't mean to preach. But one day, you might look back and regret the kind of people you killed yourself to keep content. I know how shitty that feels, and I just want better for you. For *both* of you."

The three of us sat in silence for a good 30 seconds. The television continued to alert us that it was Sasha's turn to bowl.

"I'm kind of not feeling bowling anymore," Sasha confessed. "Anyone else interested in a venue change?"

Rox smiled. "I thought you'd never ask. I know just the place."

You never do know the things that stay stuffed up Rox's sleeve on any given day. After an hour and 20 minutes of driving across dark Tennessean creation, the three of us arrived at a gravel lot just outside Appalachia. Halfway through our trek, exit signs and streetlights began to disappear as we ventured further outside the realms of civilization and electricity. The lone source of light was the white beam from the car head-lights, but it could only illuminate about 20 yards ahead of us. The rest of the site was completely engulfed in darkness with the exception of a few million shining stars above us.

"Rox," Sasha said from the back, "if you took us here to kill us, can I call my parents to tell them which cousins to give all my clothes to?"

"Ilya, did you remember to grab that salt off the table?" Rox asked.

"Yes," I mumbled dumbfoundedly. The packets were in my back pocket.

"Excellent, let's go!" Rox exclaimed, before jumping out and foraging into the back abyss that lay ahead of us. It wasn't long until their small figure escaped the confines of the car headlights and they completely disappeared from sight. It was extremely eerie seeing them evaporate into the darkness.

"So . . . what are *you* hoping your epitaph reads?" Sasha asked.

"*Was willing to follow his friends into darkness,*" I said before climbing out.

"That was rhetorical, Ill!" Sasha shouted from inside the car.

I knew we were completely safe, but it felt cruel providing Sasha anxiety that extended beyond the merits of good adolescent hijinks and merriment. I opened the car door, took her hand in mine, and led her into the darkness where Rox awaited our arrival.

Once the headlights behind us automatically shut off, we were completely engulfed in pitch black. Sasha let out a scream. When she used the flash on her phone to light our way, we found Rox sitting on the ground. Or rather, sitting on the edge.

"Rox, what the hell is that?" Sasha quaked, seizing my arm in a tight squeeze.

As I leaned in and glanced over Rox's shoulder, my center of gravity instantly gave way, and I had to use Sasha to balance myself. We were standing atop an empty, abandoned reservoir, the full depth of which remained a mystery cloaked in complete darkness.

"Ill, gimme the salt," Rox said.

"Rox, where are we? How far down does that go?" I asked.

"C'mon, the salt please," Rox said, holding their hand out.

I took a few seconds to process my surroundings and regain my balance before reaching into my back pocket. I grabbed a salt packet and placed it in Rox's hand. They tore the packet open and poured the salt into the palm of their left hand with an ease that suggested they had done this numerous times before.

"Ready for this?" Rox asked enthusiastically.

Neither me nor Sasha gave a reply. We opted instead to continue clinging to each other for warmth, balance, and dear life.

Suddenly, Rox's left arm sprung back and lunged forward as the salt flew from their hand and into the darkened abyss. After three or so seconds, a cluster of bright sparks appeared in the air with a loud *BANG! BANG! BANG!* that echoed through the dark abyss. It sounded like the tiny bang snaps you would throw on your driveway on the Fourth of July.

Sasha and I were both startled out of our wits and nearly fell to the gravel floor.

"What the hell was that?!" Sasha shouted.

"That, Sasha, was a scientific experiment in the combination of sulfur and sodium," Rox replied jovially.

"This is a sulfur reservoir?" I asked.

"*Was*," Rox replied, "but they botched the cleanup job. Meaning there's sulfur in the air on cold nights like tonight."

"Are you saying you took us an hour into the dark, freezing woods to make stuff explode over an empty pit of darkness? And this was your idea of *fun*?" Sasha asked.

"Wanna go back to bowling?" Rox asked.

"No, I really don't. Gimme some salt, Ill," Sasha said.

The three of us laughed as I reached for more salt packets from my back pocket.

After 15 or so minutes of breaking the record for the biggest and loudest explosions, we ran out of salt packets. The silences between the *BANGS* and flashes of yellow and white were filled with laughter and screams. The fun kind of screams.

"I win!" Sasha cheered. "My explosions kicked your guys' explosions' ass!"

"Bullshit!" I shouted.

"Don't be a sore loser, Ill," Sasha said with a smirk on her face. "Coach says accepting loss respectfully has more honor than accepting victory like a jerk."

"That didn't stop you, did it?" I quipped.

"Okay, fair," Sasha said. "I'm a shitty winner. I've come to embrace it."

The three of us had been so caught up in the competition that we barely noticed the significant drop in temperature since our arrival. It couldn't have been any more than 40 degrees. Snippets of fog left our mouths with every breath and syllable.

"What do winners get in this game, Rox?" Sasha asked as she folded her arms in for extra warmth.

"I don't know, I've never played it with other people before," Rox said.

"How about a free cup of hot coffee at Shelly's to warm you up?" I said.

Sasha's eyes widened with excitement. "Say less!"

The three of us made our way back to the car as our shivers and shaking became more intense the closer we got to warmth.

We arrived at Shelly's around 10:30 p.m. There was a large gathering of motorcycles in the parking lot. Christmas lights were strung across the windows coated with condensation. The mass of blurry figures motioning behind the glass signified that business was booming for Shelly's.

Once we entered the diner, we were stunned by an inexplicable sight. Twenty or so bikers covered in tattoos were helping Audrey decorate for the holidays. Some were even dancing to holiday tunes on the old-fashioned jukebox while others were wrapping decorative boxes to go under the tree. It was like something out of *MAD* magazine.

"Hello, kiddos!" Audrey barked as she hung ornaments on the tree. "Get yourselves some cocoa while it's hot!"

Once she had finally snapped out of her trance, Sasha made her way to the self-serve kettle sitting atop the counter next to a plate of holiday-themed cookies. Miraculously enough, our usual booth next to the old radiator was open. Rox grabbed a handful of cookies and stuffed them in the pockets of their peacoat before we made our way to the booth.

"So where will you go, Sash?" Rox asked before sipping their coffee.

"What do you mean?" Sasha replied before biting into her Santa cookie.

"Earlier tonight you said you wanted to travel before going to college, where exactly were you thinking of going?"

"Oh, well honestly . . . I don't know yet. I know kids usually go to Budapest or Italy but honestly, I wanna go somewhere you wouldn't think to go. I don't wanna go somewhere touristy. I wanna go somewhere that challenges me."

"*Challenges* you?" I asked. "What do you mean?"

"I mean that I see traveling as a serious currency and it's not something I wanna waste. If I do finally get the time and money to travel, I want to make it count for my growth. I want to see governments better *and* worse than my own. I want to wake up in a place where I don't know the language at all. I want to come back as a completely different person. I never want to see the US the same ever again. I've been cooped up in Podunk Anthem too damn long."

I asked, "You wanna shake the dust of the crummy little town off your feet and see the world?"

"Yes, exactly! How did you just take the words out of my mouth?"

"I didn't," I chuckled. "Frank Capra and Jimmy Stewart did."

"Who?"

"They made *It's a Wonderful Life*!" Rox said. "That's where the quote is from."

"Oh," Sasha said. "Well did they make it out of the crummy town and see the world?"

"Sadly, no. They had to stay in their hometown to take care of the family business."

"Good Lord, that sounds *miserable*," Sasha said.

"But the moral of the story is you can find love and happiness right in your backyard if you look hard enough," Rox said.

"Fat chance," Sasha said. "I've been looking all my life, and other than a few friends and teachers, I'm fed up with scouring the town of Anthem just for someone to make me feel like I matter. How soon until love and happiness find *me*? Why am I always the one on the hunt for it?"

"Anthem is just a small sliver of what the world has to offer, Sash," Rox said. "You'll find the right place and the right people, and the timing will amaze you."

"Well, for the time being, the people I have aren't *too* bad." Sasha smiled before taking a sip of her cocoa.

"Here's to the people we have now," I said, raising my mug of cocoa for a toast.

Rox and Sasha repeated the toast in unison and raised their mugs to *clink!* before we each took a drink.

"What about you, Rox?" Sasha asked. "What's your escape plan?"

"What makes you think I'm gonna escape?" Rox said.

Sasha and I glanced at each other with surprise and suspicion.

I said, "Don't tell me you're planning on *staying* in the fascism capitol of Tennessee?"

"And what if I am? Would that be so terrible?" Rox asked.

"It's not terrible at all, Rox," Sasha said, "but I think what Ilya is saying is . . . out of all the people we know who would make Anthem their permanent home —"

"I never said *permanent*," Rox interrupted. "But what if me leaving is exactly what Anthem wants? What it *needs*?"

Sasha and I made eye contact once again, this time suspicion was replaced with pure bewilderment.

"*Needs*?" Sasha asked dumbfoundedly.

Rox said, "Here's how I figure: Anthem has been the top supplier of kids to Revival for the last 20 years. Revival's entire business model relies on the idea that trans, queer, and nonbinary kids are outliers. It's infinitely easier to vilify an outlier. Children fear the most what they can't put a face to, like the bogeyman."

"So you're the bogeyman in this scenario?" Sasha asked. "Ilya too?"

"No, but we *might* represent what people in Anthem don't yet understand."

"No offense, Rox, but I think Anthem understands us just fine," I said. "People like Pastor Neary might come off as allies who are with the program, but looks can be deceiving."

"Then we call them on their bullshit," Rox said. "We stay. We become fixtures of the town whether they want us there or not. We stab the heart of Revival itself by becoming associative with the fabric of the town it depends on. We become neighbors with residents, we share their grocery stores and gas stations and restaurants."

"Rox," Sasha said, "you weren't born to treat yourself like a monkey wrench. You're not a weapon. You're a human being."

"Not to them, not to the people who keep the gears of Revival lubricated with ignorance and fear year after year."

"Rox, with all due respect, *fuck* Revival. *Fuck* Anthem. *Fuck* Erick Neary. *Fuck* the great state of Tennessee. Fuck anyone who sees you as not human or a threat or whatever. You deserve so much better. You deserve to be in a place where you're appreciated for your strengths and what you offer people."

"And what exactly do I offer people?"

"Authenticity, the thing people fear the most *and* need the most. Someone like you being your most authentic self."

"Someone like me?"

Sasha mumbled, "Well . . . I mean . . . like . . ."

"You mean *nonbinary*?" Rox asked.

Sasha flushed with crimson red. "Y-yes, nonbinary."

"It's okay." Rox smiled. "You're not getting canceled."

"Okay, good," Sasha said with a breath of relief.

"Do you still have it?" I asked.

Rox smiled.

"Have what?" Sasha asked.

I replied, "One day when we were in the sixth grade, Rox locked themself in the stall of the girls' bathroom. They were locked in there for hours but refused to come out."

"Why?" Sasha asked.

"They said they couldn't go surrounded by girls," I said, "but when I stood outside the girls' bathroom and suggested they go to the boys' bathroom, they didn't want to go there either. It was like they were . . ."

"Stuck," Rox said. "Stuck between two opposing worlds, like a custody battle where neither parent wants you. It was . . . terrifying. I still remember those green stall walls."

"So how did you get out?" Sasha asked.

"The scale," Rox said with a smile.

"The what?" Sasha asked.

I said, "Rox said they felt stuck between the bathrooms, but even as a sixth grader, I knew what they actually meant. In an instant, I swiveled my bookbag from around my back, took out a piece of looseleaf paper, scissors, and markers and started drawing."

"Drawing what?" Sasha asked.

Rox and I locked eyes and smiled. In one singular glance, Rox and I reminisced across the course of an entire friendship.

"A scale," Rox said, "with 'boy' on one side and 'girl' on another."

"Like . . . a *gender* scale?" Sasha asked.

"And my name was in the very center," Rox said, "in case —"

"In case neither boy nor girl suited them," I interrupted, "they could always circle back to themself. And every day for an entire year, the school day wouldn't officially start until Rox pointed onto the scale how they felt. Sometimes it was closer to boy, sometimes it was closer to girl, sometimes it was dead center."

Sasha's eyes began to water. "A road map."

"A what?" I asked.

"You drew Rox a road map back to themself," Sasha said as she reached to wipe a tear away with her sleeve. "That's so *beautiful*."

I had never seen the scale in those terms before, "Yeah, I guess that's kinda true."

"And little did Ilya know he saved my life that day," Rox said. "For the first time in my life, somebody took me seriously. I wasn't scolded for being confused or desperate for attention. I wasn't getting called a freak or a weirdo."

"You two need to stop before I become a blubbering mess, I'm fucking serious," Sasha said.

"But not all kids are lucky to have road maps, most of the kids at Revival don't have directions back to themselves at all. They're . . ."

"Lost," Sasha interrupted.

"Yes, exactly," Rox said. "And some kids are so lost, they go the rest of their lives without finding themselves again. It's like . . . you find shadows of yourself against the fog, but it's never truly *you*. You're so . . . *blinded* by what you were fed and taught by other people that you can never see yourself clearly. It's a waking nightmare . . . and for countless people, there's only one way to wake up."

"And those people usually end up on my mom's watch," I said.

"Exactly," Rox replied.

"Like Brent?" Sasha asked.

Rox took a brief couple of seconds to ponder their reply. "I've thought about Brent Cushman a lot, and we might never know what really happened. It might have been Revival. It might have been Pastor Erick Neary. Maybe it was a little bit of both. Or maybe we did him no favors making him out to be fit for canonization at so young an age. Maybe Anthem is to blame for filling his head with grandeur and expectations. Maybe we should have given Brent time and space to decide for himself who he wanted to be. We may never know . . . and maybe we don't deserve to. It's possible it's a conglomeration of factors to blame for his death and not one singular person or thing."

"Yeah, I guess," Sasha replied curtly. "I still don't like that pastor. He gives me the creeps. There's something in his eyes that makes me physically unwell when I see him."

Suddenly, I felt a vibration in my pocket. It was most likely Mom calling me about curfew. I had to think of a good excuse fast, and for a woman like Carol Burkhart, good had to be perfect.

But the name on the screen didn't read *Mom*.

It read *Jordan*.

"Is that my girl Carol?" Rox said. "Tell her I said hi."

"It's not Mom," I said, "it's Jordan."

"Jordan?" Sasha asked.

I swiped to answer. "Hello? Jordan?"

"Dude, I need you. Please come to the hospital." He sounded out of breath.

"The hospital?" I stuttered.

Rox and Sasha looked at me with deep concern.

"It's Jozie."

I could feel my blood go cold and my chest hollow out.

"What happened? Is she hurt?"

"It's not just her . . . it's her friend from camp . . . Ryan or whatever."

"You mean *Rory*? Her *pen pal*? What happened? What did he say?"

The line went silent. Suddenly, there was the sound of muffled sobs.

"He's in a psych ward, Ill. And so is Jozie."

Nineteen

"WHAT ROOM DID JORDAN say?" Sasha asked while frantically pressing the elevator button.

"333," I said.

I'm convinced the slowest type of elevator in the world is the hospital elevator.

"What are we supposed to say?" Sasha asked. "I've never dealt with anyone who —"

"Take it from me," Rox said, "it's not what you say, it's how you make her feel. Talk is cheap, don't give her the usual bullshit platitudes about 'not being alone.'"

Sasha asked, "Do we know why Rory . . ."

"No," I said, "but that's *not* our focus tonight. That's Jozie."

DING. We had reached the second floor.

"My heart's breaking for her," Sasha said. "She's the sweetest girl I've ever met in my life. She didn't deserve this."

"Nobody deserves this," Rox said.

"How about Neary?" I sneered. "If we find out he had anything to do with —"

"Ill," Rox interrupted, "you said yourself our one focus tonight is Jozie. If that's gonna be your agenda tonight, do us a favor and wait in the cafeteria. Get a soda while the two of us tend to our friend."

"She's my friend too, Rox," I said.

"Then *act* like it," Rox commanded before the elevator door finally opened. "This is where we get off. If you can't leave your conspiracies about Revival and that creep Neary here, take them with you and go somewhere else."

Rox and Sasha immediately bolted out of the elevator door and turned a corner. After a few brief seconds of painful deliberation, I followed.

Once the three of us stopped to catch our breath at the end of the corridor, we saw Jordan squatting along the wall of the hallway. He had his face buried in his crossed arms and was quietly sobbing.

"Jordan?" I asked softly.

He lifted his head towards us. He looked like a scared, lost child. He slowly stood up on his feet as the three of us rushed in his direction.

"Jordan," Sasha said. "I'm so, so sorry." Sasha was the first of us to hug Jordan, surprising given their last encounter ended in a slap.

"I didn't know who else to call," Jordan said. "Her parents wouldn't understand. She kept saying it was her fault over and over. I tried so hard to calm her down, but . . ."

"You made the right choice," Rox said. "She's safe here."

"And she has us," I said.

Jordan started shaking his head and a pout spread across his face. "I don't know the little girl in that hospital bed behind me. I don't know who she is."

"Yes you do," Sasha pleaded, "it's your little cousin who loves you more than anything in this world. And right now she needs you to be strong."

Jordan looked at Sasha, or rather looked *through* her, with an empty and desolate stare. He replied, "I always told myself Jozie was the strongest person I knew, and look where that got her."

Sasha gave no reply, but her eyes fell downward in remorse.

"You three should go inside," Jordan said. "It'd mean the world to her."

And with that, Rox led the three of us into room 333.

Injustice. Injustice typically felt like my lungs were being filled with hot lead. I felt injustice at Brent Cushman's funeral. I felt injustice every time I thought about his murderers roaming free. I felt injustice seeing two police officers accuse my mom of abuse. But they all paled in comparison to the stomach-churning nausea I felt seeing Jozie Flores, the sweetest, most loving human being in existence, in a hospital bed wearing blue gripper socks.

The look in Jozie's eyes when she stared up at the three of us is something I'll never forget. Gone was the spark of bottomless giddiness and curiosity. Gone was the flame that burned desperately to befriend and to love others. It was the look of someone who had themselves fooled for too long. The look of a child who finally realized they could no longer mend their parents' failing marriage with a handful of dandelions they picked from the backyard.

Rox instantly threw themself into the bed and wrapped Jozie in their stubby arms. Jozie made no noise for the first few seconds but then began to break into sobs. Ugly sobs. Coarse sobs. It was hard to tell if Jozie's light was snuffed out or if it was all a mere facade to mask something deeper. Something darker. Something more congruent with Jozie's circumstances.

"It's all my fault," Jozie quaked through her sobs.

"No," Rox said, "*nothing* is your fault, baby. Nothing at all."

"It was *my* phone call," Jozie pleaded. "If I hadn't called him, this never would have happened. He's being held against his will because of *me*."

Rox caressed Jozie's head and replied, "There's nothing you could have said that makes any of this your fault."

Jozie said nothing but continued sobbing into Rox's chest. Sasha and I could only stand and watch.

"They threatened him," Jozie said. "They said they'd come after him. I didn't know. How was I supposed to know?"

Rox stared up at me with a fierce glare, a ferocity I had never seen in all our friendship.

"Rory?" I asked. "They threatened *Rory*, you mean? Is that what he said?"

Jozie nodded and sniffed. "I just wanted to help you guys. I could tell you were really freaked out about Revival and the pastor guy, so I mentioned it to him during our phone call to see if he knew anything. He started freaking out and said they threatened to come after him and his family if he asked about Pastor Neary again."

Sasha, Rox, and I instantly exchanged looks.

"Sweetheart, let's slow this all down," Rox said softly. "What exactly did Rory say?"

Jozie wiped her nose and replied, "He was worried about Brent. We *all* were. He went to Reverend Pine's office and told him about the car drop-offs and how scared Brent would look at times. He just wanted to look out for him, y'know? He was kind like that. But the reverend told him to stop asking around about Neary and to forget about the whole ordeal, and even threatened to take him away from his family if he kept poking his nose where it didn't belong."

The understanding the three of us had previously come to about 'leaving conspiracies at the door' hung brilliantly in the balance.

"I didn't know," Jozie trembled. "He never told me. I didn't know he was in pain. I didn't know they threatened him. I just didn't know. I only wanted to help him. How was I supposed to help him if I didn't know?" Jozie instantly returned to a state of inconsolability, sobbing into Rox's shoulder.

Sasha took a seat at the end of the bed, reached for Jozie's hand. "Jozie, you weren't *supposed* to know. That wasn't your burden to bear. But Jozie, I can say with absolute certainty that you have the biggest heart out of anyone I know. I can't hope to understand what you must be going through, but I *do* know you are a fierce friend and a kind soul. If Brent — sorry, if *Rory* is in pain, then he's extremely lucky to have you to help him through it."

Tears continued to fall from Jozie's eyes as she held Sasha's hand and had her hair stroked by Rox.

Jozie sobbed, "I'm so happy to be with my friends."

Rox gave Jozie's forehead a kiss and wiped her tears away with their coat sleeve.

———

After 15 or so minutes of talking, a nurse came to alert us that visiting hours were coming to a close. Rox and Sasha immediately protested, but I successfully convinced them Jozie needed time alone. As the three of us exited Room 333, we were instantly faced with a steely-eyed Jordan standing firmly in our way.

"Did I hear her say *Neary*?" Jordan asked with an unnerving intensity.

Sasha said, "Jordan, not here. Not right now."

"Bull-fucking-shit not right now," Jordan said. "If that fucking creep laid a finger on her, I'm gonna peel —"

"Jordan," Rox interrupted cooly, "this is not the time nor the place."

"I'm going there tonight," Jordan fumed. "I'm driving to his house tonight and I'm gonna —"

"You're gonna *what*, Jordan?" Sasha asked. "Piss him off again? Send him back to our school to terrorize us again? Once wasn't enough?"

"No. Because this time's gonna be different. This time I'm gonna *kill him*. For what he did to Brent, for whatever he did to that old bastard Nathaniel Holtmeyer, and for what he did to my baby cousin and her friend. Somebody has to stop him, and it sure as shit isn't gonna be the police or the great state of Tennessee." I recognized the look in Jordan's eyes. It was an immovable, mania-fueled incentive.

"Fine," Rox said curtly. "Kill him. Give the Christians their zillionth martyr and throw yourself into jail for life while you're at it. Make it so you never see your little cousin without a sheet of bulletproof glass between the two of you ever again."

"Fine. I don't care. If it means Erick Neary and that piece-of-shit reverend are both burned to ashes and buried once and for all. If it means they can't hurt another child with their propaganda and brainwashing. It's fine with me. I can take it."

I can never tell if I automatically become more level-headed when somebody else is spiraling, or if it's simply a matter of comparison. Maybe both.

"Jordan," I said, "we can still take them down *together*. We can keep asking and gathering evidence. We can keep digging and sticking to facts. But if what I *think* is true turns out to be, Neary and the reverend will find a way to lock you up and possibly all of us with you if you so much as *spit* in the direction of his house. Trust me."

Jordan gave no reply, but the intensity in his eyes began to die down.

Rox gestured to Room 333. "That girl in the hospital bed is going through hell, *please* don't make her watch the only family member who cares about her get thrown behind bars. Because it *will* destroy her. Believe me."

"Fine," Jordan said tonelessly. "But you three better have a plan."

"Don't worry, we do. I promise," Sasha said.

We do?

———

It was a quarter to midnight once we returned to Anthem. Sasha and I knew we both would have hell to pay when we'd walk into our homes and try to explain our staggering breach of curfew. I couldn't speak for Rox, however.

"What the hell were you thinking making a promise to Jordan?" Rox asked sternly from the bench seat behind us.

"I had to say something," Sasha said. "He was going insane."

"All the more reason to have not made a promise. Of the billions of places on the planet to *not* make a promise to someone, a hospital is at the top of the list."

"He was threatening to commit *murder*, Rox. I had to snap him out of it somehow."

"Well congrats, you succeeded. You successfully promised a bloodthirsty Jordan that we had a plan to take down one of the largest church syndicates in the country by ourselves with the Anthem police breathing down our necks and God knows who else. Speaking of which, I was hoping you could find it in your heart to fill both Ill and me in on your plan since I take it we're both pivotal players. It'd be ever so courteous."

Sasha was silent. I had my eyes on the road and could not turn to see her face.

"Sash?" I asked. "*Do you* have a plan?"

Sasha remained silent for five or so seconds before saying, "We leave for Revival tomorrow. We look for evidence pointing to any foul play. We play it smart."

"Negative," Rox said. "We're already on Neary and Pine's radar. We'll be made the minute we show our faces at that compound."

"Then we sneak in when the time is right," Sasha replied. "We go when the place is empty and find the reverend's office."

"And look for what, exactly?" I asked as I turned off State Street.

"Any correspondence between him and Pastor Neary that shows they've been in cahoots. Something that can make them complicit in Brent's death."

"You really think that's something you can *prove*? You honestly think the two of them plotted Brent's grooming and demise over *Gmail*?" Rox sneered.

"Fine," Sasha said. "*You* were the one who spent a summer there and you're the one who knows the lay of the land. What would *you* do?"

Rox took a few seconds to ponder, then replied, "Pine is smart. He's been the dean at that shithole for over 30 years. That means *practice*. He wouldn't leave anything to chance. His greatest asset is what we don't already know and can't look for."

"What does that mean?" I asked.

"It means if we actually make the idiotic choice of going there, we'll have to —"

"We'll have to look for something we don't know exists," Sasha interrupted.

"That makes no sense," I said. "How can we look for something while *not* knowing what we're looking for? It's complete nonsense."

"If there really is something in that asshole's fortress worth protecting, he's already planned out the scenario of a couple of idiots like us breaking and entering like it's Watergate. The only possible smoking gun in his office wouldn't look like a gun at all."

"It would be hiding in plain sight," Sasha said.

"Yes, exactly."

The faint embers of a plan began to burn in my mind the more I listened. But as humankind has learned billions of times in our existence, rationale is hardly a substitute for a plan's efficacy on the day itself.

I said, "So . . . we drive to the camp under the cover of darkness and . . . what . . . park in the lot like we're early for a tour?"

"No," Rox said, "we can't use the main roads. Pine and his toadies have them tapped with sensors for any and all arrivals by car, and if that wasn't enough, they have security cameras in the trees along the road. Those woods are Pine's domain."

"So we can forget about driving?" Sasha asked.

"Not necessarily," Rox said. "There's a backroad along the creek counselors would use to sneak off into the town for parties. We'll have to park a distance away and walk the creek."

Usually, I would feel my anxieties quell the more a plan began to take solid shape, but this plan would be the exception if ever there was one.

"So we're *actually* doing this?" I asked without an ounce of condescension.

Neither Rox nor Sasha gave a reply. The question hung in the air for what felt like an eternity. The humming sound of the car engine felt boosted by 1,000 percent.

"Yes," Sasha said with unwavering authority. "I didn't just make a promise to Jordan, but to Jozie and every kid who ever had the misfortune of being sent to that hellhole. We'll meet outside of town at midnight tomorrow, so make sure you each get enough sleep. We're leaving for Revival and we're *not* coming home empty-handed."

The amount of sternness and passion in Sasha's voice was astonishing. It was clear from her delivery that the experience at the hospital stirred something deep inside her. Perhaps it was something new, or perhaps it was something that had been there all along and simply needed the proper friction.

"Damn, Dehwar," Rox quipped. "We'll make a gay-loving, pronoun-using, antiestablishment radical out of you yet."

Once I had dropped Rox and Sash off home, I pulled into my own driveway somewhere not quite north of 12:30 a.m. Planning our storming of the gates of Revival along with Sasha's rousing speech evoked a plethora of emotions in me, and they were almost enough to stave off the dread of having to face Carol Burkhart seated on the couch with her legs crossed, awaiting my overdue arrival home. Almost.

I made a frenzied dash for the front door in an effort to stave off any instinct to stay in the car to further delay the inevitable. But once I entered the living room, I found Mom asleep on the couch in her nurse scrubs. I had forgotten she had a graveyard shift last night and had most likely been passed out all evening. I was instantly flushed with a wave of relief and was about to take the victory with me to bed, but was transfixed on Mom. Something about seeing the people we love most sound asleep tilts our perspectives in odd, inexplicable ways. I thought about how hard she must have worked the night before. I thought about how guilty she would feel tomorrow morning having realized she missed her opportunity to ask me how my day was, something she usually spent the whole day excitedly waiting for. I thought about whether she would be at work tomorrow at midnight when we'd be making our way to the one place she never wanted me to end up. A place she fought so vigorously to keep me away from. A place whose victims she had spent her entire career tending to, whether it be alcohol poisoning, overdosing, or self-inflicted wounds. I thought about whether or not the chances of me and her being separated would increase depending on whether or not the three of us would find anything even resembling a smoking gun tomorrow night.

And finally, I began to wonder what life would feel like if she *had* been awake when I came home. What it would feel like if she asked me about my day and I was able to tell her about all the fun I had with my two best friends. What it would feel like if we made plans to see a movie tomorrow night, should she be able to get off call. What it would feel like to joke about the townsfolk of Anthem living and breathing the ongoing football playoffs. What it would feel like to have nothing to talk about and to sit in awkward but peaceful silence. What it would feel like to compliment her amazing cooking if she had been awake to make dinner. What it would feel like if she could see in my eye that something was wrong and the two of us talked about Revival and Neary and Brent and Jozie and Rox.

But as I stood there perfectly petrified in place staring at my mom sleeping in her scrubs, I realized that *my* story wasn't *that* story. And whether that was my fault, Brent's fault, Rox's fault, Jozie's fault, Pastor Erick Neary's fault, or Reverend Pine's fault, I couldn't say for certain. Maybe our stories shouldn't be measured by the faults and choices of others. Maybe that's how we lose the focus and the plot.

Mom suddenly turned in her sleep, and I was snapped out of my trance. I decided to heed Sasha's advice and made my way to bed.

Twenty

THE SCHOOL DAY WENT by in a rigid, robotic daze. The world where pop quizzes and worksheets held any weight seemed to lose merit in the past 48 hours. I was waiting to hear from Mom whether she was working the graveyard shift to better gauge my chances of sneaking off at midnight without a hitch. But the entire day, I racked my brain with one burning question: how does one find something they don't know exists? In what rational world does that game plan result in a favorable outcome?

We would have to keep an open mind. We would have to think the way Pine thinks. What were his priorities? What was his endgame? The cloak of mystery and enigma that blanketed Pine and Neary continued to work to their advantage. I suppose if our plan tonight had a somewhat tangible objective, it would be uncovering the cloak. But where would we grasp the edges? How hard would we have to pull? And most importantly, were we prepared for what evils lurked underneath that thrived in darkness?

I pulled onto the gravel lot of the dollar store just outside of town at exactly a quarter til midnight. The streets were cold, dark, and empty. I was parked in place for a whole minute before Rox emerged from the shadows around the corner of the building in a blue faux fur jacket. They had dyed their hair pink and fashioned a shoddy bowl cut. They climbed into the passenger side, and we began our wait for Sasha's arrival.

"Any trouble with Carol?" Rox asked, adjusting their heat vent.

"No," I replied, "she'll be in scrubs until 7 a.m. at the earliest."

I knew better than to ask Rox the same question. They never seemed to have an issue with curfew or any parental compliance for that matter; the choice to ship them off to Revival notwithstanding, of course.

We continued to sit in silence for five or so minutes before Sasha's headlights finally emerged half a mile from the store. It wasn't until the gravel lot was illuminated by her headlights that the irreversible gravity of the situation finally dawned on me. It felt like the second before going under for surgery when the nurse tells you to count backward from 100. Sasha parked a few spots from us so as to avoid suspicion, but after flicking off her headlights, I could see the silhouette of her head stay in perfect place for no fewer than 15 seconds. Her face was cast in shadow, yet I made out her disposition perfectly because it was my own. We three were standing on a diving board in the dark, too scared to look down. And even if we could bring ourselves to do so, there was no telling how shallow the water was or if there was an ounce of water in the first place.

Finally, Sasha emerged from her car and made her way towards us. Her pace was sluggish yet frantic, and her eyes never left the ground. The *THUMP* of Sasha closing the car door behind her brought a sobering avalanche of reality crashing down on us. Nothing was said. We each exchanged glances with one another which seemed to communicate enough. But nothing any of us could say or do could change our destination. Some small part of me spent the day hoping the plan would have developed a clearer sense of direction or even rationale by this point, but there was no such luck or divine intervention. From this point on, we were entering Pine's domain. We would spend our morning at the mercy of the dwellings of nightmares and trauma, with no adults by our side to take our hands when it frightened us most.

"Let's go," Sasha said. "I have a promise to keep."

I switched the gear shift, and suddenly the sound of gravel under the tires was replaced with the smooth surface of asphalt.

Hundred … ninety-nine … ninety-eight … ninety-seven …

"The creek is just up here," Rox said, gesturing out through the windshield.

We had spent 20 minutes forging through the dark Appalachian woods without a lamppost or streetlight in sight. The dizzying array of oaks and firs that towered over us blocked out the stars and moonlight. It felt as if the trees and darkness were enlisted in Pine's devious plots to further keep his works under wraps from the civilized world.

"Here is fine," Rox said. "Park on the grass."

"Here?" Sasha asked. "We're in the middle of nowhere."

"Yes we are, and if we want to be out of Pine's radar, *that's* the bare necessity," Rox said before opening the passenger door and climbing outside into the darkness. Sasha looked at me through the rearview mirror with eyes fraught not with anxiety, but uncertainty. Suddenly, she followed Rox's lead and exited the vehicle into the pitch-black void. I sat in the driver's seat but didn't move. I stared outside the frosted windshield at Rox and Sasha who began to chat as small gusts of fog emerged with each syllable they spoke. As I sat there and watched my two best friends chat about God knows what, a realization dawned on me. It had to be us three. It had to be tonight. Nobody else in the world had the agency we had to uncover Revival and Neary and their fiendish schemes. The cycle of dread and hopelessness would continue from this point on if we turned around now. If it wasn't us three tonight, it would never happen. And there were no other two human beings in the world I would rather want by my side.

I flicked off the ignition of the car and thrust myself into the darkness. But this was a special brand of darkness. This was a darkness that thrived off ignorance and complacency. This was Reverend Pine's darkness.

"How much further?" Sasha asked, using the flash on her phone to guide our way.

"Not far now," Rox replied. "Once the creek turns left, we'll find the road. Then it should only be 15 or so minutes."

Clinging onto the white flash on Sasha's phone for any semblance of light was doing very little for the self-esteem of the group. We each grasped onto each other for balance as the forest floor sloped and dipped randomly. We could only make out the ground in front of us in increments of five feet at a time. It felt like we were playing some horror game on the computer without the comforts of the off button or the light switch.

"There's the road," Rox said, pointing ahead.

Sasha lifted her phone up and illuminated a lone street that cut through the overwhelming conglomeration of forest. As much as I wanted to be relieved by the sight of the road, the way in which it brazenly trailed further into the darkness filled me with a deep dread.

"Not exactly the yellow brick road," Sasha quipped. Nonetheless, Rox led the crusade onward along the creek until we reached the empty street.

"This would be an opportune moment to discuss strategy," Rox said.

"Oh, *now* would be the opportune moment?" Sasha asked.

"Ilya and I will go inside. Sasha, I want you outside on patrol duty in case Pine wants to burn the midnight oil. You'll text us the minute we get any company."

"Outside . . . *alone?*" Sasha quaked.

"Yes," Rox replied, "if only one of us goes inside, there will be nothing the other two can do to save them. But if two of us go in —"

"They'll have a fighting chance," I interrupted.

"Yes, exactly. And Sash, you'll have an easier chance to escape so long as you can retrace our steps."

"Right, retrace my steps in the dark woods while being chased by fanatics. Sounds easy enough," Sasha said condescendingly.

"I'm not the one who made a promise to Jordan," Rox said. "You're the reason we're in this mess in the first place."

"*I'm* the reason?" Sasha sneered. "Are you fucking kidding me? Am I the one who invited an old man to coffee and triggered him so severely he wound up in a hospital? Am I the one who got the police involved?"

"No," Rox said calmly, "but the promise you so selflessly gave Jordan is the one thing keeping him from going on a murderous rampage. That means we have a responsibility to keep him from making that pastor a martyr and himself a lifer in the process."

"Jordan was running hot, there's no denying that. But if he really was plotting to drive to Neary's house and legitimately *kill* him, nothing we do now is gonna stop him. And beyond that, we have no evidence that Neary has a damn thing to do with this place. On the miraculous off chance that we storm that hellhole, find a smoking gun in plain sight, and put Pine *under* the jail, what if Neary walks away unscathed? What then?"

Rox replied, "What was that about Pine going under the jail? I liked that part."

"What if it's not enough? The first dean went to jail 30 years ago and what happened? Someone else took his place. What if Pine is just a puppet being strung along by someone *worse*?"

"And what if that someone is Neary?" I asked.

"What if that's the connection?" Sasha asked. "What if Pine and Neary were working *together* to groom the new generation of Revival?"

"You mean Brent?" I asked.

"That would explain why they threatened to take Rory away from his family when he started asking questions," Sasha said.

"And why Neary threatened us *personally*," I said.

"Exactly."

Rox said nothing.

"Do you think . . . *he's* the one who tipped off the cops?" I asked. "It still doesn't make sense how a pair of police officers showed up to my house knowing about our talk with Nathaniel the night *before* it became an official report."

Before either Sasha or Rox could reply, the dead silence of the forest was broken.

Hummmmm.

The sound of a car engine. The three of us instantly halted in our tracks. The sound was unmistakable, but the car itself would not present itself. If it weren't for Rox and Sasha stopping, I would have guessed for certain I had finally gone insane.

Hummmmmmmmmmmmmm.

A burst of blinding white light emerged from behind us. The three of us whipped around to find an old green station wagon only 20 or so yards behind us. The high beams were too intense for us to see who it was that sat behind the wheel. Until finally, the engine stopped humming and the lights went dim. Sasha's hand trembled as she lifted her phone's flash in the direction of the car and its unknown operator as they emerged from the vehicle.

The flash reflected off a pair of glasses. I recognized the square shape of the lenses. I distinctly remembered the pair of cold and lifeless eyes seated behind the lenses the day I sat in the administration office of Blount High.

The eyes of Pastor Erick Neary.

"Oh my God." Sasha quaked. "Oh my God. *Oh* my *God.* This can't be happening."

But it *was* happening. Pastor Erick Neary and his station wagon stood in the center of us and civilization. All that was visible in the darkness was the face and person of Neary cast in white light. It felt like a waking nightmare. A hot wave of panic overtook every ounce of my body. A panic intertwined with survival. A panic that felt naked and primal. I felt like the child making a sick game of dashing up the basement stairs pretending to be chased by an evil force. But I hadn't reached the final step on time. My left foot was seized in the ghost's cold grasp.

The evil force finally won the race.

"Here's what's gonna happen," Neary thundered in a sinister baritone. "Us four are gonna take a long ride and talk."

"How did you find us?" Sasha asked.

Neary said, "If you three walk into those woods, I can no longer guarantee your safety. You need to come with me now if you know what's best for you."

"You killed Brent Cushman," Sasha shouted. "I would rather starve in the woods alone than come anywhere near that fucking car."

"I know you three are *convinced* you know what the hell is going on, but believe me when I tell you you *don't*." Neary began slowly treading his way towards us.

"Stay back," Sasha shrieked. "Don't come any closer."

Neary stopped in his tracks. "I'm not gonna hurt you. But I'm not gonna let you go into those woods, either."

I barked, "You followed us from town, didn't you? You've been following us this *entire* time, haven't you? Did you follow us here last time? How about when Jordan and I met Nathaniel at Shelly's? He knew you by *name*, asshole."

Neary's eyes filled with the same menacing intensity as the day in the administration office. "You three are getting in the car and that's that. I'm asking you kindly *not* to test me."

"No," Sasha said sternly.

Neary tilted his head and stiffened his jaw. He darted straight for us as his nostrils flared open and closed and his hairy, burly arms stretched out.

"Get away!" Sasha screamed as she reached for Neary's face.

"AAAGHHHH!" Neary howled in pain as he buried his face in both his hands. He stumbled backward and fell on his right side, wallowing in pain. Sasha had scratched him across his cheek. It wasn't until Neary was on his side that I noticed a gun holstered on his belt.

"Holy *shit*," Rox said. The three of us were frozen in place.

"RUN!" Sasha yelled.

Suddenly, the three of us were barreling down the road without any light. Bitter cold air stung my lungs with each heaving breath I took. The only sounds were the frantic thumps of our shoes against the asphalt.

"It's just up here!" Rox shouted from up ahead. A faint orange glow beamed through the trees. Suddenly, the silhouette of the awning and the roof of the Revival main building materialized as the three of us instantly froze in our tracks and worked tirelessly to catch our breaths.

"What the hell do we do?" Sasha asked breathlessly. "We're pinned between Pine and a pissed-off Neary, it's dark and freezing cold, the cops are probably on their way —"

"Shhh!" Rox interrupted. "Get a grip and *focus*. We stick to the plan. You said yourself that we're not leaving empty-handed, so we won't."

"You really expect me to wait out here *alone*?" Sasha asked.

I personally didn't take solace in the idea of a gun-toting Pastor Neary finding the girl who left him a permanent scar alone in the forest.

"Alright," Rox said. "All three of us will go in. We can split up and cover more ground."

"This was a mistake." Sasha quaked. "This is all my fault. If I never made that stupid promise to Jordan —"

"More forces than one brought us here tonight," Rox said. "Let's not waste time arguing which one needs the most blame. We have work to do."

"How do we get in?" I asked.

"Boiler room," Rox replied. "It's where I snuck off to smoke. I had to crack the window open and never once was it locked when I went back the next day."

"Can we all fit?" Sasha asked.

"Let's not waste time hypothesizing," Rox said before setting out for the building. I slowly turned to Sasha and saw the fear in her eyes illuminated by the glow of the orange streetlights that lit the parking lot. Despite the complete lack of feeling in my hands, I reached out to grab Sasha's hand and held it in mine. We gave each other a faint yet assuring nod, and together we made our descent towards the main building of Revival Church Camp.

Sasha and I circled around the northeast corner of the building and found Rox propped on top of a gray junction box jamming a window open. With the help of me and Sasha on each foot, Rox fed themself through the rectangular aperture of the window and made it to their feet. We were in. Sasha was able to squeeze through the window with hardly any difficulty despite her height and build. Finally, it was my turn to complete the breaking-and-entering hat trick. I stood atop the gray junction box, took Rox and Sasha's hands, and slowly the two were successfully able to feed me through, despite my hoodie getting caught on the railing and riding up to my belly button.

"Okay," Rox said. "Ilya and I will take Pine's main office. Sasha, I want you to check the gymnasium and dorm rooms if they're unlocked."

"Got it," Sasha said.

"We meet back here in 15 minutes. That's 3:30. If any of us get split up and run into trouble, pull a nearby fire alarm. That'll be the signal to evacuate."

"What if we can't reach one?" I asked.

"Scream," Rox said. *Scream*. That one singular word seemed to hang suspended in the air as everything else surrounding it froze in time.

"Let's go find a smoking gun," Rox said before making their way to the door.

The hallways were dim but not completely dark. It reminded me of doing Christmas pageants at school at night and how odd it felt seeing the usual classrooms and halls not alight with sunshine.

"Pine's office is this way," Rox said. "Sasha, make your way to —"

"Make my way to the cafeteria and dorm rooms, got it," Sasha interrupted, but not maliciously. Rather, it was a tone of anxiety-riddled determination. As Sasha made her way down the hall, Rox led the two of us in the opposite direction. I had the sickly sensation that Pine would be standing on the other side of every corner we turned waiting for us. I can't describe the feeling, but I couldn't shake the idea that Pine was watching us the entire time.

"Here we go," Rox said as they sped up their strut. They planted themself directly in front of a wooden door with a tall, rectangular window bolted inside of it that provided a glimpse inside the darkened office. Rox reached for the doorknob and slowly tested it but found it wasn't mobile.

"Is it locked?" I asked stupidly.

Rox reached for their back pocket and withdrew two bobby pins. They further cornered themself into the door and began to jimmy the lock. After 10 or so seconds of jimmying, Rox was finally able to bend the knob downward and slowly lever the wooden door open. They turned their head and looked up at me, making square eye contact. Suddenly, it was Rox's eyes which were filled with fear. I could count on one hand the amount of times I saw Rox visibly scared in my lifetime. Rox didn't get scared.

But in that moment halfway between Pine's office and the natural world, Rox had the look of a scared child drawn plainly on their face. They had bravely led us unto the breach thus far, maybe now it was time someone repaid the favor. Since we had found respite from the freezing cold, I had finally gained feeling back in my extremities. I reached for Rox's hand and took it in mine. Looking into their eyes, I realized something. We weren't just here for Jordan, or Jozie, or Brent Cushman, or Nathaniel Holtmeyer, or Rory, or the countless other kids whose heads were filled with self-hatred and shame. We were there for Rox. We were there for the protagonists of Rox's stories they fought so hard to protect in their writing. We were there for the portion of themself they had to sacrifice in order to persevere for the entire previous summer.

It was at that moment that I realized there wasn't a door in the world I wouldn't walk through for the people I loved most.

Rox led me by the hand into the darkness and the secrets it harbored.

"Should I turn on the light?" I asked.

"Negative," Rox said. "We can't risk the exposure. Use your phone flash and keep it low."

Now it really was starting to feel like Watergate. I turned on my phone's flash and saw the legs of a large metallic desk. I scanned the far corners of the room and saw a handful of filing cabinets.

"There's a closet," Rox whispered. "I'm gonna jimmy it."

As Rox got to work on the closet door, I made my way to one of the four filing cabinets and reached for the top drawer. Locked.

"These are all locked," I said. Rox made their way from the closet to the cabinet and fished out the same bobby pins as before. In five short seconds, they had successfully pried the lock and all four filing cabinets unlocked. I was about to ask where they learned the trick but remembered time was of the essence. I withdrew the first drawer and found a long assortment of files and manila envelopes stacked alongside each other. The firm *clink* sound from behind let me know Rox succeeded in jimmying the closet door open. Now we were cooking with gas. I reached for a random file in the drawer and unfurled it using the phone flash to illuminate its contents. The papers inside looked like a worksheet from chemistry class more than anything.

"What is it?" Rox asked from inside the closet.

I feverishly scanned the paper and found highlighted words, one of which was so long I had no hope of pronouncing it. An *M* word.

"Ill? What's in that file?" Rox asked sternly.

"It's . . . I don't know."

"Then take a picture. We don't have time."

Suddenly, we heard an assortment of thuds coming from down the hallway. Footsteps.

"That's not Sash," Rox said uneasily. My blood went cold as the thuds came closer and closer.

"Shut the closet door! Don't make a sound!" I whispered frantically. Rox stood in place for three or so seconds before quietly shutting the closet door. I instantly shut the file, jammed it into the metallic drawer, and shut the cabinet closed. The room filled with fluorescent light as the door flew open. I whipped around and found Reverend Pine standing in the doorway.

"Son," he asked, "what in the *hell* is going on? How did you get inside?"

The seconds turned to hours as I tried to make up a believable excuse.

Finally, I said, "My car broke down in the woods, so I came here to call for help."

The look of sharp suspicion remained on Pine's face. "Son, you signed a no-bullshit clause the second you broke into my damn office. Now you have got some *serious* explainin' to do. You wanna tell me what's *really* going on? Are you in some sorta trouble? If you're not already, trust you're sure as hell gonna be."

"Trouble?" I quaked. "No. No trouble at all. I just had —"

"Don't you dare lie to me, son," Pine interrupted sternly. I panicked. "Yes . . . trouble. I was in trouble so I came here."

"Is somebody after you, son?"

Do I tell him the truth?

Pine narrowed his eyes. "Son . . . is that *pastor* you mentioned last time givin' you grief? What was his name . . . Norman?"

"Neary."

"Yep, that's it! Neary. Is he the one you're in trouble with?"

"Yes . . . yes he is."

Pine closed the door behind him completely shut and gestured for me to take a seat. "And you came to me because you needed someone immune to his small-town charms. Someone who can stay *objective*."

I sat down. "Yes . . . exactly. He threatened me and my friends. He threatened an alumnus of this place too, Nathan Holtmeyer, for agreeing to meet with me and my friend. Nathan knew him by *name*."

Pine nodded but didn't break eye contact. "Son, you'll be happy to know I already brought your concerns to the proper authorities down there in Anthem."

"You what?" I quaked.

"Don't let his sermons and diatribes fool you, son. If Pastor Neary brought even an ounce of harm to one of *my* kids, there is gonna be hell to pay. I can guarantee it."

"You can arrest him?" I asked.

"Son, with the friends I have, I can see to it that Neary's next and final congregation is nobody but his damned *cell-mate*. After what he did to Brent Cushman and that poor sonovagun Nathan Holtmeyer."

I couldn't tell if Pine was bluffing. If he and Neary were truly in cahoots, why would he be selling him down the river? Or was Pine a man who kept his friends close but his enemies closer?

Pine said, "I'm sorry for the scare he gave you and your pal at Shelly's. That had to be downright fearsome."

The glimmer of hope was about to reach its apex until it was extinguished completely by a sudden and bone-chilling realization.

I said, "Sir . . . I never mentioned we were at Shelly's."

Pine's eyes suddenly widened with the realization of what he had said. His cheeks filled with crimson as his eyes darted back and forth.

I trembled. "You knew we were there, didn't you? It was *you* who called the cops on my mom, wasn't it?"

"Son," Pine said, shaking his head, "when it comes to the safety of children, Revival doesn't leave any stone unturned. That's our *mission*."

I rose from my chair. "Bullshit. You're the one who sent the fucking police to my home. *You're* the one who sent Nathan to the hospital."

"Nathaniel Holtmeyer is a disturbed man, son."

"He's disturbed because of you people. Revival destroyed him. It ruined his fucking life. I guess some people can't hack the *adjustment phase* or whatever the fuck you call it."

"Son, I don't expect someone your age to grasp the complicated nature . . . the *nuance* of what it is we do. Our work focuses primarily on teens . . . and teens are *messy* and *complicated*. It only makes sense that our work has to be messy and complicated at times. I can't expect you to understand the type of compromise we have to make to ferry thousands of lost young souls to a better place summer after summer. If we ceased to exist, where would those lost souls go? Yes, the path *back* to God is painful. Sometimes in this life, we must *prove* our worthiness of his grace and forgiveness. But what we believe is that the pain of growth is better than the pain of staying the same. Staying lost. Staying *confused*. Sometimes to relieve a person of their pain, you must briefly introduce them to another pain. Not unlike a surgeon amputating a leg to spare further disease. *That* is truly the path back to God's love."

I said, "This isn't *God*. This isn't *love*. You don't *guide or protect* anyone. You manipulate kids. You fill their heads with nothing but guilt and self-loathing until they can't stand the sight of themselves. And then you turn around and offer them your own fucked-up cure and when they reject it, you threaten to tear them away from their families and their homes. You're the fucking *devil*."

Pine's eyes suddenly filled with contempt. "Son . . . I know this has been a confusing month for you and your friends, and I will never hope to fully understand. But you bring my life's work of protecting the youth of this state into question . . . you make things *personal*. Trust me, son, I am not a man you wanna make things personal *with*."

"I don't care," I said. "You killed Brent Cushman. You roped him into your world of brainwashing and . . . *preying* on the innocence of kids who only want someone to listen to them and love them for who they are. You're right, those kids *did* need guidance, and you gave them nothing but rope to hang themselves with. Like Rory —"

"Son," Pine barked. "You better choose your next words *wisely*. You're a hair's breadth away from ringing a bell you can't unring, and I promise you you'll regret it."

Suddenly, there was a small racket from the closet.

Rox.

"Oh dear," Pine said sinisterly. "We had company and you didn't bother telling me?" He made his way to the closet. "Far be it from me to let a guest feel unwelcomed in *my* office."

"DON'T!" I shouted. Pine shot me a smile. A bloodcurdling, loathsome smile.

But before his hand could reach the knob, the door flailed wide open. The metal doorknob thrust directly into Pine's side, and Rox escaped from the closet as he fell to the floor.

"GRAB SOMETHING!" Rox shouted.

As I darted for the filing cabinet, Pine began howling in pain and let out a series of fiery expletives. I grabbed the file I stuffed inside the top drawer earlier, and Rox and I made a mad dash out of the office to find Sash and get the hell out of Revival.

Rox began shouting for Sasha as we raced down the hallway towards the boiler room. I clung onto the file for dear life as we rounded the corners so fiercely our shoes slid across the tile floor. After what felt like an eternity of running, we finally had the boiler room door in our sights, but no sign of Sasha.

"Where is she?" I asked breathlessly.

"Don't know," Rox said. "Maybe she's waiting for us outside."

We brought our mad dash to a screeching halt at the boiler room door and opened it. No Sash.

"*Shit.*" I trembled. "She's not here."

The window was still closed shut.

Rox rushed both of us inside and closed the door behind us. "There's a chance she was closer to another exit — we can't wait now."

"We *can't* leave without Sash," I said. "I won't let us."

"She defended herself once already today," Rox said as they made their way to the window. "She's a tough kid."

But before Rox could open the window, our shadows were suddenly cast along the wall as a gust of wind met our backs. The door flailed wide open. We whipped our heads back with our fists clenched but were greeted by Sasha standing in the doorway completely out of breath.

"What the hell happened?" Sasha asked breathlessly.

I said, "Pine's behind *everything*. The cops, Brent, Rory, Nathan —"

"Let's save the info dumping for another time," Rox said as they pried the window open. We each fed ourselves through the window once again, though this time there were considerably more scuffs and scrapes as the job was rushed.

"THIS WAY!" Rox shouted as they made a break for the black forest.

———

Dawn was breaking. The forest floor was actually visible compared to when we were racing *towards* Revival and not away from it. I was so laser focused on my footing through the sloping grassy ground littered with branches and acorns, the thick fog, and the endless array of trees, I was unsure who was running to my right and who was running to my left. My senses were so usurped by adrenaline and fear, I could hardly find my bearings even with the new light breaking through the trees. The only sounds were frantic and anxious inhales and exhales and a cacophony of frenzied footsteps. It became difficult to discern which was coming from whom as the race through Appalachia became one blurry distortion of cold and dark.

"LOOK!" Sasha shouted from up ahead. "THE ROAD!"

Suddenly, the bright new morning light was cast along the street not 50 yards away from us. We still had a long way to go until our warm beds, but the sight of the sunlit road through the trees and fog symbolized freedom. I had miraculously managed to hold onto the file stolen from Pine's office even through the mad dash through Appalachia in the freezing dark.

"YES!" I shouted. "Rox, which way back to the car? Rox?"

Rox wasn't replying. In fact, Rox was nowhere in sight.

"Rox?" Sasha said. The two of us spun around in hysterics looking and shouting, but Rox had vanished.

"ROX!" Sasha shouted helplessly. "ROX!"

"Did we lose them?" I asked.

"No," Sasha quivered. Suddenly, the color drained from her face as she stared back into the very woods we were escaping. I followed her eye back into the forest and instantly felt the air bolt out of me when I saw what she saw.

Rox was frozen in place some 30 yards away. As the fog passed through, I saw a pair of legs dressed in black pants standing directly behind Rox. The fog cleared and revealed Reverend Pine standing directly behind Rox. In one hand he had Rox's pink hair clenched in his fist, in the other . . . a gun pointed directly at Rox's temple.

"Oh my God." Sasha trembled. "He has a *gun.*"

Pine's voice boomed through the trees and fog. "Son, this life is too damn short for silly misunderstandings like these. How about you and your friends come back with me, and we sort this all out? Howsabout it?"

Rox struggled in his grip as tears strolled down their cheeks.

"DON'T YOU DARE FUCKING HURT THEM!" Sasha shouted, her voice cracking.

Pine shouted back, "I've spent my whole life fighting anything and anyone that stood between me and my mission to protect God's children. When you decided to break into my office, accuse me, and steal from me . . . you positioned yourself between me and my mission."

I shouted back, "You're pointing a *gun* to the head of a child, Pine. It's what you've spent your entire 'career' doing. You haven't molded a *single* child into God's image in that time, just your own."

Rox continued to squirm in Pine's grip before he angrily straightened them back into position. "Son, I know common sense is anything *but* common at your age. But you have something of mine, and I have something of yours."

"DON'T DO IT, ILYA!" Rox shouted as they continued to squirm. Pine pressed the gun to Rox's head not in fury, but in petty frustration. Like it was a slight inconvenience.

"You're a smart kid, Ilya," Pine said. "I know this past month has been hell for you and your friends. I'm willing to chalk all of this up to . . . *adolescent rascality* if you return what's mine. Do the right thing, son."

"DON'T LISTEN TO HIM, HE'S LYING!" Rox shouted.

"Give it back." Sasha quaked. "Ill, give him the file *back*."

"HE WON'T LET ME GO, ILL!" Rox belted. "TAKE THE FILE AND GET BACK TO THE CAR!" Once again, Pine pressed the gun further into Rox's temple.

Growing visibly irritated, Pine shouted, "Now's *not* the time to test my resolve, son. It's a battle I've won time and time again. Don't be stupid."

Sasha said, "Ilya, have you lost your mind?! Give him the fucking file before he blows Rox's head off."

"He won't," I said, unsure of who I was trying to fool the most.

Pine's brow was lowered in a state of sheer impatience. "TEN . . ."

"RUN!" Rox screamed through sobs.

"ILYA, GIVE IT BACK!" Sasha shrieked.

Pine belted, "NINE!"

Suddenly, Sasha yanked the file from my grasp. She sprinted a few paces and chucked the file across the forest floor in Pine and Rox's direction.

"NO!" Rox shouted, their sobs becoming heavier.

"Okay, you have your file back, asshole," Sasha yelled. "Now let Rox go."

But Pine simply smiled and maintained the gun's position on Rox. "See? Was that so hard? We can be rational adults after all."

"LET THEM GO!" Sasha shrieked.

Pine began shaking his head. "Still . . . I can't help but feel as if we all got off on the wrong foot here. It only seems right that we take this conversation back to my office, and we can work to come to a *better* understanding. One that suits us *all.*"

I screamed, "PINE, YOU SON OF A BITCH! YOU HAVE YOUR PIECE-OF-SHIT FILE, NOW LET THEM GO!"

Pine shook his head. "It doesn't seem right to leave things on this sour note. I'd much prefer we air things out to clear my conscience."

"You don't *have* a conscience, asshole," Rox said. Pine pulled Rox's hair backward as they let out a shriek of pain.

"STOP!" Sasha screamed. "We'll come with you, please just don't hurt them!"

"NO!" Rox shouted. "HE LIED ALREADY, HE'S LYING AGAIN!"

Rox was right. Pine called our bluff once already.

Pine shouted, "My generosity *and* my patience are running thin, kiddo. FIVE . . ."

I knew if we three went back with him, we'd never see our homes again. I would never see Mom again.

". . . FOUR . . ."

I was scrambling to form a plan but was drawing complete blanks.

". . . THREE . . ."

Rox thrust their elbow squarely into Pine's ribs. They got out from under his grasp and made a dash for it while Pine fell backward. He let out a wail of pain before he raised his gun directly at Rox's back as they ran away.

"NOOOO!" Sasha shrieked.

BANG!

A gunshot pierced our ears and echoed through the forest. Rox tumbled face-first into the forest floor with their arms to their sides.

"ROX!" Sasha yelled in a bloodcurdling screech.

But Rox wasn't moving. They remained perfectly in place with their face nestled in the grass and fallen pine needles. There was no movement. No twitch or sign of a twitch. Sasha began to sob uncontrollably and suddenly dashed towards Rox before I grabbed her by her shoulders. We both fell to our knees as I held an inconsolable Sasha, repeating Rox's name over and over through hoarse sobs. I could not process what was happening, or rather what had just happened. The sight of Rox lying lifelessly on the forest floor seemed to crystallize itself like a painting. Their complete lack of movement only fed the sensation that time was frozen completely still.

Sasha continued to wail and howl as memories with Rox began to flash in my mind. This *couldn't* be where our story ended. We were supposed to travel places. We were supposed to see who would get their story published first, or who would get their book adapted into a movie first. We had a plan to meet at Shelly's at least once every year, even into adulthood, no matter how rich and successful we had become to compare notes and swap story ideas and prompts. We were supposed to grow into weird elderly people who encouraged teenage rebellion and chaos.

But all those plans and all those dreams were lying dormant on the forest floor, completely immobile. Rox was cut off before their prime as if a beautiful story was cut off halfway through the prologue.

But suddenly, Rox's body jolted upward. They glanced down at their chest and stomach looking for blood, but their shirt and coat were completely spotless. Sasha let out a painful, euphorically relieved gasp. Rox whipped their head in Pine's direction, and I could see he was gripping his left shoulder while awkwardly seated on the ground. He withdrew his hand. Blood. Pine had been shot in the shoulder. But how? The gun was pointed *squarely* at Rox when the shot rang through the trees.

Pine then glanced up from his fresh wound and bloodied hand to his right. I followed Pine's glare into the tree line. Some 30 yards away, another handgun was suspended in the air, pointed directly at the reverend. Smoke floated from the barrel. Attached to the gun was a burly, hairy arm. Attached to the arm was Pastor Erick Neary.

Sasha and I continued to cling to each other with white knuckles, but neither of us made a sound. Neary maintained his position, pointing his handgun squarely in Pine's direction as smoke gravitated from the barrel. Rox frantically rose to their feet and made a mad dash in our direction as Pine continued to stifle the blood from his left shoulder.

"RUN!" Rox belted as they raced past me and Sash. Sasha and I remained frozen in place, crouched on the ground for five or so seconds before finally snapping out of the trance. The three of us raced to the road.

"There's Neary's car!" Rox shouted from up ahead. The green station wagon was parked only a few paces ahead.

"Are you crazy?" Sasha shrieked.

"Have any quicker escape options?" Rox said.

The three of us made it to Neary's car and thrust ourselves inside on either side. But the driver's seat was vacant.

"Why the hell aren't we moving?" Sasha shouted from the backseat.

"Neary should be right behind us," Rox said from the passenger seat.

"You're seriously gonna let that creep drive us through —"

"It's not him, Sash," I interrupted. "It's Pine. All of it is Pine."

Suddenly, Neary emerged from the tree line and rushed towards us. It wasn't until he opened the driver's side door that he was close enough for me to notice the massive gash running from the bottom of his left eye to the corner of his lip. Sasha's doing. Neary thrust the car into ignition, and we sped off into fresh daylight.

The car ride was silent. Neary focused on the road as we three kids worked tirelessly to catch our breaths and regain our sanities.

Sasha said, "What the *hell* are we supposed to do now? Where are we supposed to go? Pine probably has police knocking down our doors right this second."

"Not likely," Neary said remarkably calmly.

"Care to elaborate?" Sasha sneered.

Neary took a good 20 seconds to ponder before replying, "Pine's spent the last three decades cultivating Tennessean law *and* Tennessean press. That type of power and influence comes with the condition of keeping your hands clean at any cost."

"Meaning?"

"Meaning Pine's position is too delicate for him to risk a trial involving me and you three geniuses."

Sasha said, "He can say it was a kidnapping. He can spin some tale of him heroically throwing himself between you and us and —"

"He *won't*," Neary interrupted. "Trials are bad for business. There are three decades' worth of kickbacks and gag orders that have stood between Revival kids and taking the stand in court."

"You mean like Nathan Holtmeyer?" I asked.

Neary made eye contact with me through his rearview mirror. It was the same steely-eyed look as before but without the usual flame of anger. It was a look of pure exhaustion.

Neary said, "Nathan deserved to live out the rest of his lonely life in peace. You had no business getting him involved in this bullshit crusade of yours."

I snapped, "He knew you by *name* . . . and we deserve to know how."

"I don't give a single damn what you *think* you deserve. You're roping innocent people into your mess without giving a thought to the consequences."

"Did you threaten him? Did you strike the very fear of God into him like you did me and Sash?"

"No, absolutely *not*."

"Then how did he know your full name? And why did it nearly send him to an early grave?"

After what felt like a full minute of silence, Neary spoke. "Nathaniel . . . was my *counselor*."

"Your *counselor*?" I asked dumbfoundedly.

Neary said nothing. It wasn't until Rox whipped their head back in my direction and I saw their sheer, unadulterated look of shock that I finally realized what he meant. My jaw fell. My lips dried up.

Sasha stuttered, "You mean . . . *you* were a Revival kid?"

Neary kept his eyes on the road. In the rearview mirror, I could see his cold glare as his eyes filled with what looked like a painful yearning.

He said, "My mother left my father and I when I was only three. She didn't bother leaving us a note or anything. As my father opted to drown himself in self-pity and Jack Daniel's, there was a silence throughout my childhood. An *absence* of praises and celebrations usually reserved for a child. But in that silence . . . God spoke. He was the only force in my life I didn't have to . . . *kill* myself to earn the validation of. I clung to God, or rather, He clung to me.

"My sophomore year of high school, I was appointed the parish liaison of my school. I was the spiritual leader of my class, leading prayer before football games and final exams and things like that. Before I even knew the names Pine or Revival, I was perfectly acquainted with God's love and the impact it could have on others. God was in no need of being further pitched to me.

"One day, I was approached by a classmate of mine named Jesse Evers. It felt odd for a junior to come to a sophomore for guidance, but as always, I was eager to help in any way I could. He said he was in desperate need of confession and being forgiven. He looked haunted and hunted. When I asked him what terrible thing he had done, he told me. He was attracted to men. *Just* men. He said he'd been praying every single morning and night for the past two years for the feeling to stop, but it was only getting stronger with each day. He said he was certain the devil was working inside him . . . and was *winning*.

"I had heard about homosexuality in the news, in class, and at church. I knew it was seen as sheer evil and an abomination. But as Jesse broke down in front of me, I could only see someone lost and unseen. I knew what that felt like and didn't want it for anyone else in this world. I was able to talk Jesse down and worked desperately to convince him that God's love was unconditional. I could tell I was the first and only person in his life who made being attracted to other men out to be anything other than wickedness. The glimmer of hope in his eyes that his life was still worth living was unmistakably God.

"Then he kissed me. He cradled my head in his right hand as he pressed his lips to mine. I had never been kissed. I had never been held. It felt like —"

Neary's eyes welled up with tears as he cleared his throat. "It felt like coming home. Like something being returned to you that you never knew you wanted back so desperately. I came to crave the feeling more than anything else, more than eating or sleeping. Jesse and I met at his house every possible day we could after school. I was certain I was gifted Jesse by God at a pivotal time in my youth when I needed him most. But one day when we were cuddling in his bed, his mother walked in on us. She instantly broke down in tears in the middle of his doorway. I'll never forget the sight of her clinging to the wooden threshold as she became burdened by the knowledge that her son liked to kiss and hold boys.

"Jesse's parents met with the principal of our school and demanded that I be removed as parish liaison and expelled. Before I could process what was happening, I was watching in real time how my liking boys was costing me my passion for introducing my classmates to God. The only thing that gave my life purpose and kept me from feeling like a hollowed-out husk of myself. The principal, who had witnessed firsthand my passion for faith and service, was adamant in finding a compromise that would keep me in school while satisfying Jesse's parents' bloodlust for the kid who dared put his body on their son. He suggested Jesse and I enroll in a summer camp for young wayward men. But Revival was just beginning to lick its wounds after the PR disaster it faced during that time, and I knew the place was wrought with corruption and abuse. But the principal assured me the proper heads rolled and that 'Christian values' were back in control.

"From the first time I watched Pine open his ugly mouth, I knew he had taken the usual dogma of hate and simply repackaged it for the upcoming 21st century. But my peers were smitten with him. Pine represented something boys who liked boys were desperate for . . . a voice that wasn't shaming them or screaming at them simply for existing. Pine brought a charm and an empathy to his speech that had kids convinced he was their friend. Seeing the gullibility and innocence of children being exploited by a man hiding behind a bible was almost enough to deter me from my faith. Almost. I was unmoved by Pine's snake oil spiel, and he picked up on it instantly. I could tell he kept one eye open for malcontents and dissidents like me.

"The first night of camp, I was invited to his office for individual counseling. The second I walked inside, Pine stretched his hand out and had a bright smile on his face. He said he had heard a lot about me and was aware of my role as parish liaison at school. I can't explain what happened, but the more Pine spoke, the more calm I felt. The more willing I became to open up and share. Not long after I sat down in his office, I began telling him about my mom walking out on me and my father. I told him all about Jesse and the kisses we shared. All the while, Pine didn't break eye contact with me for a single second. It felt like he had waited his entire life to hear my story. Little did I know, the entire time he was plotting. He was piecing together his blueprint to fuck me upside the head.

"I had learned later on that Jesse was being given individual counseling of his own. As the summer went on, I noticed a change in him. He was cold to me. He refused to talk to me or even acknowledge me. It wouldn't occur to me until much later that it was Pine's meddling with my psyche, but at the time, I was completely alone. Jesse went from being the only person in the world who I felt truly saw me for who I was to being a reflection of something inside me I was an idiot for unveiling to the world. The foxholes I had dug in the far reaches of myself to hide from self-loathing had become Pine's playthings. Jesse was no longer home. Pine had taken my only feeling of home and . . . and . . ."

Rox interrupted, "He turned home into hate."

Neary tore his eye from the road and gawked at Rox. "Yes, *exactly*. How did you know that?"

Rox said nothing.

Neary said, "But one day, near the end of the summer, Jesse cornered me. He completely broke down. He told me Pine had threatened to take him away from his parents unless he iced me out. I held Jesse in my arms as he cried and cried. In that moment, it became clear to me that God was being twisted and corrupted just the same as He was before the trials and the PR hell storm that befell Revival. Jesse and I agreed then and there to bring Pine to justice.

"With the scandal still being fresh in the minds of reporters and journalists, our report to the police picked up steam quickly. But it wasn't long until testimonies weren't lining up and the burden of proof became more and more staggering. The case ended before it had even begun. But Pine had saved his most genius move for last. With the Tennessee press hounding him for answers, Pine decried our suit as 'a cog in American culture's ongoing war on Christianity.' Suddenly, my efforts to put Pine behind bars ended up being his most formidable defense against any dissenters and cynics. It ran with every election cycle. It became the rallying cry of nearly every conservative hell-bent on keeping the gears of conversion therapy spinning . . . and it all started with me. After that day, I never heard from Jesse ever again. His parents were uncomfortable with the idea of us sharing a high school together and moved him.

"God and Jesse Evers were the only people in my life who I felt loved by, and Reverend Pine tore each one away from me. The big man upstairs and I were squared away just fine before Pine used his bag of tricks on me and so many others like me. But my faith clung to me like a disease. I've spent the last 10 years teaching others the word of God, not knowing if I was supplying them with the agency to hate me and want me dead. Until just over a year ago, I met a young man who reminded me of myself as a teenager. I always tell young people to be a pencil in God's hand, and this kid was one if ever there was."

"You mean . . . Brent Cushman?" Sasha asked.

Neary went silent. The tension in the car was suffocatingly palpable.

He said, "Brent wasn't a stranger to the reputation that preceded Revival. He simply could not distract himself from the possibility that God and His love were being used to hurt others. It lit a fire deep inside him. He was a firm believer that faith could and should be coupled with queer and trans-affirmation. I tried my best to steer him as far away from Pine as possible, but he was relentless.

"So finally, I agreed to provide him with counsel as he signed up to be a counselor for a summer. Like any idealistic politician, Brent was hell-bent on changing things from the inside for the better."

Rox interrupted, "And like every idealistic politician, he was met with a bludgeoning dose of reality quickly."

Neary said, "Exactly. I should have foreseen Pine seeing the optimism in Brent as a weakness to exploit. But after the first month of the summer, something in Brent changed. He was slow to speak. The fire in his eye was gone. I kept telling him over and over that he could walk away at any time, but he felt doing so would be casting doubt on his devotion to God's work. But I knew the closer he was getting to Pine, the more of Revival's sickly underbelly he was exposed to. He just wouldn't say as much."

I asked, "Why didn't you go to the police?"

Neary replied, "Let me ask you this, have any of you had any unpleasant run-ins with the Anthem police recently?"

"Yes," I said. "Two officers came to my house the other night. They knew about Nathaniel . . . before it was even reported."

Neary shot me a glance through the rearview mirror.

"Pine told the police," I said.

"Pine *is* the police," Neary said. "Revival is one of the last standing testaments to the idea that being gay or transgender is reversible . . . or at the very least unsettled. Do any of you geniuses know how much money was spent on anti-LGBTQIA+ laws last year from churches? Over $200 million. Places like Alliance Defending Freedom that work around the clock to curb queer and trans rights are indebted to places like Revival. With Pine supplying politicians and pundits with all the evidence they need to sing the praises of conversion therapy summer after summer, and combine that with kickbacks from his friends in the foster care system for his annual donations of 'at-risk youth,' Reverend —"

Rox interrupted, "Reverend Pine is the most powerful man in the state of Tennessee."

"Correct. There's not a badge between the borders of Tennessee that doesn't go through Pine. If your grandmother is pulled over for a broken headlight, he'll know about it before she does."

Sasha said, "So what can we do?" But her words were met with silence. It was clear none of us had any idea how far down the rabbit hole we would go. Corruption. Bribery. Kickbacks. It was making my head spin just trying to remember where it all started.

Rox said, "Ilya, what was in that file you took?"

I had completely forgotten about the file. All my memory could serve for the time being was some complicated word that starts with *M* and some chemistry logo.

I muttered, "It . . . it was some chemistry paper. *Meta* something."

Suddenly, Sasha fished her phone out of her pocket and began frantically scrolling.

She asked, "Methylenedioxy?"

"Yes . . . that sounds right. How did you know?"

She held out her phone towards me, and on it was a photo of a label bearing the exact word highlighted in the file.

I asked, "Where did you find this?"

Sasha replied, "It was in the cafeteria cabinets. I had to jimmy the lock open with a meat cleaver. There were tons of paper envelopes with this label and others that looked like different medications."

Rox said, "Ecstasy."

"Ecstasy?" Sasha asked.

"Methylenedioxy is what you find in drugs like molly or ecstasy. It causes the brain to increase the feel-good hormones like dopamine and endorphins. It makes you feel euphoric."

Euphoric. For some reason, that one word stuck in my brain.

I asked, "Rox, what did you see in his office?"

"I found a safe. It had an old dial, so cracking it wasn't an issue."

"What was inside?"

"Some paper, a handful of opened envelopes, and a flash drive."

"A flash drive? With what on it?"

"How am I supposed to know? All I know is his office was filled with locked filing cabinets. If he wasn't gonna take a chance leaving it in a locked filing cabinet in his own office, there's gotta be something on it not meant for prying eyes."

Sasha asked, "Why didn't you grab it, then?"

"Once Pine shut the office door with us inside, I knew an exchange was gonna be our only chance at escape if he got us, and he did. If we were caught with the flash drive that morning in the woods, it would have been back in Pine's hand and would never see the light of day again. As far as I can guess, Pine's ignorance of the fact that I even *know* a flash drive exists is our greatest weapon at the moment. But if we go back, we'll need to beef up our numbers."

Neary hissed, "Being the only legitimate adult in this car, I feel morally and somewhat spiritually obligated to put this crusade of idiotic proportions to a permanent end. The man put a *gun* to your friend's head, and you've decided you're not satisfied?"

"I agree," I said. "No way in hell am I letting any of us back into these woods. This is Reverend Pine territory."

"May I remind you two that the same psycho who held Rox at gunpoint and attempted murdering them is the exact same man who oversees the care of thousands of children every summer? Did that somehow slip your mind?" Sasha fumed.

Neary replied, "I already had one child die on my watch at the hands of that demagogue. I'm not letting three others join him just because they wanna cosplay as revolutionaries."

As Neary's car turned a corner in the woods, my car finally appeared down the street. We were halfway home.

Sasha said, "If you knew Pine was so dangerous, why didn't you warn us to stay away?"

Neary chuckled. "Y'know, it's funny you say that, because if memory serves correctly, I *did* warn you in no uncertain terms. You're the ones who refused to listen."

Neary parked directly across from my car. The dawn had broken into a bright morning.

Neary threw the car into park and leaned in. "I know you kids think you've seen the world at its worst. You're convinced you're jaded and desensitized from it. But it would amaze you to learn just how much you've benefited from the protection of adults in your lifetimes. When you enter these woods, that protection goes away. I know you have good intentions, but in this world, good intentions are no substitute for knowing when you're out of your depth and believe me, *you are.*

"So here's what you're gonna do: you're gonna go back to school, you're gonna learn trig and biology and whatever other crap, you're gonna graduate and take pictures, and then you're gonna *leave Anthem.* You're gonna put Reverend Pine in your rearview and forget about him. And maybe in time, his evils will catch up with him. But you'll have to stay alive long enough to see it. If you keep playing with fire in this way, there's no guarantee you will."

I needed no convincing, but Sasha was beside herself with anger.

With nothing else needing to be said, the three of us lazily exited Neary's station wagon into the chilly and sunny morning air. I expected to feel a massive wave of relief having reached my car after cheating death, but I mostly felt deflated and defeated. I finally learned the truth of Revival and Reverend Pine but somehow felt worse than when I started. I wondered if maintaining the mystery would have been better for my health in the long run.

As I put the car into ignition and began our odyssey back home, I was trying to rationalize the fact that I put my best friends' lives in danger. I was trying desperately to find any and all justification for the fact that we entered and escaped the lion's mouth, but not before giving the lion a taste for our blood. What if Neary was wrong? What if Pine made one simple phone call and ensured none of us three would ever see our families ever again? How far did his authority stretch? What repercussions had to be faced after pissing off the most powerful man in the state?

Twenty-one

"WE HAVE TO GO back," Sasha pleaded. "We have to get that flash drive."

"Absolutely out of the question," I replied. "Putting your lives at risk once is enough for me."

We were an hour outside of Anthem.

Sasha said, "Rox, you're the one who hacked the entire computer system of Blount High when you were just 13. Can't you hack your way into Pine's computer?"

Rox replied, "I tried this summer. Wall-to-wall encryption. It's like Fort Knox even from inside the building itself."

"Then we have no choice but to go back," Sasha said.

I asked, "Sash, may I remind you that if it wasn't for our new friend the pastor and his stellar marksmanship, Rox and possibly us two would be dead in the woods?"

Sasha shot back, "Can I remind you that countless kids including Brent Cushman are dead because of Revival . . . and that there are even more to come if he stays in power? How many gay and trans kids have to become convinced they're the fucking devil before it becomes enough?"

I replied, "There are countless people in the world doing the good work to remind those kids that they're perfect just the way they are, and they don't put themselves in danger to do so. And even if we're stupid enough to go trotting back into that compound expecting to walk out with a flash drive without a hitch, Pine will still have his hands on the strings. The last time a handful of kids were stupid enough to go after him, they ended up handing Pine the exact precedent he wanted."

Sasha said, "Ilya, that was almost *30* years ago. It was an entirely different world back then. Think about all the progress that's been made in that time. If someone blew the whistle on Revival today, it would turn a helluva lot more heads than it did in the '90s."

Sasha was making a valid point, but it would take more convincing for me to willingly drive my friends back to the place where I had to watch one of them be held at gunpoint.

She said, "And if Pine really does hold the key to every courthouse and precinct in Tennessee, then we go to the press. We don't give Pine that chance to get out in front of us. We take the fight to *him*. If we can take down Pine, dominoes will fall. People will wake up to the irreparable damage that conversion therapy does to young people. We can win in the court of public opinion."

I said, "Half of public opinion already knows, and the other half either doesn't care or is glad it's happening. People like Pine have stopped whispering the quiet part years ago. PR disasters are a dime a dozen these days, and anything that won't put Pine behind bars will most likely put him in the running for state governor and us in jail."

Sasha snapped, "But this is *bigger* than us three. It's bigger than Jozie and Jordan and Rory and even Brent Cushman. This is about not letting another kid be convinced they're gonna fucking burn in hell because of who they are or who they love. It's about stopping a special kind of evil that's specifically designed to shame and bully innocent children."

We passed the rusty sign that read: ANTHEM CITY LIMITS — POP.: 9,000

Sasha was speaking the truth, but it was nothing I didn't know already. All I wanted to envision was the three of us graduating from Blount High and putting Anthem, Tennessee, and the whole smoldering mess behind us once and for all. But just like Pastor Neary said, we had to live to see the day.

I said, "You two are the best friends I will ever have. I don't know what I would be without either of you. Please, *please* don't make me find out."

My mother always said that our struggles make us who we are. In fact, one could argue that we ourselves are indistinguishable from the hardships we have faced and the wisdom they granted us. I like to think that my struggles through discovering my sexual identity have shaped me into somebody resilient and self-aware. But struggles don't just gift us with flowery wisdom and life lessons. They burden us with knowledge too. Knowledge of just how unfair and unjust our circumstances can become in the blink of an eye for no reason whatsoever.

I spent the following week after our Bay of Pigs at Revival contemplating who I would be without the knowledge of Revival and people like Reverend Pine. Who I would be if I didn't know that one man wielded the fate of law and legislature in Tennessee. Who I would be if I was unburdened by the knowledge that Pastor Erick Neary had his faith in God all but demolished because of Pine. Who I would be if I didn't know that families could be torn apart and lives could be ruined at the discretion of one man with unchecked influence and power.

But I was equally as haunted by all that I didn't know. I didn't know the sheer magnitude of Revival's reign of terror and how far it stretched. I didn't know the span of generations that suffered the shockwaves of one child being convinced loving someone of the same sex would land them in a lake of fire. I didn't know what Brent Cushman learned that drove him to so dark a place that he drank himself to death and, in doing so, laid waste to the morale of an entire town.

I tried desperately to follow Neary's advice of going back to my life and counting down the days when Anthem and Revival could be put in my rearview. I tried as hard as I could to focus on class and tried even harder to convince myself that anything I was being taught merited my attention in light of what I had been through the past two months. I started focusing more on potential colleges. I began asking myself the big questions of who I wanted to be after graduating high school and what type of work I wanted to commit my life to. I knew I wanted to fight for human rights but had to narrow down a path. I wanted to win legislative victories for queer and trans rights, but I know I didn't want to be a politician.

I was debating whether to pick a college local or far distance while I was rummaging through my school locker during passing period when out of the corner of my eye, I saw a familiar figure.

I asked, "Did you make flashcards for zoology?"

Sasha curtly replied, "Don't."

"Don't what?"

"Don't act like I'm here to talk school with you."

"What else is there to discuss?"

"I'm not here to debate with you, Ill. Rox and I are going back, and we're leaving with that flash drive."

I sighed. "Pine is gonna have you both made the second you step foot in those woods. Hell, he probably has police watching our every move right now. If either of our cars leaves Anthem, he'll be the first to know about it." I shut my locker and was completely stunned by what awaited me on the other side.

Sasha was wearing a hijab. A beautiful, dark-blue hijab decorated with the pins her little cousins made for her. She was picture-perfect.

She asked, "Do you like?"

I stuttered, "It's perfect."

"Thanks."

I was no longer looking at the Sasha I used to know. This was somebody new. Somebody altered irreversibly.

I said, "I'm happy you didn't wait until college."

Sasha replied, "I guess I don't want to get to college just to look back and regret all the things I could have done but was too scared to."

Sasha's tone made perfectly clear what was being said between the lines.

I pleaded, "If we're stupid enough to go back into the lion's den, there's no guarantee we'll even *make it* to college. If we aren't killed, Pine will put us in jail or pull enough strings to ensure no college accepts us. He can ruin us like he has countless others before us."

"Don't tell me you're actually siding with Neary."

"And what if I am? Do you honestly think Pine isn't watching the security camera footage of us breaking in right this second? And even if we did miraculously make it out alive with a flash drive, the contents of which are a complete mystery to us, and we manage to make a trial out of it, what happens when Pine pulls enough wool over the jury's eyes to dismiss it? What if we just end up proving to the world once again that places like Revival can continue to fuck up kids without the slightest repercussion? What's gonna be different this time?"

"This time you'll have me," a familiar voice from behind said. Jordan.

"How's Jozie?" I asked.

"Better," Jordan said. "She's holding on to the idea that her best friends are gonna be waiting for her with open arms once she's released. Will they?"

I replied, "If we really are *stupid* enough to go back to Revival and under Pine's eye, maybe not."

Never had Sasha and Jordan been more united in a disposition than now. In both their eyes, I saw a desperate yearning for me to take that leap of faith.

"I'm sorry, guys. But enough people have been hurt because of me. I already can't forgive myself for the fact that I put a gun next to Rox's head —"

Sasha interrupted, "You weren't the one who put the gun to their head, *Pine* was. And he deserves to rot in jail for it."

I simply shook my head. "Guys, we're *teenagers*. We can't afford to put even more of the weight of the world on our shoulders. Don't you remember what Perdun said about us just being children? If karma really does exist, Pine's evils *will* catch up with him eventually, and we can live to see the day it finally comes crumbling down around him. But in order to do so, we need to stay alive and keep out of trouble. We need to keep our heads down."

Sasha nodded as if she understood, but in her eyes, I saw defeat. A sense of hesitant conceding. It made me physically sick having to snuff out the flame inside her which was burning to right a terrible wrong. It went against every moral and ethical instinct in my body. But if it meant keeping us safe from Pine, I would do it a hundred times over.

Sasha said softly, "I've had my head down my *entire* life. I've spent years having to tuck away and hide the things that made me who I truly was. For *years*, I've had to convince myself again and again that my faith wasn't a burden. Every outfit I've picked in the morning before school had to be a give-and-take of who I *wanted* to be versus who I *had* to be in order to survive. But until I saw our friend being held at gunpoint by someone who wouldn't suffer consequences for it, I was stupidly convinced I was doing the right thing. It didn't take me until I saw Rox sprawled out on the ground to realize that by concealing who I was, I was *enabling* people like Pine. My silence and my squeezing myself into small corners in the wall is exactly what people like Pine need to thrive."

I replied, "You said when the day would come that you'd wear a hijab to school, it wouldn't be for other people."

"And it's not. I'm not wearing this for you, for Pine, or for any of the small-minded morons at this school."

"Then why are you wearing it?"

"Tomorrow, we're going to Revival and we're not leaving without enough evidence to put an end to Pine once and for all. I'm going to need all the courage I can get. Allah will provide. *Fi Sabilillah.*"

"*Fi-what?*"

"It means 'in the cause of Allah.' Baba taught it to me when I was little. He taught me that saying it would always make me strong. He always said that taking a stand only —"

"Taking a stand only matters when it's somewhere no one like you has stood before."

"Yes . . . how did you know?" Sasha asked.

"Your baba told me in Nashville. Except you're wrong about one thing."

"What's that?"

"He didn't teach you . . . *you* taught *him*."

Sasha's lip formed a half smile. Mine did the same.

She said, "I'm not asking you to storm Revival with a massive rainbow flag in hand. I'm just asking you to consider what you would be willing to risk to make the world a safer place."

"The world is gonna keep turning with or without me."

"Then ask yourself what you'd be willing to risk for your *friends* because they're heading out tomorrow with or without you. And you've let your heart break over and over trying to get to the bottom of this shitshow. You deserve to see this to the end. I wouldn't even be trying to convince you if I didn't think it would bring you even the smallest amount of peace. You're a good person, Ill, and good people deserve to have their kindness rewarded."

Jordan said, "Sash told me about the pastor guy being a Revival kid. I may not know a lot about this stuff, but Coach Beauchamp says we should all strive to stay kind in a world hell-bent on hardening us. It sounds like that's what this pastor guy has done, and I just figure he deserves some peace too."

I said, "I can't stop thinking about him. The fact that he suffered so much and had no help at all."

Sasha replied, "He has help now."

The bell rang. Jordan ran off. Sasha gave a slight nod and turned to head to class. But I stood at my locker perfectly in place wondering what I did to deserve the friends I had. I then began to ponder Sasha's question regarding how much I'd be willing to risk for my friends. Would I risk my life? Would I willingly risk theirs? But it wouldn't occur to me until later in the day that this was no longer just my fight. It was no longer me calling the shots.

As I robotically washed the dishes after dinner, Sasha and Jordan's words echoed through my mind. The longer they reverberated, the more they rang true. This *had* become bigger than the four of us. It had become even bigger than Revival, Anthem, Pine, and the state of Tennessee. This was about a line of generations who suffered in silence like Pastor Neary. This was about the millions of people like Neary who had to forge through unimaginable self-hatred to find their way back to a God that loved them unconditionally. This was also about those who had God torn away from them indefinitely and never found their way back.

"Ill?" I heard from behind. Mom. We had barely spoken during the entire dinner. In fact, we had barely spoken at all since the night Reverend Pine sent two of his finest to our door.

I said, "The rigatoni was perfect tonight."

Mom said, "Ill, I can't let this happen."

"Let what happen?"

"I can't be that mom whose kids feel like they have to patronize and sugarcoat everything for. I *was* that kid, and it was fucking exhausting. I want you to feel like you can tell me anything. If you're in trouble, tell me. If you fucked up, tell me. If you murdered someone, I'll grab a shovel."

Mom was getting frighteningly warmer and warmer to the truth.

I mumbled, "Mom, can I ask you something?"

"Yes, *please*."

"Why do we still live in Anthem if you hate all the adults here?"

"I don't hate *all* the adults here. Just most of 'em."

"Then why have we stayed all these years? You could work anywhere in the country. Why are we still living in Anthem?"

Mom chewed on the question for five or so seconds. Finally, she replied, "When those freaks from that camp first showed up to our door, you were only seven. *Seven* fucking years old. I went online and started looking for jobs that same night. But there was only one problem standing in my way."

"What was it?" I asked.

"You."

"*Me?*"

"You were the smartest child I knew, Ilya. You still are to this day. Too smart for your own good. Hell, you figured out Santa didn't exist a year before you were toilet-trained. I knew you would immediately ask why we were leaving, and beyond that, I knew no bullshit answer I gave would suffice. And when I realized that, I realized something else."

"What?"

"I wouldn't be leaving Anthem for you, I would be leaving for me. I knew I'd be taking you away from your friends and your life, and starting over at your age would be hell. And yet, all of that paled in comparison to another realization I had that night."

"Which was?"

Mom's eyes filled with tears. "I didn't want you to spend your life thinking you were the reason we were always on the move. Us getting the hell out of Dodge is exactly what these assholes wanted after your presentation in class, and I refused to give them that. This town was too stupid to realize how much they lucked out getting a kid like you, and as badly as I wanted to punish them for it, I couldn't bring myself to punish *you* in the process."

I asked, "So . . . we stayed to punish *them*?"

"No," Mom said, "we stayed . . . because I wanted to raise my son to believe there was nowhere in this world where he didn't belong."

For the rest of the night, Mom's, Sasha's, and Sasha's baba's words echoed through my mind. All my life, I never considered the possibility that I belonged in Anthem. It always felt like I had tunnel vision towards grabbing a diploma and putting Tennessee in my rearview. But the more I listened to the ones I loved, the more it felt like I was here for a reason. Then, slowly but surely, that reason became brazenly clear. If my friends were going to right an unrightable wrong, they weren't going alone.

I reached across the bed for my phone on the nightstand and texted Sasha:

I'm in. When and whose car?

Twenty-two

DÉJÀ VU WAS IN full effect. We met in the same parking lot at the same time. A considerable amount of chips were put on the possibility that Pine wouldn't think we were stupid enough to simply press replay on our previous plan. The only thing keeping it from feeling like we were stuck in a loop was Jordan's attendance and borrowing Sasha's neighbor's car in case the cops on Pine's payroll were watching. Sasha, Jordan, and I sat and idled until 11:58 p.m. when Rox emerged from around the dark corner of the dollar store like they had the other night. Once they joined the two of us, I asked the million-dollar question. "So . . . what are we gonna do differently this time so one of us doesn't get a gun held to our head?"

Rox replied, "This time we know exactly what we need and exactly where it's hidden. Our biggest obstacle now is getting Pine out of his office for long enough to make the switch with *this*." Rox fished out a small red flash drive from their jacket pocket.

I asked, "Okay . . . so how do we guarantee he won't be in his office waiting for us?"

"He'll be in the electric room working to get the power back on."

"How do you know that?" Jordan asked.

"Because one of us will go in before the others to ensure the grid is down."

". . . Alone?" I asked.

Rox said nothing. The desperation of the situation began to fully rear its head.

I said, "Okay, fine. Then what are we waiting for?"

"Him," Rox said.

We glanced up and saw a pair of headlights rolling into the parking lot. I instantly recognized the headlights from a stretch of street deep in the woods. Neary.

"Oh fuck," Sasha said. "Is he here to stop us?"

"Just the opposite," Rox replied. "It took a *lot* of convincing, but I knew we weren't the only ones with demons to face in that hellhole."

Neary parked his car and sat in place. He was dressed in full pastoral regalia.

"Let's go," Rox said before exiting the car. Sasha instantly turned off the ignition and followed Rox to the pastor's station wagon. It took her remarkably less time to leave the car compared to our last venture to Revival. Jordan had a look of bewilderment on his face and took 10 or so seconds to ponder God knows what before exiting the car. It was time to take a stand where no one like us had stood before, but what I couldn't be sure of was whether it would be the *final* time somebody like me ever would.

———

We drove in complete silence on the dimly lit highways. Our destination, our mission, and the stakes involved were too palpable for further conversation to be warranted. I began to wonder what would happen should we prove successful. I wondered if it really was possible to put Reverend Pine behind bars once and for all. But then I started to envision all the ways our plan could go horribly wrong in an instant. If we weren't shot and killed, would we be arrested? Would Pine pull the proper strings to tear us away from our families? Would our parents be arrested and we'd be put in foster care? Would I ever see Mom again?

I knew my thoughts would only venture into darker and darker territory the more I hypothesized, so I tried to focus on the mission at hand.

Sasha looked to the pastor and finally broke the silence. "So . . . has anyone ever confessed really messed-up shit to you, like murder?"

I asked, "Seriously, Sash?"

Neary was slow to reply. "We have a duty to protect the seal of confession at any cost."

Sasha replied, "Right, I totally get that . . . but what if a serial killer started to confess all his crazy killings and said he was gonna kill more? Wouldn't you have to do something?"

It finally dawned on me that Sasha was desperate for distraction, or else she wouldn't be rattling off such asinine questions like a child in Sunday school.

Neary replied, "Yes . . . I've had murders confessed to me, but they were mostly vets who had to kill in combat. I've also given counsel to prisoners who were doing time for murder."

"What's it like meeting with prisoners?" Jordan asked.

"The same as meeting with lawyers, doctors, business owners, fathers, mothers, and children. The only difference is the orange jumpsuit."

"How's that?" I said.

Neary was again slow to speak before replying. "While I was in seminary, I was taught that the potential for atonement was the same in *all* souls, the sinners and saints alike. It was one of the main reasons I loved the church and felt so passionately about my faith. But not everybody seemed to agree."

"How come?"

"During my first visit to a prison in Pikeville when I was in my twenties, I saw a prisoner beaten within an inch of his life in the cafeteria. I'll never forget the sound of the lunch trays being used to batter in his head as the guards blew their whistles. What I learned later on was the prisoner was convicted of first-degree murder. But not just any murder . . . the starvation of his own child. He and his wife were too busy scoring meth to be bothered with feeding the child that it wasted away in its crib. When I returned to seminary and told my mentor, he shared with me a bit of clerical wisdom that I'd never forget."

"What was it?" Jordan asked.

"When someone is sent to prison for hurting a child . . . God turns his head."

I felt shivers crawl down my spine and through my arms. Somehow, discussing prisons and murder was doing only so much to whittle down the tension as we neared Appalachia.

Rox said, "You were sent to Revival against your will. You suffered Pine's wrath for an entire summer. You witnessed firsthand God being used as a tool for abuse and shame. You visited prisons and witnessed carnage and the lowest form of human depravity. How did you still end up a pastor?"

Rox's staggering line of questioning was met with complete silence. Before the silence became insufferable, Neary finally said, "Pine's method is fully contingent on the idea that loving God and being gay are mutually exclusive. I spent 20 straight years making the journey back to myself over and over and over again. But Pine's *teachings* were still perfectly intact all those years. If I didn't hate the part of me that loved other men, I hated the part of me that still needed God. But it wasn't until I was 30 that I realized they could not only coexist, but one desperately needed the other. I could only embrace God's love to the fullest if I accepted all that he made me to be."

"Even the part of you that was gay," Sasha said.

"Yes, exactly. Pine's method is reserved specifically for a teenager's gullibility and incessant need for love and validation."

Suddenly, Neary turned his head to Rox.

Neary asked, "What did Pine have reserved for *you*?"

Rox stared directly back at Neary while taking a drag of their cigarette.

Rox said, "Sending me to Revival was the only sign from my father that he even knew I existed. But believe it or not, I was actually *excited* to go. Three months in nature with kids who were just like me, some of whom might actually be nonbinary too. I had heard the stories and the rumors since I was in elementary school, but I figured it was all made up by bored teens with nothing better to do than to scare each other with ghost stories. The first day of camp, Pine asked to speak with me privately. He said he was eager to have a camper like me who could teach him about the new and upcoming generation. He asked me countless questions about my gender experience and why I changed my name, and I was beyond happy to fill him in. He was the first adult in my life who was actually interested in what I had to say about . . . *anything at all.* I was starting to feel like I had finally found a place where I belonged.

"But the next day during his first official sermon, he began ranting about how God will welcome His children to His kingdom, but that His children are only descendants of Adam and Eve. Nobody *in-between.* He said any kid who meddled with God's design was an abettor of Satan himself. The kids looked at me with disgust, even the ones who I knew were nonbinary too. That night, I realized in my bed what I was too stupid to realize in Pine's office. That while he was wearing that shit-eating grin and showing such keen interest in my gender, he was plotting. He was *scheming.*"

With each streetlamp we passed, orange light fleetingly illuminated Rox's face. Their eyes were empty. "The only two things that sustain the sawmill of Anthem are church and sex. There's been no port in the storm for me since I was a child, except for *Rox*. My *name.* I never wanted to wear a suit at prom. I didn't want a bathroom. I wanted a name that felt like . . . my *bed*. Something that didn't judge when you wanted comfort. Something that didn't mollycoddle you when you needed understanding. A name. A bed. *Roxanne.*

"It was the wooden cradle I felt protected sleeping inside, until Pine and his ilk rammed hammers into all four sides of it and made splinters. How I came even mildly close to understanding myself is exactly what they used to punish me and anyone like me. They weaponized me. They made me *complicit* in their efforts to make children forget who they really are through deceit and whatever else. As long as Revival still welcomes thousands of kids each summer, *Roxanne* will be used to shame, bully, and marginalize."

"Not after tonight," Sasha said. "We're gonna bring Pine and anybody who aided and abetted him to justice once and for all. But for what it's worth, I'm so sorry you were all alone."

Rox replied, "I actually wasn't alone, not entirely at least. There was one person this summer who actually talked to me and made me feel like I wasn't a monster."

"Who?" Sasha asked.

"Brent Cushman."

The rest of the car ride was silent.

———————

"Right here should be fine," Rox said. We parked considerably closer to the edge of the forest compared to our last visit to ensure a better chance of escape.

I said, "So I take it the boiler room window is bolted shut by now?"

"Almost certainly," Rox replied. "We'll have to switch up our entry point."

"How do you figure?" I asked.

Neary switched the car off.

"The sewer," Rox said.

"The *what*?" Sasha asked.

"Before modern plumbing made its way to the Appalachian Mountains, man-made tunnels ran directly to the source. When they built Revival in the '70s, they built the boiler room with a manhole in the floor to the tunnel for easy access. Counselors used to sneak off to party there before it was found out by the staff and shuttered off."

"So . . . we have to crawl through a dark and empty *tunnel*?" I asked.

Rox said, "If I know Pine like I think I do, every possible entrance and exit of that building is bolted shut. This is our best and *only* option if we want in."

The five of us exited the station wagon into the bitter cold and dark. Sasha used the flash on her phone to guide us into the same woods we miraculously escaped with our lives from only days before.

As we made our descent through the towering trees, Rox said, "The tunnel entrance is about a mile outside of the camp at the edge of the creek."

"A *mile*?" Sasha asked.

"If we hurry, we can get underneath the boiler room in under half an hour. Once we get inside, one of us will split off to kill the power grid. When the power is off, that'll be our cue to head to Pine's office while he's busy turning the power back on. We'll have until the power is back to grab the flash drive and make the switch. Jordan, I want you on lookout in the hallway until we snatch the flash drive. We meet back in the tunnel underneath the boiler room."

"So . . . who's gonna split off alone to shut off the power?" Sasha asked.

The five of us froze in our tracks. It wasn't until we stopped trudging that I realized how freezing cold it really was. But the more we waited for a volunteer, the more time we wasted.

I said, "I'll go."

"Don't be a hero, Ill," Sasha said. "Now's not the time."

I replied, "I'm not giving Pine another chance to hold a gun to my friend's head. You three are safer together with *him*." I gestured to the gun on Neary's side.

"Ilya's right," Rox said. "We *would* be safer with Neary."

"Then it's decided, I'll get the power off and meet you guys in the tunnel."

Sasha's face was dimly lit by her phone flash, but I could clearly see the trepidation in her expression. So far, there was no element of the plan that appealed to her. Nonetheless, Rox continued to lead the five of us along the creek to the sewer tunnel.

A running back, a nonbinary nicotine addict, a Pakistani volleyball star, a pansexual aspiring author, and a pastor all take a hike in the woods . . .

It wasn't until a minute or so after volunteering that I realized exactly what I had signed up for. First, I would need to know the path to the power grid by memory. Second, I would have to navigate the darkened hallways of Revival all alone without using a flashlight lest I give away my position. Third and finally, I would risk running into a gun-wielding Pine with every corner that I turned. I would be walking through a living horror video game. These abject fears did anything but subside as we neared the gaping mouth of the sewer tunnel. The entrance stood at about eight feet tall. The interior seemed to run off into an infinite and vacuous dark abyss sandwiched between graffitied cement walls.

"We're walking through . . . a *mile* of this?" Sasha quaked.

"The quicker we're in, the quicker we're out," Rox said. Once again, they were at the head of the foray as we slowly made our descent into the dark and cold abyss.

"Ilya, let's talk the electricity room," Rox said as their voice echoed through the tunnel. "How well do you remember your tour?"

The tour felt like ages ago.

I stuttered, "A little bit . . ."

Rox replied, "A little bit will have to suffice. Once you leave the boiler room, you're gonna turn right and head for the cafeteria. After the first corner you turn, there will be *three* doors to your left. Using *these*" — Rox withdrew two hairpins from their pocket — "you're gonna jimmy the lock of the *middle* door. Got it?"

I said, "The middle door to my left, got it. But I'm not sure I know how to jimmy a lock."

"Use the flat end of one of these first, then use the second pin to find where the lever pivots. Once you're inside, there will be a red switch along the box. That's the switch you'll press to shut off the entire grid. There might be a backup grid that powers on."

"It's funny," I said. "They can afford a backup grid but can't afford basic air-conditioning in their gym."

"Air-conditioning?" Rox asked.

"Don't you remember the gym being scalding hot? When Sash and I visited, we nearly passed out from heat exhaustion."

"I never went to services, I always ditched to go smoke."

Neary said, "Revival has been flush with cash from donors across the country for decades, I doubt keeping the A/C on is a headache for them."

"But during the tour, they said it was too costly to replace their A/C system. Why else would it have felt like a brick oven?" Sasha asked.

I said, "Pine told us that kids experienced a 'closeness to God' bordering on euphoria during the services in that brick oven."

Jordan said, "Yeah, and Jozie echoed as much. I wonder if it wasn't just hysteria from the heat."

Our march through the tunnel continued on, guided only by the lone light of Sasha's phone flash. I was certain her phone battery was running low by this point.

Suddenly, a ladder made of rebar bolted into the cement wall appeared. Directly above the final step was a circular manhole. We made it.

"This is it," Rox said, halting directly in front of the rebar ladder. We were standing directly below Revival Church Camp, and for all we knew, Pine was standing on our heads.

Rox said, "Ill, you first. You remember the way?"

I stuttered, "The *middle* door to my *right*. Use the pins to find where the lever pivots."

"No . . . it's the middle door to your *left*, remember?"

"Oh . . . right. My *left*. I got it."

Jordan, Sasha, Rox, and Neary all stared at me. It was clear my lapse in memory didn't instill confidence.

"Don't worry, Ill, you'll remember," Sasha said. "I know you will."

I gave a half smile and nodded. With nothing else needing to be said, I began my ascension upward. The rebars were as cold as ice. I used my right palm to lift up the manhole lid, which was equally as cold as the rebars. Once I put my shoulder into it, the lid finally propped open and upward.

"Don't make too much noise," Rox whispered from below.

It took all the strength of my right arm and shoulder to lift the manhole lid gracefully enough to seat it on the floor softly. I used the last ounce of strength I had left to push the lid across the floor as slowly and quietly as I humanely could. Once the hole was uncovered, I shook the strain from my right arm and thrust myself through the floor into the boiler room.

We were in.

———————

Rox's instructions repeated in my head as I exited the boiler room and turned left. Wait, was it right? No, it was left . . . wasn't it? I closed my eyes and took a deep breath to clear my mind. Suddenly, I remembered. Turn *right*. The middle door to my *left* once I turned the first corner. As I slowly shut the boiler room door behind me, it began audibly creaking. In a panic, I shut the door as quickly as I could.

THUMP.

The sound of the door shutting echoed through the halls. My heart skipped at least two beats. How could I be so stupid? If Pine was in the building, he almost certainly heard it. I tried to put the possibility as far out of my mind as I could and began pacing down the hall. Once I turned the corner, I found the three doors Rox said would be to my left. I immediately withdrew the two hairpins they gave me and began working on the middle door. But the sweat from my fingers caused one of the hairpins to slip out of my grasp. It fell to the floor and skidded underneath the door.

Fuck. Fuck. *Fuuuuck.*

I didn't know how to jimmy a lock with only one hairpin. I barely knew how with the luxury of two. With the clock ticking, I jammed the lone hairpin in the lock and frantically began jimmying. The sweat on my fingertips prevented me from keeping a steady grip. I wiped my hands on my hoodie and continued jimmying away. My breaths were becoming heavier. My knees felt weak. The plan was collapsing.

But finally, the chrome doorknob twisted completely. The door propped open. I nearly fell to the floor with relief. We were halfway there.

Click.

A noise from behind me caused me to stop in my tracks. My blood turned frozen cold. I stopped breathing. It was the indistinguishable sound of a gun being cocked.

"I don't see an electrician uniform on you, son."

Pine.

My arms trembled as I raised them above my head. I slowly turned around and was met with the sight of Reverend Pine pointing his gun directly at my chest. His left arm was inside a black sling from Neary's gunshot.

He asked, "Where are our pals this time? Let me guess, unlike you, they actually had a brain cell to spare and elected to stay home?"

I said nothing.

Pine's eyes widened. "No, they're *here* . . . aren't they? Y'all split up like the Scooby gang, yeah? Smart."

Suddenly, he closed in on me and brought the gun within an inch of my chest.

He said, "You're not gonna tell me where they are, and that's okay. Because I already know. But maybe you can help me understand why they sent their brightest to the *electricity* room of all places. How could the electricity factor into such a brilliant scheme?"

I couldn't give away their position. We would all be dead by dawn if I did.

I mumbled, "It's just me . . . I'm all alone. I was looking to see if there were any clues inside. I didn't know it was the electricity room."

Pine nodded, but I saw in his eyes he knew I was full of shit.

He said, "Let's take a looksie, then, shall we? See what we find," and gestured to the room with his gun. Every instinct in my being was screaming at me, telling me if I walked inside that room, I wouldn't be coming out. Pine put the tip of the gun squarely between my shoulders and forced me through the door. I saw the grid box and the red switch that Rox said would be on its side.

"Press it, son," Pine ordered.

He knew. He understood the plan perfectly. I stared down at the red switch and knew once I pressed it, all our lives would be over. Rox and I would never be famous writers. Sasha would never see her little cousins ever again. Neary would never preach the word of God ever again. It was all my fault. I was the one who led us here. I was the one who spent months obsessing. I was the sole reason I had a gun being pointed at my back by the most powerful man in Tennessee.

Suddenly, I felt the tip of the gun at the back of my head. In a panic, I reached down and pressed the switch.

Black.

From behind me, I heard, "Now howsabout a reunion with our friends?"

Pine held my left arm in an airtight grip as we marched down the empty halls. The gun was pointed firmly in my left side. The backup generator had kicked on and lit our way to his office where Sasha, Jordan, Rox, and Neary unknowingly awaited us.

Pine said, "Now let's see . . . if I were a little piece of evidence meant to put the mean ole reverend under the jail, where in my office would I be? My desk? My filing cabinets? My closet?"

I kept my mouth shut. If I was going to die, what difference did it make?

He said, "Come to think of it, the safe in my closet looked a little out of sorts last time I checked. I guess your little friend made herself at home during our little chat, huh?"

"*They*," I snapped. "It's *they*, not her."

Pine chuckled. "Well, I'm sure you've been itching to know what's inside since *they* told you about it, no?"

I stayed silent.

"A *key*, son, a *key* is what you and your friends are after."

Rox never mentioned a key.

"A key to *what*?" I sneered.

"*Justice*," Pine said. "Except it ain't your regular Kwikset."

"A flash drive," I said.

"Ding ding ding! Correctamundo! It might be small, son, but it unlocks more than you can imagine. It gives me eyes and ears when and where I need 'em most."

"You mean like the police you sent to my house?"

"Oh, you mean ole Sandra and Dale? The three of us go *waaaay* back, and let's just say that these days, they have a tendency to take me at my word. In fact, once we link up with our good pals, I might just ring them up to join us. Of course, I'll have to ask your friends for the flash drive back so I can cross some t's and dot some i's before they get here."

I sneered. "So that's how you tear kids away from their families? You break your way into the system and make up lies?"

"It's a dark world, son, and it's only getting darker. Kids have always come up with the damndest things since the dawn of man, the only difference now is no adult is there to smack 'em back into reality when they need it. The ground beneath our feet has been shrinking the past decade, but we've refused to give up the ship. If you think you and your ragtag bunch of bleeding hearts are gonna be the ones to stop us, you're even stupider than I thought."

We turned a corner and both saw Jordan on the lookout. I froze in my tracks, but Pine yanked me forward by the arm. I couldn't bear to see my friends' faces when they saw me with a gun in my back. Jordan glanced up at the two of us, and the color left his face. Pine withdrew the gun from my back and pointed it directly at Jordan.

"Jordan?" I heard Sasha say from inside Pine's office. "Any sign of Ill?"

Jordan raised his arms in the air and began breathing heavier and heavier. Pine made a gesture with his gun for Jordan to reply.

Jordan said, "Yeah . . . he's coming."

The three of us stopped in the doorway of his office. Sasha and Neary were rummaging through one of the filing cabinets when they glanced up at us. Sasha smiled once she saw me, but her relief immediately turned to terror when she saw Pine. Tears began to fill my eyes as I felt my heart shatter.

Rox emerged from the closet. "I got it, let's hope Ilya didn't —"

Pine instantly withdrew the gun from my side and pointed it directly at Rox. They let out a shriek and dropped the flash drive.

"I'm gonna be needing that, sweetheart," Pine said.

"Rox, don't," I pleaded. "The flash drive gives him access to —"

"SHUT UP!" Pine shouted before he pointed the gun back at me. Gone was his faux pleasantness and cheeriness. In his eyes, I could only see pure, unfiltered hatred. He pointed the gun back to Rox. "Give me that flash drive right this goddamned second, or I swear you're not gonna believe what happens next."

Rox instantly reached for the flash drive and picked it up from the floor. They darted towards Pine and placed it in his hand.

Pine said, "See? We can be *reasonable* people here, can't we?"

Rox circled back and rushed to join Sasha, Jordan, and Neary by the filing cabinets. Sasha held Rox in her arms.

"So far, nothing's happened that cannot be undone. Well . . . apart from this little number," Pine chuckled and pointed to the shoulder he was shot in. "But Roxanne, that's your *real* name, isn't it? I remember you, you were one of the brightest we've ever had, Roxanne. You helped us more than you can imagine."

"Oh you're going to *hell* hell, you freak," Sasha fumed.

"But Roxanne," Pine said, "I'm willing to bet not all the adults in your life *see* what I see. I bet your mom and dad don't see the bright and intelligent person I see."

Rox said nothing. There was pure scorn in their eyes.

Pine held the flash drive in the air. "But *this*? This can change that, Roxanne. This is all I need to ensure you go somewhere where you are *loved* and *appreciated*."

"Don't listen to him, Rox," I said. "He's lying."

Pine made his way to the laptop on his desk and inserted the flash drive. He opened the laptop lid and began typing.

He said, "Your folks don't deserve you, Roxanne. *Anthem* doesn't deserve you. They've done nothing but confuse you and fill your head with lies. But we're gonna take care of that right now. After I finish my work here, your folks are gonna pay for how they've hurt you. I promise you'll never have to worry about them again." There was nothing any of us could do as Pine did away with any chance Rox had of a seminormal life. Whatever kind of diabolical work was happening behind that computer screen was responsible for thousands of children being ripped away from their families, guilty of nothing but showing their queer or trans child the love they deserved.

Suddenly, Pine's eyes narrowed downward in confusion. He stopped typing. He began clicking a key over and over and over again. He turned his head towards the flash drive to ensure it was fastened, but the small white light on its side signified it was.

"It's not working," Pine said.

"On the contrary," Rox said. "From what I can tell, it's working *perfectly*."

"How's that?" Pine asked.

A fiendish smile appeared on Rox's face. "A beacon flash drive is a remarkable thing. It can send packets of information through the airwaves in seconds. Y'know what else is remarkable? A rubber ducky."

"A rubber *what*?" Pine belted as his face turned crimson red.

"A rubber ducky flash drive. It might look inconspicuous to the eye, but it can hack into any mainframe in just 30 seconds. But you know what's more dangerous than a rubber ducky?"

Pine looked both bewildered and mortified.

Rox said, "When a rubber ducky *meets* a beacon. Then, any hacked files can be sent to whatever preordained IP addresses are plugged into the drive."

Pine thundered, "You better start making some goddamn sense *now*."

Rox replied, "Every email and file you've ever saved has just been sent to every news outlet and civil rights attorney in the country, as well as the FBI and ACLU. Since the closest FBI headquarters is in Knoxville, I'm assuming you have . . . *three* hours before you get raided?"

Panic filled Pine's eyes. For 10 straight seconds, he sat completely stunned as he dumbfoundedly stared at his laptop screen. It was then that I realized Rox's rubber ducky drive was never just a decoy meant for the switcharoo. It was the complete downfall and undoing of Reverend Pine's legacy in a matter of seconds. The look on his face as he sat and watched every ungodly skeleton in Revival's closet become public property filled me with an otherworldly sensation.

But the sensation was short-lived. In an instant, Pine rose to his feet and lifted his gun-wielding arm in Rox's direction.

I shouted, "NOOOOOOOOOO!"

But as Rox's eyes widened with panic, Sasha reached across them with her fist fully clenched. In one swift motion, she knocked Pine squarely in his jaw before he could get the shot off, and he went tumbling down, fumbling the gun in the process. Before I could process, Rox frantically grabbed the gun off the floor and had it pointed squarely at Pine with both their hands on the grip. They held the gun not two feet away from Pine's ugly mug.

"You . . . *morons*," Pine barked. "You don't know what the hell you just did."

"We ended your life, asshole," Sasha said. "We made sure no kid suffers because of you ever again."

"Do you know how many underprivileged kids we feed and shelter each summer? *Thousands*. Where are they gonna go now? You don't think they're gonna end up somewhere worse after tonight? You think it's gonna be any different wherever they end up in the world? Homeless, jobless, and on the street? You wanna 'save kids' so goddamned badly . . . you just signed a hundred of their death warrants."

Rox sneered. "I would rather be homeless and dying on the street than your guinea pig."

Pine stared up at Rox and looked hell-bent on gouging their eyes out with his bare hands.

Pine said, "You *kids* . . . you wanna save the world and sing fuckin' 'Kumbaya' with hands held across the globe. You cry and you *beg* for help but you're too goddamn stupid to accept it. You scream all the livelong day about change, but it's too *triggering* for you when you realize what it takes. You wanna save the world . . . you can barely save yourselves. You're one lone-wolf classmate with his daddy's assault rifle away from collapse, and when that happens . . . I'm gonna laugh. Then you'll finally understand what the world really is, but at that point, it'll be too fuckin' late."

Rox maintained their position and aim. Their eyes were fully fixated on Pine but didn't demonstrate an ounce of fear. Rather, they conveyed a calculation taking place in Rox's mind. I could only hope to know what was happening inside of it.

Rox said, "Pastor . . . in the car, you said that when someone who hurts a child goes to prison, God turns his head."

Neary said nothing but continued shielding Sasha and Jordan. Suddenly, tears began streaming from Rox's eyes. "When a man dedicates his life to taking thousands of beautiful, funny, kind, and intelligent kids who are perfect just the way they are . . . and *destroying* them all while cowering behind a crucifix . . . when a man like *that* goes to prison . . . what does God do then, I wonder?"

Sasha began quietly sobbing to herself. One singular tear fell from Neary's left eye from behind his glasses.

Rox said, "Reverend, I don't know if there is a hell and quite frankly, I can't be sure you're going to it. But as you well know, there are plenty of hells in the natural world as it is. So just in case you really are gonna be rewarded for your years of service in heaven, I'm gonna send you to hell on Earth . . . *personally.*"

Rox lowered the gun to their side. They wiped their tears away with their coat sleeve and slowly made their way to the door.

"Let's get the fuck out of here," Rox mumbled.

But as Rox, Jordan, Sasha, and I gathered in the doorway, we noticed there was one group member missing. We looked up and saw Pastor Neary with his own gun pointed squarely at Pine. He had merely switched places with Rox.

"Neary . . . what are you *doing*?" Rox asked.

"I've envisioned this moment every single day for *30 years*," Neary trembled, "and never once did it involve a courtroom."

Rox said, "Neary, you pull that trigger and you make him exactly what he wants to be: a *martyr*. Don't give that to him. Prison will take care of him a million times over."

But Neary was undeterred. Pine suddenly began smiling as Neary continued to point his gun squarely between his eyes.

Neary shook his head. "He's not going to prison. He's smiling that shit-eating grin because he knows the *exact* people and the *exact* money he put in place are gonna be there to save him just like they have the past 30 years."

Sasha said, "If you kill him now, *that* becomes the narrative. Not the lives he ruined, not the kids he tormented into an early grave, and not the families he destroyed. You have to trust that the world has changed in all that time."

Although Neary maintained his position, his arm began trembling. His exhales became sterner. "You aren't capable of love for anyone in this natural world. I'm not convinced you even love yourself, and yet you are so fucking full of ego and self-hatred that now I realize . . . you know full well you're not going to heaven. But you don't care about heaven and you sure as shit don't care about hell because you know that's exactly where you're headed.

"You don't care about God or Satan . . . you just wanna feel big enough to be worthy of their conversation. You knew you couldn't warrant their attention with love because you are fucking *incapable* of love, so you opted for hate instead. But you're an intelligent man, Reverend Pine. You hate people in that special way only intelligent people can . . . *amicably*. With *charm*. With a smile and a bible in hand."

More and more tears streamed from Neary's eyes. "Even as a stupid, mindless teenager, I loved God more than you ever will. And you fucking *tore* him away from me just like you did countless other children. I've spent the last three decades believing a God couldn't possibly exist because of you, until one day, a young man walked through my office door. His name was Brent Cushman, and I knew from our first conversation that he was a godsend. And you took him away from me, and you took him away from his classmates, his school, and his town."

Sasha clung to my arm as she sobbed, and I was crying along with her. Neary began slowly nodding. I was certain the trigger would be pulled in the next five seconds, and all our work to right a terrible wrong would be undone. Pine would be a martyr, and justice would never be served.

Neary said, "And you're gonna stand trial for his murder and the murder of countless others, you son of a bitch." He lowered the gun to his side, or rather, he thrust it to his side unwillingly. The smile left Pine's face. His expression twisted into confusion but then melted into stark realization. Horror befell him as Neary made his way to the four of us huddled together in the doorway. We gave one final glance to Pine, who remained on the floor, before turning to exit into a new world. Whether it would be a better world remained to be seen.

Twenty-three

DAWN WAS BREAKING. I laid in bed and stared up at the ceiling as rays of sunshine broke through my bedroom window. The adrenaline from our final visit to Revival still pumped through my veins. I didn't know how to feel or what to think. What if Sasha was wrong? What if the world hadn't changed enough to make someone as powerful as Pine fully pay? What if whatever contents sent from Pine's laptop weren't enough? What if we had merely provided Pine with all the tools he needed to pull off the greatest PR stunt of the decade?

Had we really changed or solved anything? Or had we simply uprooted the very lives ruined by Revival we sought to avenge and exposed them to further scrutiny? I began to debate if the path to hell truly was carved by good intentions, but suddenly I heard a vibration from my nightstand. It was a text from Sasha.

CHECK TIKTOK NOW

I dashed to my TikTok app. The first live video at the very top of my For You Page depicted a long hallway, a hallway I distinctly remembered being walked down with a gun to my side just hours before. There was a cluster of people with cameras flashing and boom mics waiting at the end of it. Suddenly, two men in black windbreakers turned the corner with another man sandwiched between them. It was a perp walk. As the bulbs of cameras began manically flashing in every direction, the three men neared closer and closer. In the center of the trio, Reverend Pine walked with his hands behind his back. A cacophony of questions and expletives began raining down on Pine from the crowd.

By the same evening, the story was the top trending topic in the country. Social media feeds overflowed with personal testimonies from Revival alumni, young and old. The next day at school, 12 different vans from news stations across the country were scattered across the parking lot. Random students were being interviewed by news anchors in the hallways. It was complete and utter pandemonium. It was the liveliest Blount High had been since Brent Cushman's death. By noon, classes were canceled, and students were sent home to snuff out the feeding frenzy.

———

The trial commenced only a week later in federal court. The judge was certain public discourse would erode the integrity of the jury if too much time passed, and the trial was moved to state court. One of the most damning pieces of evidence, which proved to be Pine's ultimate demise, started with the letter M.

Methylenedioxy. Campers who felt a euphoric closeness to God during sermons were not feeling divine intervention, but rather a mixture of Methylenedioxy and Gatorade. The trial revealed that Pine and his ilk were putting their spin on the Pavlovian method as the euphoric highs campers felt after enjoying a drug-laced refreshment were met with a crushing low the next morning. It stumped nearly anyone following the news how thousands of kids could be lured into drinking the same drink until they learned of the gym's A/C and its convenient failure to function properly.

Pine's final verdict read like that of a mob boss. For 30 years of infliction of mental and bodily harm onto minors, child enticement, child exploitation, racketeering, tax evasion, illegal drug use and possession, trafficking, cybertheft, expungement, extortion, and negligent homicide, Reverend Pine was sentenced to Riverbend Maximum Security Institution in Nashville for 40 years without parole.

———————

"You're *leaving*?" Sasha asked.

Pastor Neary was packing the contents of his office into various cardboard boxes. I recognized the *Pietà* in the form of a ceramic figurine as he packed it away.

"There's a campus minister opening in Minnesota," Neary said as he continued packing.

I said, "But you've lived in Anthem your *entire* life."

"I've *resided* in Anthem my entire life, but I haven't lived in that time once."

Sasha asked, "But don't you wanna stay somewhere where your work is needed most? Gay and trans kids in Minnesota seem pretty well-off, by comparison."

"I'm not going for *them*," Neary said.

This shut both of us up.

"You're going . . . for *you*?" Sasha asked.

Neary stood quietly for a second or two. "Your friend . . ."

"Rox?" I asked.

"Yes, Rox. When they told us about . . . 'sleeping in a wooden cradle with splinters . . .' I realized how much living a double life was killing me. The courage your friend has to live as no one but themself . . . the *strength* it takes to do that in a place like Anthem left me a long time ago. You kids still have a future to build and fight for, but for old farts like me, that gift was forfeited years ago." Neary resumed packing.

Sasha said, "I'm sorry . . ."

"Sorry? You have nothing to —"

"I'm sorry for what you went through. You were put through an unimaginable hell, and there were no adults there to save you. I can't imagine what that's like."

Neary nodded and suddenly smiled. "It's funny . . . there were no adults to save me this time either. Just a couple of batshit-crazy kids."

After that day, I never saw Pastor Erick Neary again. But I did think about him every single day. It was easier for me to understand why he had to leave for Minnesota the older I got. I realized it wasn't just something he needed, it was something he deserved. For someone whose faith was tested so cruelly and unnecessarily for so long to continue on as God's unconditional servant, only the calmest and most peaceful waters should have awaited him. Unlike me and Rox and Sasha and Jozie, Pastor Erick Neary wasn't given the luxury of a brighter and better tomorrow. Neary's better tomorrow came and passed him by like it had so many others his age. Generation after generation of pain becoming politics and devils disguising themselves as devil's advocates. I later realized the privilege of the moment in history I shared with my friends and the responsibility it came with.

One day during my senior year of high school, I received a letter in the mail from Duluth, Minnesota. I opened the envelope and found a wedding gift registry. Pastor Erick Neary had finally found his calm waters, and his name was Owen.

Twenty-four

"YOU COULDN'T FIND THE bisexual flag?" Jozie asked.

"They were all out at the store," Sasha said. "They had pan and lesbian though!"

"The bis are a resilient bunch, they'll survive for now," Rox quipped.

The first-ever meeting of Blount High's first-ever LGBTQIA+ student group was about to be called to order by its fearless leader, freshman Jozie Flores.

It wasn't until I turned around to grab more duct tape that I realized the room had been filled with no fewer than 30 kids. Jordan was using his college lunch break to help his little cousin by working the sign-up table and passing out nametags.

"Okay, that should do it for now. Let's get this show on the road!" Jozie exclaimed, clasping her hands together. Chairs had to be pulled from nearby classrooms to accommodate the number of founding members. Once the commotion had died down, all eyes turned to Jozie.

With a bright smile and tears in her eyes, Jozie took a long look around the room and spoke. "James Baldwin once said, 'It took many years of vomiting up all the filth I'd been taught about myself and half believed before I was able to walk on the earth as though I had a right to be here.' Our choices make us who we are. I chose to spend more time obsessing over old TV shows than studying for tests. I chose to dress in ways that would make my classmates cringe or worry about my sanity.

"But never once did I *choose* to like girls. Never once did I *choose* a life of convincing myself over and over that this wasn't a phase and that I wasn't just succumbing to some type of peer pressure, which is what my mom and dad would have preferred. Because if I knew liking girls meant I would have to sit in a reserved seat away from my grandparents on what could possibly be their last Thanksgiving, I wouldn't have chosen it. If I knew being bi meant having to tell my future girlfriend she could only be introduced at family weddings as my 'plus-one,' I wouldn't have chosen it.

"Kids outside of this room will never know what it's like to try on prom dresses not knowing if you and your date are gonna fuck up the most magical night of your classmates' lives simply by walking the carpet together. They'll never know what it's like having to brace yourself for getting out of the shower because the body you see in the mirror is not your own. We may never know why liking someone of the same gender or being a different gender has caused us, in some way, to shrink ourselves down. We may never know why straight kids get to worry about where they're going to party after prom while we worry about getting to our cars safely.

"But I look around and see so many brave and beautiful faces today, and I know in my heart I've never been prouder of being who I truly am. I never chose to be bi, but I *did* choose to forge through an ocean of self-hatred and hopelessness for four years because I knew one day, I would stand in the sun as the person I was always meant to be: myself. The girl who likes girls and hates superhero movies.

"I'd like to share a prayer I wrote: *If the decision to live my truth wounds me, let the brunt weaken with each time I decide. If living my truth invites reproach and shame, let me live to see the day when it invites love. And if somebody hates me for who I love, may I take solace in the fact that it is no longer my own hatred that I must suffer.*"

"A NUMBER OF MONTHS ago, I read in the newspaper that there was a Supreme Court ruling which states that homosexuals in America have no constitutional rights against the government's invasion of their privacy. The paper states that homosexuality is traditionally condemned in America & only people who are heterosexual or married or who have families can expect those constitutional rights. There were no editorials. Nothing. Just flat cold type in the morning paper informing people of this. In most areas of the USA it is possible to murder a man & when one is brought to trial, one has only to say that the victim was a queer & that he tried to touch you & the courts will set you free. When I read the newspaper article I felt something stirring in my hands; I felt a sensation like seeing oneself from miles above the earth or looking at one's reflection in a mirror through the wrong end of a telescope. Realizing that I have nothing left to lose in my actions I let my hands become weapons, my teeth become weapons, every bone & muscle & fiber & ounce of blood become weapons, & I feel prepared for the rest of my life."

— David Wojnarowicz, artist and AIDS activist
(1954–1992)

LGBTQIA+ charities
for your consideration

- Advocacy & Services for LGBTQ+ Elders (SAGE) sageusa.org

- Affinity Community Services affinity95.org

- The Attic Youth Center atticyouthcenter.org

- The Audre Lorde Project alp.org

- Black Trans Advocacy Coalition (BTAC) blacktrans.org

- Center for Black Equity centerforblackequity.org

- Genders & Sexualities Alliance (GSA) Network gsanetwork.org

  Lambda Legal lambdalegal.org
- Out & Equal outandequal.org

- Point Foundation pointfoundation.org

- The Trevor Project thetrevorproject.org

About the author

DANIEL BISHOP (HE/THEY) has been deeply entrenched in the fight for social equity and queer/trans empowerment for the past decade. Since he was a sophomore in high school in his rural Illinois hometown, Bishop has been outspoken in his fight for fairness and equality through civil activism and organization in both local and national politics. Both his passions for justice and mental health awareness have led him to pursue a master's degree in clinical mental health counseling, and he is currently training to be a licensed professional counselor in the state of Missouri.

Twitter: @stanchips
Instagram: @danieljbishop
TikTok: @danbish99

Thank you for reading *My Teeth Become Weapons*! If you enjoyed the book, please share it with your friends and family to support the indie author community.

Every review can help a new reader find this book, so please share your review online!

www.ingramcontent.com/pod-product-compliance
Lightning Source LLC
Chambersburg PA
CBHW022006310726
48972CB00006B/1540